ALFRED'S JOURNEY

Bella Veil

EDITED AND PUBLISHED
BY PETUNIA BLUE LLC
PRINTED BY LULU.COM

ISBN 978-1-329-98729-6

All Rights Reserved
Printed in the United States of America

Epilogue

As I wrote this book I reflected and remembered times that we had and shared together. I have written this book with tears, joy and remembrance. My grandfather, Alfred Barder Reid came to this country with nothing but the clothes on his back and little money. I am very proud of him.

Writing this book started out as a labour of love but now I am finding out that with admiration, love and joy it is more of a tribute to a wonderful husband, great father and grandfather. It is not just about a man who brought me up, and taught me about life but about a man that preserved all odds to survive and leave his home to start a new one in a different country that he has always loved and admired Canada.

He went to war, worked and built his own empire. He loved his family and took great care of his wife and children and my brother Malcolm Jr. and myself Bella. I am very grateful that my grandparents did not leave us aside as we see so many people do today. This is not just a tribute to Alfred Reid but, a legacy he has left behind.

On September 27,1991 Alfred Barder Reid passes away in the hospital in his sleep. Oh, my, did I cry and my mother was beside herself. His sons and various grandchildren were also there but the one child that bothered me the most was my daughter Cindy. Although she was older and understood more, she was still mourning the death of her great-grandmother and now her great-grandfather as well. To this day I still ask him and my grandmother Anna for advice. It was hard for me when they died. It was not just losing grandparents but losing a set of parents. It was heartbreaking for my daughter, my mother and I. Alfred Reid was not just some man he was our lighthouse in a storm, our teacher, our father, our grandfather even mentor at times. He was loved and cherished by his family. Especially by me and my mother, his baby girl Lena. He had created a bond with three generations and we all felt his love and encouragement.

 He lived his life and never wavered from his course. He always knew what he wanted and where he was going. He instilled in us to be kind. courteous and to believe in the power of God and prayer. Alfred Reid was a self-made man and he left behind a legacy only I could write about. You see he was a father to me too and I miss him and Anna every day, for they gave my brother and I their hearts as well as their home.

 At times, it was hard to put words to paper and relive some parts of my life, but in the end, it was all worth it because my grandfather Alfred Reid and grandmother Anna Reid were the two most honest and loving two people

I have had the utmost pleasure to know and be related to them.

Dear readers I hope that you will enjoy reading about a man that even with all he had to endure, he still could show love and compassion for his family and mankind. Yes, it is also with great pleasure and respect above all that I write about not just any man, but a man; my grandfather who instilled in me the values of life and how I should always be a lady and hold my head high...

Alfred Barder Reid was a man who came to Canada as a young man after being smuggled onto a boat as a child and making his way as he went along. Fighting and surviving two World Wars and coming home to his family that soon became five generations. To this day there are still Reid great-grandchildren and great-great-grand children being born, and they should also know of their heritage and about the man and woman who started it all. Yes, Anna and Freddy had their share of hard times as well as good times but, through it all they still had each other.

Childhood

He was born August 4, 1890 in Kingston Jamaica. His mother, a pretty mulatto colour girl with very pretty hair was named Louisa. She was born to a slave mother named Mabel but, they simply called her Granny. Louisa's father was a plantation owner.

His father, John Barder Reid, was the plantation owner's son and was very smitten with Louisa McFadden. Even though she had a last name she was still a servant and "concubine." Alfred's grandmother and mother both worked in the Big House. They were among those of a lighter skin colour. The lighter you were the more likely you would work in the Big House.

Louisa had four children, three boys and one girl. The boys were named Alfred, John Jr. and James. Her daughter was named Melvina. Alfred the eldest of the boys grew up on the plantation with his siblings, and was the most adventurous of the siblings. He liked to make jokes and pull pranks.

His grandfather, the owner of the plantation, was a spiteful, mean drunk of a Scotsman with a big bushy beard. He would get drunk and go looking for Alfred to take out his frustrations on by repeatedly abusing and torturing young Alfred. Grandfather Reid liked tying him up by his thumbs to the back of the chair, and make him sit there for hours at a time. He thought this to be a great punishment and he would call him, "Little Black Sambo." This was very scary for Alfred to endure. His Granny would try and save him from the horror and abuse whenever she could.

Alfred would ask his Granny, "Why does my grandfather Reid hate me so much?"

She would reply, "Because you are more like your mother than your father."

"What do you mean by that?" he would ask.

Granny could only reply, "It's because your skin colour is not the same as your brothers and sister.

"Why should that make a difference," said a scared and frightened five-year-old boy. He didn't understand the reasoning for such meanness from his grandfather. How do you explain to a child that he is not loved or wanted because his skin colour is different?'

They tried to protect him as much as they could, but at times it was impossible. Old Man Reid would drink a lot of Jamaican rum and his native Scottish whiskey. When he would get like that it was always a good idea to stay far away from this crazy man.

There were nights when Old Man Reid got drunk and would yell and scream for Alfred by calling out the pet name he had for him.

"Where is that Little Black Sambo bastard," he would shout like a roaring wind. "That bastard child has ruined my family. I want to teach him a lesson."

It was terrifying for young Alfred to hear, for he knew what was about to come his way. Alfred would try to hide from him but, he was not always successfully.

It's believed that Old Man Reid hated the fact that his son had children with Louisa. This made him angry to no end. But even as Louisa loved her children, she tried to love John Reid too. On the plantation, there were no big love affairs, nor marriages between servants, slaves, and masters. This didn't change the Old Man's attitude toward them being together. Although it was not a convenient union somehow it had its moments and they found ways to make it work.

Despite all that, Alfred still had a very loving mother and Granny. He also had a good relationship with his siblings; especially with his older sister Melvina. Once in awhile they would skip chores and housework and just run free in the sugar fields and sometimes in the woods. It was from his fear that Alfred got the idea to hide in the sugar cane fields and learned his love for rock candy.

Alfred said to Melvina with joy, "let us go out in the sugar fields, and find some sugar to make rock candy."

"I don't think so Alfred that we should play there," says Melvina her being the eldest and more sensible.

"But why can't we get rock candy? It is so sweet and good, it's our favourite candy of all," he says.

It was a safehaven for him at times, when he could get away from the abuse and meanness of his grandfather Reid. Whenever it was possible to escape his tormentor Alfred felt at peace and freedom.

Sometimes their two brothers would join them and then they could gather up as much sugar as possible to make their favourite candy. John Jr. and James were little devils and both were very lucky not to know the wrath of Old Man Reid. How far his hatred could go and to what measures he would let it. It was strange that he would never hurt Alfred's siblings. He would spare them, as they looked more like his son than Alfred did. Yet when Grandfather Reid was not drinking which was rare, he would also leave Alfred alone.

As for Melvina well, she was sort of his favourite because she resembled his sister Mary back in Scotland. So, for Melvina's sake this was a blessing in disguise. However, she hated the way Alfred was treated and hated it even more when she couldn't stand up for him or say anything in his defense. She always felt helpless when Alfred was being abused or beaten. Melvina would try to hide him too but, when she couldn't she'd tend to his cuts and bruises.

His Granny would try and save him by saying he was not around. Old Man Reid would say, "Granny you had better not be lying to me. If I find out you are, it will be worse for the little bastard."

Granny would answer back, "I wouldn't lie to you Old Man." Granny could call him that because they went back along ways. Heck they were almost kin. Some days it was sheer heaven living on the plantation. Other days were not so pleasant, filled with hard work and no respect.

When the Scottish people came to Jamaica they came for the sugar cane and metal bauxite which is a form of alumina used for metal purposes. The metal looks like a clay rock, and is the world's main source of aluminium. This mineral was to become a very profitable source of monies for the owners of these mines. The men that were able worked the bauxite mines and some did sugar caning too. Along with the trading and selling of sugar, there was also coffee and rum. The country was also famous for its Blue Mountain coffee.

While the growing of sugar cane and mining of bauxite were still on the market; rum was used mostly for trading and some selling whenever possible. The trading was so good that some plantation owners were known to be wealthy and very prosperous.

When the Spanish came to Jamaica they brought with them African slaves as well. They would mingle with the Jamaican people, thus some becoming slaves or "servants."

Some of them worked the fields, while others the Big House. They tried to take over, but lost to the British.

They also brought bananas and chocolate. The exporting of banana was embraced by the people and sold like crazy. It was it was very similar to the plantain which is Jamaica's native banana. Although they look the same they taste totally different.

The 'freed Jamaican's' as they were called because they were either baptized or had a last name which meant they were free men. Some had jobs either in the mines, as ship crewmen or traders; while others worked the plantations for money. It was the freed men who could trade only certain things. They could buy for themselves but trade and sell very little. They felt they shouldn't be bossed around by the Scots. Some took to the Black Market just to survive. At times, this proved to be a great problem for the Scottish traders. This would go on for many years and some traders were known to be violent and some even killed behind their wanting to control trading. It was a hard life for some but, for others they simply tolled through it all.

Even with the threat of bananas being traded and sold by some freed men this didn't hurt the Reid plantation. Old Man and John Reid were not worried for the time being, as they were still secured with their trades and plantation. Business went about as usual and for now the plantation slaves would not starve.

Old Man Reid would often say to his son, "Aye John, the plantation is doing well now. However, I fear that these freed men are becoming more abundant and soon the Big House plantation and our home might be in danger."

"What makes you think that father?" said John.

Says his father, "I see that with these bananas and coffee being traded by the freed people and some selling of rum, I fear if this keeps on it will ruin us. We must not let t them sell and trade too much at any cost."

John ponders for a bit and tries to see his father's point of view. Yes, John thinks to himself, it may be harder than they think, but then again coming to this country was not easy either. John would sometimes wonder why they ever came to pursue the trading of sugar cane and bauxite alumina. He thought it to be a nonsense idea, but his father thought different.

They had to get use to the weather. The heat alone would make the Scots people very irritable at best. They also had to understand the language that the people spoke amongst themselves called Patwa. It derives from a Creole and Jamaican dialect. It was a way to create their own language if you will. It sounded like singing or marbles at times by the formation of their mouths and words together.

The Scottish people also had a harsh sounding tone to their voices, it was called a Brogue. It was a very different dialect to the Scots as the Brogue to the Jamaicans. The

Scots thought that they could introduce the Jamaican people to a better way to speak but they kept their Patwa.

This combination and the thought that Reid plantation might go under was the making of the Old Man's increased reign of terror. The heat, the people and the trading would eventually take its toll on the Scottish people. As for John Jr., he didn't mind the weather to much or the women but, it was the men he had problems with. He was hopeful that they could endure anything coming their way.

As time went by Old Man Reid continued drinking heavily as Scots do and abusing and beating poor Alfred whe n he felt like it. Alfred's Granny and mother did their best to always be by him except when they had to work in the sugar fields or in the Big House.

John Jr., his father was a little nicer to Alfred as he didn't abuse or beat him, but he did not pay much attention to him either. It wasn't that he was a heartless man it was that he did not acknowledge these children as his by marriage.

The slaves and servants were also known to say that John Jr.was a little kinder to them and didn't treat them badly like his father. Everyone knew that Louisa held a special place in his heart, and it was her more so than their children. This made Old Man Reid crazy with madness. However, the more he protested, the more John Jr. could be found with Louisa.

Catholic Missionaries

The Catholic missionaries came to Jamaica to have a religious order. They wanted the Jamaican adults to attend church and the children to attend Sunday school. For the slaves and servants to attend church and the children to attend Sunday school they had to first be baptized and give last names. The Scots were a religious bunch of people, which were mostly Catholic but, they were against the baptism.

The women who couldn't get their masters' last name were happy that at least the children would have them to attend Sunday school. The masters, their sons and overseers also had to give use of their last names, especially to the servants and concubines. Slave children also were given last names. The names were taken from the bible. If they refused to be baptized they were not permitted to attend the House of the Lord, nor his Sunday school.

For some of the Jamaican people it was a confusing procedure and they didn't like to be told what religion to practice. The idea behind this was that the Missionaries believed that without religion in their lives their souls would not go to Heaven but, to be damned to Hell for eternity.

The baptizing in the end proved to be a good thing, in the years to come, church records were kept of all or mostly all the baptisms. This allowed the slaves and servants to trace back to your family tree.

Some of the Scottish men tried to get around the decision of the Catholic Missionaries. The Missionaries didn't like the fact that the men would mate with the servants and slaves. Because such mating produced children, the Missionaries wanted to save their young souls before they were damned. You can bet that Old Man Reid was not too pleased by this Missionary decision. He hated the idea of Louisa's children having to bear his last name.

This of course would end up with Old Man Reid hating and despising Alfred even more and continuing to beat and abuse him. Sometimes his sister would lay awake at night and try to think of ways that she could hurt and abuse Old Man Reid the way he tortured Alfred, even though he treats her alright at times.

But sadly, all she can do is tend to his cuts, bruises and welts, and dry his tears. For she was only a few years older than Alfred and was just a child herself.

"What the hell is this thing, you say they must be baptized and by what laws," says the Old Man Reid as he addresses an assembly of his peers.

"You know the Missionaries have been after us to baptize the slaves as well as the servants and more so the ones with children if they are to attend church and Sunday school. It's been posted in the trading posts and all over town," says plantation owner Angus McLeod whose plantation was over in St. Ann.

He was smaller in statue than the Old Man with red hair and freckles, which came out in the warmer climate. Though he didn't wear a beard he did have a handlebar moustache. His plantation grew coffee and plantain as well as sugar cane.

"Aye Reid," says Andrew McDonald, "it was a request that came straight down from the Archbishop himself and as we know the church always wins."

The McDonald plantation which was over in Montego Bay grew sugar cane, yams and a little bauxite mining too. Mr. McDonald was not burly or small, but his stature was in between. He had light brown hair greying at the temples like the temples of Old Man Reid, but Old Man Reid has a few greyer hairs than Andrew McDonald.

After some of these baptismal there would be a feast with some yams, they would make candied in sugar. The slaves would make cakes and pies, and cook King Fish and Akee. Some of the men would get drunk on the rum while the children would enjoy rock candy. The people would dance and sing of freedom and of Jamaica. Sometimes the men drank too much rum and had a hard day's work ahead of them with massive hangovers.

Sometimes Old Man Reid would get drunk himself and wander down to the slave and servant's quarters, wanting to join in the festivities. The slaves and servants were alarmed to see that the Master wanted to join the party. Some were not pleased at all, others just stood in astonishment. John, his son would have to go and bring him back home to their house.

"Father you must not mix with the slaves and servants when they are having their baptismal feasts. You know they feast as we do amongst themselves."

"But it's my plantation. I own all this land even the land they live work on. Its mine, I TELL YOU, IT IS MINE!!" The Old Man was furious as ever and stubborn as an old goat.

"Yes father, this is true, but you know as of late more and more are being baptized every day," says John.

Not only did Old Man Reid not have a say in the decision to have the Jamaicans baptized, but he could not even join in the festivities on his own plantation. Plus, the fact that he and his son had to give their last name to Louisa's children. However, Louisa kept her maiden name, for this was her father's dying wish.

Old Man Reid would give John a lecture all the time for going to see Louisa. He would say to him, "John Barder Reid, why don't you send away for a nice lass from Scotland?"

John hated to be called by his Christian name Barder. He would glare at his father and walk out the door straight to Louisa's arms and bed. The old man hated John having children with Louisa, but there they were for all to see.

Even though his grandfather Reid made living on the plantation a hard way to go, they still lived a decent life. They lived in a mud and grass thatched house. Some of the hut homes had outdoor kitchens and everyone had an outhouse. But all in all, the plantation life wasn't so bad as other plantations around them. Considering how the other slaves and servants talked about the living conditions on their plantations the Reid plantation was good by far.

The baptizing decision was working fine for awhile. Louisa's children went to Sunday School even though the older boys skipped a lot from Church and Sunday School. Old Man Reid also attended church as did his son John on occasion. If Alfred got caught and Old Man Reid heard about this, it was for sure that Alfred would be getting a beaten for skipping Sunday School to go play marbles.

The McLeod plantation is a wee bit smaller and not as big or as some would say as profitable as the Reid's. The McDonald's was a medium size plantation and it prospered a little more. But they all managed to make a decent profit at the end of the week.

This was the only life that some of the slaves and servants knew. Some were taken from their homes, others just left to fend for themselves. In a way living on a plantation meant survival for some and was better than starving. It was a hard life but they survived the best way they knew how. No matter the size of the plantation, all slaves and servants and their children had to be baptized. This was mandatory and had to be respected. After all, the Archbishop himself from Canterbury, England was the person in charge of making this decision.

You see the Scots and the Irish at that time were under the British Rule. McLeod didn't protest to much as he thought this would save him a place in Heaven. He was a foolish man at times when not to drunk from drinking rum. McLeod was hard a Master but not as hard as Old Man Reid. McLeod rarely beat his slaves and servants. He didn't believe in that they should be hurt physically. Instead he would put them in a "Hot Box" with no food or water for days at a time, depending on the crime committed. This in no way was a better form of punishment but it was better than living on the McDonald plantation.

Yes, the McDonald plantation was not a good place to work or be if you were spirited or had your own opinions kind of person. He hated when he was talked back to or disrespected. On the McDonald plantation, he demanded respect and loyalty from all his slaves and servants baptized or not. He treated all who worked for him as lower forms of human beings. This truly offended the slaves and servants. They felt that he had no right to treat them this way even if it was the rules of the plantation. But if they protested they would be beaten or whipped. They all learned very quickly to stay out of the way of Master McDonald.

McDonald was a man that felt he should be in competition with Old Man Reid. It was an idea that he would make his life goal. But Old Man Reid's servants never protested too much for their Master did not whip them like McDonald. Old Man Reid did not like seeing his slaves and servants with welts. Alfred's poor treatment was an exception.

A few of the surrounding plantation owners were jealous of the Reid plantation. But this did not fluster Old Man Reid at all he liked the feeling of being the best plantation owner in the colony. For the moment, Old Man was not worried and kept his plantation and Big House that way.

There were times that the servants, and many the cooks of the house, would go and shop in the markets. Since fish was abundant for them, the only other meat they would purchase was beef and chicken.

The McLeod plantation is in St. Ann, Jamaica while the McDonald's is in Montego Bay. Not only were they far apart and their plantations were not managed the same at all. Some of the slaves and servant would trade stories at one of the baptismal feast at the other neighbouring plantations. The stories they would mostly talk about were their Masters and what they have been up to, and who was whose latest concubine. Yes, the slaves and servants from the other plantations would get together during a feast time and socialize and gossip about everything under the sun. They were happy at these times and enjoyed being with friends and family.

 The conversation of baptizing soon became old news and the people started to accept it. Even though the Jamaican people were being ruled under the British Rule via the Scots and the Irish, they kept to themselves as much as possible and still spoke Patwa.

 As he got older, Alfred would say with pride and respect that he was a Jamaican first and a British subject second. This was 1890 a century coming to a close, things changing countries being evaded and ruled by others. It was a scary time and they did what they had to do to survive all the changes happening. A new century was about to begin and there was also talk of abolishing slavery.

 However, with the British invasion of Jamaica they would have slaves, servants and mate with them. The children would range in colour from an almost coffee colour to mulatto to high yellow as they would call them as they were almost but, not quite white. As the years went by the mixing of the blood line produced different shades of Jamaican's and other races.

 Today you can see the different blood lines when visiting the country of Jamaica.

The Jamaican people persevered through all the hardships and struggles, yet they never wavered from their true self. Jamaican's are a proud people and always will be. As the years go by they all try and live in harmony. And the because of the nearby plantations slaves and servants feasting together during the baptizing feasts some of them would mate too. This mating was a common thing among the slaves and servants of the surrounding plantations as they were always working or helping with the harvest at one plantation or another. This at times made it hard for them to be at the same plantation and truly be together. Some of the plantation owners were not too keen on the idea of their slaves and servants mating with the freed men, for this brought about slaves and servants leaving their plantation especially the women who were not concubines. It was a way for the women that were slaves to be able to leave and never look back. The owners tried hard to put a stop to it but to no avail were they successful. John just stood by and watched he sort of understood why the slave women would want to leave. It was a way for some to have a resemblance of a family life.

Louisa and her family were safe under the protection of John Reid. He was so smitten with Louisa that he couldn't let any harm come to her. It was a true union for John and Louisa even thought he didn't show any type of affection to their children. He would always be cordial with them and

Granny, for he knew this is what Louisa wanted. And he knew she would be happier and more complying. With this being the case, he also had to protect her children and Granny too. This made Old Man Reid upset, frustrated, and furious all at the same time. John told him that this was the way it was going to be. For now, Old Man Reid swallowed his words, but that would not be the end of that. Yes, John knew his father would try and intervene somehow but until then John would enjoy his time with Louisa and hope his father would eventually calm down.

This was wishful thinking on John's part, his father was letting him think he won, but John knows only too well to what lengths his father will go to get what he wants. John also knows that getting in his father's way when he is like that is just asking for trouble.

Even though some of the unions between slaves, servants, and their Masters made some of them feel they were almost in a relationship. The time came for John and Louisa to understand this is all they would ever have. This was not the case for all the unions between slaves, servants and their Masters. Some could say there was jealousy at the Reid plantation, because of Louisa being the concubine she had more privileges than most in her position. Granny and the children benefited from this arrangement too.

But despite all this Louisa secretly hoped and prayed for more from John Reid. Even though the church recognized baptismal, they didn't press for marriages among the slaves and servants, because some of the Scots and the few Irish still had families back home.

You see the reason behind the Church's decision to baptize the people was because it was a way to keep count of everyone on their plantation. Eventually the freed men and women would try and stop the church and the Missionaries from taking over.

Because of this the slaves and servants who were concubines could try to make a better way of life for their families. It was not so easy as one would think, to be a slave or servant nor even a concubine. But as time went on the people adapted and all was well for now.

This would be a way of life for many Jamaicans that were slaves, servants or concubines. The church and missionaries thought that making them Catholics would enrich their lives for the better. But the people who were the freed ones, didn't care much for the idea of being told how and who to pray and believe in.

These were hard times for all not only being a slave or servant, but the plantation owners also, they had to be careful not to let their slaves and servants mix together and eventually mating, especially with the freed men it would ruin the female ratio on the plantations. This would cause some plantations to lose their workers and slaves, or some gain more workers and slaves.

This practice really put a cramp into Old Man Reid's plans for his plantation and its future. For he protested against the baptizing and the concubine unions. This came all down to the church and missionaries trying to bring Christianity into their lives. It was to become a way of life for many and they had to adapt to survive.

During all this Alfred was growing and becoming more apt at dodging Old Man Reid whenever he could. Although it was still hard at times to stay out of his way, he still had his Granny and sister even his mother at times too. Alfred still ran and hid in the fields and woods, it was his place of freedom and peace, a safe haven if you will. His sister would still tend his wounds and bruises, and dry his tears. Although this was all she could do she still felt so sad for Alfred. And she still despised the Old Man Reid she would always be her little brother's protector. He still felt the awful wrath of his grandfather Reid, but because of this treatment he received it made him a stronger man in the years to come and a little less trusting too. But through it all it was his life and he had to learn to live it to survive in this world.

The Scottish Mission Church was behind this entire baptizing ordeal. Old Man Reid was not having any of it at all. He tried to protest it in church and at the Town Hall meetings but, no one paid him any mind. They knew that the Archbishop was having his way on this matter like it or not.

The freed men and some women were baptized because they had last names and some were set free by their Masters. While others bought their freedom, so hence the name freed people.

The Church endured them as Parishioners. So now because of this the Missionaries wanted the others, such as the slaves that were coupled with a freed person or servant that had children from unions that were made of Master and servant, slave and servant and servant and servant. The Missionaries thought this to be an unholy act against God.

So now the Missionaries are trying to convince the people that this is the right thing to do. The plantation owners were not for this at all, especially Old Man Reid he hated the idea from the start. It was a sure way to stir up trouble. Now Reid knows that his neighbors to left, the McLeod plantation and to the right the McDonald plantation. The McLeod plantation was of a medium size, but truly holding their own. Angus McLeod himself was a man of medium stature; he had red hair and a big mustache to match. He also was a fair plantation owner and as ruthless as the two men with him.

The other gent was Andrew McDonald. He was sort of a stocky build. His plantation was not as big or as thriving as McLeod or Reid. Yet he was in the same circle of people as them. He still had slaves and servants as they did, but not as many and his plantation was smaller too.

But even so the three men were what some would call friends who are, sociable and cordial with each other. They are the only plantations that were not badly in danger yet.

The Missionaries proposal to the Archbishop for the baptizing is making Old Man Reid nervous. He is not thrilled with the idea that the Church and Missionaries might win at this. The Missionaries were adamant about wanting the baptismal to be performed. They believed that this was the only way that the souls of the slaves and servants, would not be damned to Hell for eternity. They also wanted the children of the plantations to attend Sunday school. This was playing havoc with the nerves of Old Man Reid, but even thought he was a member of the Church he could not sway the Missionaries from their objective. He was even considering speaking with the Archbishop himself when he came to Jamaica for the meeting and discussion about the baptizing of servants and some slaves. Old Man Reid didn't want to have to speak with His Eminence, but if this is what it would take then so be it.

Yet the Old Man knew in his heart that he had to be polite and cordial with the Archbishop. He certainly did not want to upset the Archbishop, Missionaries nor the Church, by being forceful and commanding. He had to find another way to approach this situation. He thought of asking his fellow plantation owners about what their thoughts were on this matter.

"Well I think that this is all the working of the church, and the Archbishop and let us not forget the Missionaries too," says Andrew McDonald. He disliked the church decision to have servants and slaves baptized so that they can fill the coffers with money for the church.

"Aye true as may be, it is not a true and sure thing you say Andrew McDonald?" asks Angus McLeod, as he sits and listens quietly pondering their words. McLeod considers himself to be a bit of a Christian you might say, and was not keen on confronting His Eminence the Archbishop.

"You are such a scared little man when it comes to the church are you not McLeod?" says McDonald as he so much likes to ruffle McLeod's feathers.

"Now, now lads let us not bicker among ourselves we must stick together, and figure out how to make the Scottish Mission Church see our point of view," says Old Man Reid as he looks at them both with questioning eyes.

There was silence for a moment. "What do you think then lads if I alone ask the Archbishop and the Missionaries if they would reconsider their want of baptismal for the servants and slaves?"

"Well I am not sure how he would receive you Reid and I would really worry about you with him too," says McLeod with a weary look to him and his voice.

"Well I for one think it to be a wonderful idea and I am behind you all the way Reid," says McDonald as he grins while playing with his mustache.

The next day the Old Man Reid made the long and hot trip to the Scottish Mission Church in town. On the way, the Old Man was thinking of what and how to speak with the Archbishop once he got there. He was not looking forward to speaking with the Archbishop of Scotland. This weighted heavily on his mind, for he would be talking with a man of God. Either way it had to be done. He had to hear his side too, not just do as the church sees fit. The Old Man was also hoping that he could convince the Missionaries that this was a bad idea. As he approaches the church he starts to sweat a little and have dry mouth.

"Good day Your Eminence, and how are you feeling this fine hot day?" says the Old Man Reid.

"Just fine Mr. Reid and how may I help you today?" says His Eminence hoping to be able to help Old Man Reid.

"I was wondering if the matter could be reversed for this baptizing of servants and some slaves. It is not normal for a church to make such decisions and side with the Missionaries," says Old Man Reid trying not to sound angry with his voice.

"Well my Mr. Reid all I can say on the matter is that the church and the Missionaries have made their decision and I must abide by it and that is where I stand on this matter," says the Archbishop as he looks over at Old Man Reid.

And with that Old Man Reid departs and heads back to the plantation. As the Old Man makes the trip back home to tell the lads, he still cannot believe that the Archbishop sided with the Missionaries. He could not bring himself to even think that His Eminence would even consider such a proposal of this kind.

When he arrives home, McDonald is first to question. "Well what did His Eminence have to say about our refusal to this baptizing matter and how did he look when you mentioned it to him?" as he sided with Old Man Reid from the beginning.

"Well lads, it was like this, the Archbishop said to me that this was the decision of the church and the Missionaries and he could not and would not change it. So, lads I think we are stuck and have nay a choice in this at all," says Old Man Reid with heavy heart and not liking the words coming out of his mouth.

"Now you know this was a possibility that the church and Missionaries would win over and we would have to succumb to their decision and there it is we have no choice at all, so now where do we go from here?" says McLeod as he thinks of himself as a Christian man of sorts and has a better understanding of the church and its' laws. Something that Old Man Reid and Andrew McDonald would find out for themselves one day.

In the meantime, they still had to contend with the baptizing of servants and some slaves. This was very hard for the Old Man Reid to accept as he hates the idea that now, Louisa and her children could now have his surname all because his son John Jr., decided that he wanted children with his Concubine Louisa. So now the baptismal were taking place every second Sunday in the church. Also, the church wanted the baptized children to attend Sunday school. This was not a favourite pass time of Alfred's as he hated Sunday School and would rather be with the big boys playing marbles and eating rock candy. But Alfred had to be careful if he got caught by his grandfather Reid, he was sure to get a beating and tied up by his thumbs to the chair for hours. His sister Melvina would try and save him from the Old Man Reid, and when she couldn't she would tend to his cuts, bruises and sometime welts.

This baptizing matter had Old Man Reid more riled than he was before and when he drank it became worse and started to show in the way he would treat some of the servants and slaves. This scared some of the servants and slaves for they feared he would treat them like he did poor Alfred. When he got that way every slave and servant tried to stay out of his way. John saw his father acting strange because of the church decision to baptize the servants and some slaves.

But even so this would prove valuable later through the years that people could find their ancestors through the church records of their baptismal. In the long run, one could say that this idea of the church and Missionaries to have the servants and eventually all the slaves baptized in the Scottish Mission Church was a good idea. Yet the Freed men were not in favor of this baptizing matter the church was proposing, they were Freed men and did not want to be told who or what God to pray to. They to tried protesting but their words fell on deaf ears, and the church won out again. As the time went by the church continued baptizing and teaching Sunday school to the children on the plantations. The surrounding plantations had miss giving's about the baptizing matter, but they too did not get very far as the church stood firm and that was that.

It was hard for the three Scottish plantation owners as they though being Scottish themselves might have a bit of weight, but that was not the case here and so on the baptizing went and they were powerless to do anything against the Scottish Mission Church.

This was the making of Old Man Reid resenting the idea that he had no choice but to give his surname to John's children with Louisa McFadden, all four of them. He didn't mind to much for Melvina, but all the same he didn't want the boys to bear his surname at any cost.

Some of the other plantation owners were feeling the same after awhile and wished they had said something sooner too. This was a bit to late thought Old Man Reid, where were they when he needed them. Now they want to rally up the troops when it is too late to do anything of any kind.

The matter was closed and the church and the Missionaries were not budging from this matter at all. For now, they just had to sit back and let the church baptize their servants and slaves and the children for that was what mattered to the Church. The baptismal was valid as far to say that the reason everyone thought was this baptismal church law was passed because of less attendance at church. But it was because the church coffers were empty and this did not please the Archbishop in any way. He preferred his church coffers to be plentiful always no matter the circumstances. This was not known to the plantation owners till later and then it would be too late to retaliate at all. Now while the church recognized baptismal it did not recognize marriages of any nature between master, servants or slaves, so therefore they had Concubines. This was to be a sort of union and the church wanted these children especially to be baptized. For they knew of some of the slaves and servant's fathers of these Concubine's children, and they could easily find their fathers to give the children their surnames.

But it could prove to be hard to do at times, as some of the fathers moved on or left to go back home to Scotland or Ireland. Some Irish men stayed, but not too many and most of them left when the Scottish came and took with the British.

Louisa being a concubine was given certain privileges more than just a mere servant or slave, this made some of them very jealous towards her. Even so she and Granny would reap of these privileges and made sure that Louisa's children benefited too. Granny was one of the first to embrace the idea of the baptismal, she was a big believer that God truly exists. This was a dream come true for Granny, as she thought now her soul was going to Heaven and she was going to meet her Maker. She would sing hymns from the church that she would hear every week that she attended.

This not marrying of "Concubines" and "Masters" was a matter that Louisa did not like, and she tried to bring it up with John Jr., but it always fell on deaf ears. She would wait for the next opportune time, but sadly for her it never came again. The reason for this was that the church recognized the union between freed men and freed women, and this was not fair play in Louisa's eyes.

This meant that the church had its' own views of things as they perceived them. This was not what God intended. The Missionaries preach in church that all men and women and children are created equally.

This was her life and for the children and Granny she would accept it for now. Some of the servants and slaves accepted the baptizing of their children. They would even celebrate with a feast for those who were baptized. There would also be singing and dancing.

Since they had very little access to meat and poultry the men and boys went out fishing in their boats and brought back as much as they could. The women and girls would then prepare and cook all the food. The girls who wee not attending to the smaller children were helping by picking plantain and bananas. Digging up yams and preparing them for the celebration they were to have.

At times, the surrounding plantations would also join in the festivities and celebrate with each other. This made for more food and of course more rum for the men. It was a joyous time for some to be had. Some did not feel the need to celebrate as they saw this as a ploy that the plantation owners were concocting.

The celebrations at the Reid's plantation were the best by far. They had better plantain, yams and bananas and of course let us not forget rum. The slaves and servants in way of provisions were not left to starve. Some plantation owners only gave their servants and slaves the bare necessities.

It was a well-known fact around the plantations that the Reid plantation, was the best if you could be strong skinned and put up with the Old Man Reid. Some were brave enough, others were not enough to try.

The celebrations were something all the plantation servants and slaves looked forward to, even some owners. This one-night Old Man Reid is drinking as usual and smoking his cigar, listening to the celebration of another baptismal. This was like a slap in the face to him. The way his slaves and servants were celebrating, and they know full well that he was against it from the start.

The more the celebrating continued the more it became louder and this was making the Old Man Reid angrier by the minute. This made him drink more and when he couldn't take it anymore he decided that enough was enough. He got up from his chair and made his way to the door, and stumbled a bit down the hill to towards the servants' and slaves' quarters. There he saw how much fun they were having and then it hit him, these heathens did not even invite him. The Master of this plantation, the owner of all this and some of them too. He was not having any of this at all.

He looks around and bellows out, "YE HEATHEN KNOW THIS MY LAND, PLANTATION AND I OWN

ALL OF THIS. DO YOU UNDERSTAND AND YOU DON'T INVITE ME. AYE MAY YOU ALL BURN IN HELL!!!!"

Granny approaches him and says, "Well, well now Old Man Reid, I'm sure everyone on the darn island heard you. We here are not deaf, just praising the Lord and our loved ones that were baptized. Too bad you were not invited but, I see you're drunk and not thinking right." With that she turns and walks fast to the Big House. Looking for John Jr., she finds him with her daughter Louisa.

Granny says to John Jr., "Sorry to bother you sir, but your father is drunk and acting the fool again. Some of us are scared sir, not me personally, but the other slaves and servants are."

"Well first Granny, you can call me John Jr., okay and second, where is my daft father now?" says John Jr., with a bit of a smile on his lips.

"He be down near the slaves' and servants' quarters, and hollering about us not inviting him to the celebration," says Granny. She looks at her daughter for guidance with speaking to John Jr.

"I'm sure John Jr., will go fetch his father and everyone can relax again," says Louisa hoping to help the situation.

"Well that would be very kind of you and I truly appreciate it. Thank you, John Jr.," says Granny with hope in her voice. You see her fear was not only for the slaves and servants but, also for her grandson Alfred.

With this knowledge John Jr., headed to the quarters to see what kind of fuss his father was making now. As he starts to near the quarters he sees and hears his father bellowing again. He could also see the frightened slaves and servants not knowing how to accept this intrusion from their plantation owner.

John Jr., as politely as he can say, "father why are you harassing these poor slaves and servants, while they are celebrating the baptismal of their families and friend?"

"They did not invite me and so I say again, THIS IS MY LAND AND I OWN EVERYYTHING AND EVERYONE ON IT," bellowed out Old Man Reid.

"Father you must come with me now and let me take you home. We can have a celebration of our own," says his son hoping he listens and wants to leave the quarters and all that is going on there.

It was not easy at times to make the Old Man do what you wanted him to do. It seemed that John Jr. was the only one able to calm his father and reason with him. Especially when his father was drinking, which was quite often these days.

Old Man Reid hated the fact that Louisa and her heathen children were to have his surname, because John Jr., wanted to mate and lay down with her. His son was a grown man and he could not tell him how to live his life. He just hoped that one-day John Jr., would come to see the errors of his ways and come to his senses. Until then the Old Man would just try and cope with his sons' decision for now. The more the Old Man Reid protested the more Louisa and John would be together and not pay the Old Man any mind. This convenience for John Jr., was ideal in a way that he could escape his father's harsh words and relentless acquisitions of questions being hurled his way. This was especially true when the Old Man Reid was in his cups, oh how that Old Man loved his cups. He loved to drink his native whiskey and found a new love for rum.

Thank goodness, his mother was not here to witness the goings on of her only son, it would surely make her mad and hurt. However, as fate would have it that was not meant to be, for she passed away when John Jr., was a small boy of 12 years old. It was just him and his father for the longest time now and the Old Man did not want to lose him too. He tried to keep his feelings about his son and Louisa inside hoping as not to make John Jr., angry enough to want to leave the Old Man Reid alone to fend for himself.

John Jr., was his only heir to the plantation. Even though Louisa had John Jr.'s, children, the Old Man did not recognize them as his grandchildren. Louisa's children called their father, John sir, and their grandfather Master

Reid. Old Man Reid was very adamant about this and that's the way it stayed.

It was sad being a slave and a concubine even if it meant more privileges and better living arrangements. This was fine for Louisa as it meant that her children and Granny also benefitted from it all. The other servants who were not concubines, were of a jealous nature. Despite that Louisa still held her head high.

The Plantation

Old Man Reid ran his plantation with strictness. He would deprive his slaves and servants of their privileges, such as their infernal baptismal celebrations. He did this for he knew how much some of them loved these celebrations. If one messed up they all paid the price. This would affect some slaves and servants terribly. During baptismal time, everyone on the Reid plantation would be on their very best behavior.

The other plantation owners; Mr. McLeod and Mr. McDonald ran their plantations very different from Old Man Reid. McLeod ran his plantation sort of mild. He did not go for the whipping of his slaves or servants at all. He would rather punish them by depriving them of food for a few days. Giving them just water and bread like in a prison.

McDonald on the other hand ran his plantation with an "Iron Fist." For his punishment, he would put his misbehaving slaves or servants in a "Hot Box." This meant no food and no water for days at a time, depending on the offense committed.

Life on the plantations was hard for some, especially the slaves, for they were kept poor. The freed men and women, tried to influence the slaves and some of the servants to become free themselves. This would irritate the plantation owners something fierce. They tried as much as possible not to let them on their plantations as much as they could. This proved to be hard at times as the freed men and women would sometimes themselves, join the baptismal celebrations with the servants and slaves in their quarters.

This baptizing ritual the Scottish Mission Church did proved to be beneficial in regards to the plantation owners. It allowed them to keep track of the slaves and servants they had on their plantation at any given time. This would in time make it harder for the freed men to try and convert the slaves and some servants to become freed themselves. The plantation owners did not approve of this at all, but they soon relaxed when they realized that with the church record of the baptismal, it would be hard for slaves and servants to be recruited by the free men.

Old Man Reid found a redeeming quality about the whole baptizing idea. Because this meant that he still had some sort of control over his slaves and servants on his plantation. However, this would also help the slaves and servants to find their families later. It was a good day for all when the plantation owners all agreed to the baptismal and the keeping of church records.

As Alfred gets older he gets better at dodging the Old Man Reid when he would be stinking drunk. It was a game of chance at times when he eluded his grandfather, other times not so well. When he saw, his grandfather coming for him, he would run like the wind and hide as best as he could.

This was just the beginning of what was to come, they thought that everything was going quite well, and the plantations were prospering well. But this was only to last a while, for as we know all good things do come to sort of an end. The plantations were flourishing as well, the trading and selling posts were doing well too. So, everyone that traded or sold things or had a plantation were doing profitably well.

The freed men were not doing so bad but were not as prosperous as the plantation owners. They still had to struggle to make ends meet. Every day they wondered where the next meal would come from and how to keep a hut from falling apart around you. Remember that the freed men could trade and buy but, not sell. This is why most of the freed men would work on the ships and the docks for small wages. With these merger wages, they were still able to buy rum and other things too.

This was not too much of a concern for the plantation slaves and servants. Living on a plantation meant you had a home, food, and most of the time you did not have to worry how to fed yourself or your family as they were housed and feed regularly. Depending on the prosperity of the plantation some slaves and servants ate quite well, while others just had enough to eat. This was the case of the Reid plantation it was the most prosperous now and remained to be for a long while.

One day McLeod and McDonald receive telegrams saying that their darling wives are making the long voyage to Jamaica to be with their beloved husbands. They were to arrive in a fortnight on the next boat bound for the island of Jamaica and what it had to offer them and maybe help run the Big Houses so they can concentrate on other matters at hand. The two husbands sat in their big easy chairs as they read their telegrams. Both reading almost the same telegrams.

However, managing the Big House was not the only reason the two wives were making this long voyage. They had gotten word over in Scotland via the church, that the Scottish Mission Church was baptizing the slaves and especially children from the mating of concubines and Masters.

This was not a worry for Old Man Reid nor his son John Jr. For Old Man Reid was a widower and John Jr. had a fiancé named Lois, back in Scotland that was a fragile wee bit of a lass. She certainly could not make the voyage per the doctor's orders. This suited the Reid men just fine as they had enough to contend with and the bother of women folk was not a priority for them now. This left just the two husbands McLeod and McDonald, who were to have their better halves join them.

On the way to Jamaica poor Winifred McDonald got sea sick. She was a fragile wee bit of a woman, and grew up pretty much sheltered and waited on most of her life. Whereas Agnes McLeod, was raised on a sheep farm and often went fishing with her brothers. She was no stranger to the ways of the sea and all its' turbulence.

"Aye Winifred lass, you're looking a wee bit green, and a little feverish too," says Agnes with an air of concern.

"Well yes, I do feel a wee bit peaked, and cannot seem to hold any food down either," says poor Winifred still looking like a ghost.

"I say shall I go and fetch the ship's doctor, maybe he has some sea salts that can help with your sickness," says Agnes wondering if she should meddle in this.

"Oh, please do and thank you, I hope it is not an imposition for you as we hardly know each other," says Winifred as she silently hopes that Agnes will fetch the doctor.

"No problem at all, I shall return quite soon with a doctor, and he will make you better," says Agnes with a convincing voice as she could muster.

As she arrives with the doctor he looks over Winifred and examines her thoroughly and says, "Ladies what we have here is a severe case of sea sickness and we can cure it. It will take a few days but all will be fine after."

"Well doctor that is good news and I will see that she is taken care of," says Agnes as she looks over at Winifred.

"Oh, my Lord I hope this is not an imposition for you Agnes. I would hate for you to catch this and be sick as well," says poor Winifred as she starts to vomit all over herself. This was so embarrassing for her as she started to weep.

Agnes says to her, "Aye lass, stop your tears now and all will be well in a few days alright."

As the two women make the voyage to Jamaica they became friends of sorts. Now it was Aggie, not Agnes and Winnie not Winifred. After the bad case of sea sickness, they both witnessed, they had a better understanding of each other. Even though they came from different back grounds this did not make any difference to them. It would be a long voyage still and they made the best of it. Hoping that this country they were about to embark on was worth this sea sickness and the long voyage to get there.

McDonald got word that his wife Winnie, had taken ill and was being cared for by McLeod's wife Aggie. This worried McDonald for even with all his exterior gruffness, when it came to his beloved Winnie he was as soft as a lamb. Knowing that Aggie McLeod was there to help, made him rest a lot easier than he had before he got word that his beloved Winnie was okay.

They finally arrived and were not impressed at all. They were expecting a little more enthusiasm from their husbands, especially Agnes McLeod. When Winnie arrived, her husband Andrew McDonald, was happy to see that she was recovering very well from her bout with sea sickness. He owed a debt of thanks to Aggie McLeod and was not afraid to tell her.

"Aye Aggie lass, you are a grand lady to be caring for me little Winnie her, and she and I are so very grateful," says McDonald with happiness in his voice and water in his eyes.

"Aye yourself Andrew McLeod, I was doing this for my new friend of sorts, Winnie McDonald your wife. You know it was okay to help her, and she already thanked me a million times or more," says Aggie as she glances at her husband.

"Well Aggie love, I am glad to see that you both made it here safe and sound. What puzzles me is that you were not sick my dearest?" says McLeod.

"Aye you well ask my husband, it is because if you so remember I am used to the sea. Many a day's I went fishing with me dad and brothers. You see Angus my beloved, I am no stranger to the sea and this I relied on to help poor Winnie in her time of need," says Agnes McDonald with such pride in her voice.

So, they finally went to their perspective plantations. It was s shock for poor fragile Winnie, but not so much for Aggie as she grew up on a farm, so this was just a bigger sort of farm to conquer. She would thrive a little where as her new-found friend will not be able to cope with the pressure of running a Big House. She always had things done for her. Here she was doing the ordering and managing of things. With no help, she would turn to Agnes McDonald, and again ask her to help with these matters so she could cope. This would prove to her husband that she was not as fragile as he thought her to be.

Aggie and Winnie were settling in and making the best of what this new life had to offer and tried to see the pleasant side of all this. The plantations were flourishing, the Big Houses were all running to the best of their capacities, and everyone seemed to be happy and so it would remain for the time being.

Yet Old Man Reid still did not see the need for his fellow plantation owners to have their wives come here from Scotland and see what was up. He feared the wives would send word to Scotland and that John Jr's fiancé would find out about John and Louisa and the fact that she is his concubine.

Old Man Reid kept close watch over the two wives. He was especially worried about Agnes McLeod. She was a real Scottish lass and had no worries about it. She would surely tell all to whoever would listen. How she hated being there and that she was trying to fit in like her friend Aggie McLeod. On the other hand, there was weepy and fragile Winifred McDonald, who was very prone to being home sick as well as sea sick.

Old Man Reid did not like female tongue wagging of any kind. As far as he was concerned his business was his business and not for anyone else to be worried about. So, he kept these two families close in sight and made sure their wives were kept in check.

But as she considered Winnie a friend Aggie would try and make the transition for Winnie a little easier to bear. This made Angus McDonald's life easier to bear and ever so grateful to Agnes McLeod even if her husband was not happy about her arrival. At least Winnie and her husband appreciated the effort she would spend on helping poor lost Winnie cope, with being in a foreign land and learning the ways of said land and people.

The two women would bond over this arrangement and have each other to lean on. This would carry on for the rest of the time that these two women were to be in Jamaica, and stand by their beloved husbands and help them to succeed in this country. For this is where their husbands came to make fortunes and to return to Scotland, wealthier than when they left their homeland to pursue riches and wealth beyond their dreams. This would prove to be a challenge for all three plantation owners and the wives.

Yellow Fever

Not even the Scottish Mission Church or the Missionaries could have predicted what was about to happen. Everything was going on quite nicely for awhile, and everyone got a long and tried to live well with others. Then it happened, the disease that would be the worst one of the Twentieth Century. It was called the Yellow Fever. It would take the Caribbean Islands by storm and make everyone afraid of everyone.

It would be a great disaster and mayhem. Families losing family, people gone from everywhere and not coming back at all. It would be of tremendous pain and sorrow for all involved. Lives taken and lost people not knowing what to do. It would prove to be one of the worst tragedies known to mankind.

This Yellow Fever came about when the slave traders, bought over the African slaves to replace the now freed men. Unbeknownst to them the slaves and some crewmen were infected with the Yellow Fever.

It was a disease that took hold quickly causing fevers, loss of appetite, dizziness and headaches. In extreme cases this would cause jaundice, which would cause the skin to yellow which is where the disease got its name. It was a very deadly and dangerous disease.

With this sickness slowly becoming rampant, the ships and docks took precautions in making sure their vessels and docks were not contaminated. The ship yard bosses posted up signs throughout the town, stating the disinfecting of all vessels and docks in Jamaica. It read as follows:

> *"Such vessels that have brought over African slaves and produce such as cotton and bananas, woolen articles, whether personal or domestic use. Until such articles have been thoroughly cleansed and disinfected. By steam disinfecting apparatus if the vessel be provided with it. Or said articles be immersed in a solution of corrosive sublimate and water of two parts to a thousand from ten minutes to a half an hour."*

The inspecting physicians decided whether the effects of the crew and passengers were to be disinfected. All vessels were subject to be checked out and inspected before the crew could embark any cargo at all. This made for very low commodities and supplies. The trading and selling market was at a low and worry was on the agenda.

The plantation owners were starting to get worried about this disease coming to their homes and plantations and making their slaves and servants sick. They also worried for themselves, especially McDonald as his poor Winnie was a fragile lass, and surely not strong enough to make it through the disease. He truly worried and hoped to God she would be spared.

"Aye Reid, I am not sure about this disease coming our way," says McLeod as he looks over to him.

"Aye McLeod you may be right, but if it does come our way we must be prepared and hope for the best," says Old Man Reid as he smokes his cigar and drank his native whiskey.

"Well both daft it will not come this far to our side of the island, and then again the town signs say all vessels and docks to be disinfected," says McLeod with a tone of uncertainty in voice.

"You are all worrying for nothing and acting like little old ladies waiting for the worst," says John Jr. looking at them and shaking his head.

"What do you know of any such matters? You spend all of your time with that concubine so what do you know of anything," says Old Man Reid as he sizes his son at a glance.

"You may well say father, but at night I need a warm presence and my Louisa fits just right," says John Jr. with a boyish grin on his face.

"So you say my son, but the truth is you are not fully aware of what this disease they call the Yellow Fever may do us financially," says the Old Man as he takes a long drink of his whiskey, and looks around him and wonders if they know what is ahead of them and how it is going to change things.

For now, they would be aware and prepared for this death defying disease that was about to descend on them and their plantations.

Now they all thought how will we survive? "What will become of our Big Houses and plantations that they worked so hard to cultivate? These were questions that they wished they had answers to, but unfortunately they just had to wait and see what the future held for each of them. This weighed heavily on their minds as they would get together and try to strategist a plan of action before the disease hits.

It was making trading and selling harder. There was no importing or exporting of any kind till the physicians decided that the ships and docks were not infected and clean and free of the virus Yellow Fever. This would prove to be tedious cleansing and disinfecting of all the vessels and ports that were infected and or carried the virus.

The people were getting scared especially the freed men and women who had worked on some of the vessels and docks. They were worried that they would get sick or make others sick too. This was a scary time for these people, the slaves and servants were also afraid, some of the women who were not concubines mated with the freed men and worried if they encountered the deadly virus Yellow Fever. It would prove to be a powerful virus taking many lives with it before coming to an end. This was a very hard time for the plantation owners and their slaves and servants. Also, it would affect some of the white people too.

    This disease crept into the plantations of McLeod, McDonald and Reid, slowly but surely. It took over the slaves and servants especially the weak and elderly ones. The children too but not the ones under two years of age and still nursing, this for some reason saved them. As it was said the transporting of African slaves and bananas into Jamaica, was the main cause of the virus Yellow Fever.

    It was reported that the mosquitoes would infect the bananas as well as the African people. Therefore, bringing in the virus and making a home for the Yellow Fever. Once infected it took two to five days and then, there were different stages of the Yellow Fever and how it affected the Jamaican population. The living conditions of the slave and servant quarters were not of the utmost sanitary. Their quarters as they were referred to were made of mud and some brick and straw roofs. Some of the slaves and servants were known to have their kitchens outside the home as well as an outhouse. This way not the life for all servants and slaves. If you were a woman and lucky enough to be a Concubine," then you had a hut made mostly of brick and a tar like roof. This was the case for Louisa and her children and Granny. But even with all the better living arrangements and better housing, this disease did not care it just wanted to be. It would prove to be a dangerous and deadly disease.

This would be a hard disease to conquer and they were about to encounter, one of the most challenging times they have ever had to deal with.

This virus would prove to be the downfall of many plantations. Some would survive and others barely would make it through the terror of this disease. It was a trying and scary time for all in Jamaica. It did not matter if you were Scottish, Irish, or Jamaican, this disease did not care who or what you were, it just wanted to make you sick or kill you.

As time went by some of the plantations' slaves and servants would help each other out whenever they could. The disease was spreading and the plantation owners were getting very worried about the loss of slaves and servants. The disease took a hold of the adults quicker than the younger children, except for the babies who were still nursing as they had pure antibodies. The children most like to be infected were from the ages of five to fifteen years old. With these odds, it still was not enough to understand, how to defeat this disease and save many lives in the process.

This was to be a hard task to do, as they did not have a medical doctor to treat their slaves and servants.

The local medical doctors did not want or like to treat the slaves or servants on any plantation, and now this disease was rampant and many were dying at alarming any rate. With all this at hand and no importing or exporting of any kind, the plantation owners were getting very antsy and decided to have a meeting to try and figure out how to defeat this Yellow Fever once and for all.

They would call it a council meeting, and hoped that all the surrounding plantation owners would attend to give insight on the matter at hand. This was making Old Man Reid nervous mainly because, he had a suspicion that the council was about to appointment him as a mediator between them and the Archbishop. Now under other circumstances he would not flinch at the idea, but he already went up against the Archbishop and the Scottish Mission Church and their missionaries. He was not looking forward to this reunion with his Eminence in the very least.

So now he knew that McLeod could not have an audience with the Archbishop and conversant on a political or even practical level and get his point across. McLeod was a true Catholic and hard time trying to understand that the Archbishop was a Man not God.

As for McDonald, well, he was a bit of a hot head and this was not what the council needed right now. Why they would choose the Old Man Reid was beyond him, he hoped that someone else would rise up and say, "I will have audience with the Archbishop."

But no one stood up, they looked to Old Man Reid and voted unanimously for him. So now the Old Man is stuck and must speak with the Archbishop and swallow his pride. It would be days before the Old Man Reid could see the Archbishop and plead his case. This just made matters worse for the Old Man. He would brood, and get angrier by the minute waiting to have an audience with the Archbishop.

Finally, the Archbishop sends word to Old Man Reid and tells him that he accepts to see him and have an audience. This letter came just in time too, as the slaves and servants were getting sicker and sicker each day.

So, the Old Man Reid had another meeting, and told the council of what the Archbishop sent in a letter granting him an audience. This pleased the other plantation owners especially McLeod as he shall we say did not have much backbone, and McDonald for he would not do well at all.

Then the Old Man Reid decided that if he had to do this then let us get on with it. He told his son John Jr. that he was to be in charge until his father's return. The Old Man got his horse and carriage ready and left for the Scottish Mission Church to see his Eminence.

As he was making the trip there it would take two days and he kept thinking, that the last time he was going to meet His Eminence, was to ask him not to baptize the slaves and servants. Seeing as this matter is totally different maybe he would reconsider and help the plantation owners with their Yellow Fever problem. After all he thought are they not all God's children and need to be saved as they are Christians now? He was hoping in a strange way that the Archbishop might see things from his perspective. He was also hoping that not too many more slaves and servants would die before his return.

This was proving to be a long two days and it gave him time to think, and put together a proposal that even he the Archbishop could not ignore at any cost. This was proving to be a harder task than he had anticipated and oh so challenging in a way he was not familiar with and was struggling a bit with the idea.

The Archbishop on his end too was wondering, why would the Old Man Reid ask to have an audience with him again. Their first encounter did not go to well and this was disturbing for the Archbishop. Even so the Archbishop thought to himself, if this Old Man Reid can face me again after the last time, well deserves an audience with me. The Archbishop was also curious as to the nature of his request for this audience and why it is of direr need to be discussed.

The two days waiting on each side would not take long and the Archbishop and Old Man Reid, would prove each in their own way to have respect and politeness for each other as well. This would go a long way in negotiations that were about to be had. The Archbishop knew of the Old Man Reid's stubborn side and being a Scottish man himself the Archbishop had a notion of what he could expect and was ready for it. This audience was proving to be a challenge for both men concerned. How are they going to come to a conclusion, when the last time they met it was not a pleasant term. This time the Archbishop is hoping that this audience that he has said yes to, will end a good solution for everyone concerned.

In two days, these men will meet again and sit down and discuss a disease of gigantic measures that is killing people at a frightening rate. Hopefully the Archbishop and Old Man Reid can and will come to a compromising solution for all the plantation owners that are involved. It was also something the Archbishop was aware of too. He had heard from the Missionaries that the Yellow Fever has taken over plenty of slaves and servants and the plantation owners are getting very worried and some are scared.

Old Man Reid hoped that this audience would prove to be more fruitful than the last one he had about the baptizing of the slaves and servants. He was hoping this would not be brought up in conversation either. He was just hoping that this audience would be better than last time. As the day approaches, Old Man Reid is still asking himself why did he say yes.

"Aye good day your Eminence, and how are we this fine day? I have had very hot and humid trip over to see you, in hopes of discussing a matter that we both know needs desperately to be discussed and find a solution as quick as possible," says Old Man Reid with a hint of desperation in his voice.

"Good day to you to Mr. Reid, I hope this is to be a meeting of the minds, as I would like to think. I see you have a favor to ask of me, I certainly hope I can help this time," says the Archbishop as he sits in front of the Old Man Reid with only a desk between them.

"Well your Eminence it is a very big favor, and I too hope that your influence and church standing will get the job done," says Old Man Reid hoping the Archbishop and he will come to a conclusion suitable for everyone concerned.

"It's like this your Eminence, the Yellow Fever is killing off our slaves and servants, and we cannot get a town doctor to help them get better. So, the other plantation owners and myself, were wondering if that your Eminence might try and the veterinarian to help us. We had a meeting McLeod, McDonald and myself, and we decided that the veterinarian could come and cure our sick slaves and servants. We have tried to clean and disinfect the huts and the concubine make shift houses, but we still need medicine and bandages and a doctor, to monitor the disease itself," says the Old Man Reid, who sounds very desperate and scared.

"I have heard of this disease and its spreading to the plantations, we must all try and find a solution to this problem. It is hitting all the newly baptized members of the church too. Yes, you have my word Mr. Reid I shall telegraph my Superior and ask his guidance on this matter. I will get word of the results as soon as I can," says the Archbishop with hope and joy in his voice.

"That would be grand and oh so helpful we are running out of options. Let us hope that the veterinarian will want to help us heal our sick slaves and servants," says Old Man Reid as he starches at his beard.

"Aye from your lips to the Gods' ears Mr. Reid, I also know that you are here on the behalf of your fellow plantation owners. I cannot take the decision on my own you understand the church and the Archdioceses have the last word on these matters. Just as it was for the discussion to have the baptismal," says the Archbishop in his defense.

So, it was time to sit back and reflect on the conversation at hand over a glass of whiskey and a cigar. The Archbishop was hoping for a good discussion and promising outcome for all. Now that the Archbishop and

Old Man Reid had their discussion, it was time to go back and tell the other plantation owners that they all had to wait for the final word from the church itself. As the Archbishop explained to Old Man Reid, it was beyond his power to go against the church and the Archdiocese too.

Going back and trying to explain what transpired between himself and the Archbishop, was to be a challenge the Old Man did not see coming. For he believed that the other plantation owners thought he could work miracles, and make his Eminence see that these were desperate times and they needed the church's help. With this raging disease claiming too many lives and most of those lives were just baptized. He pondered at what he was to say to the council upon his return to his plantation.

He still had a half day's ride and hopefully he will have then thought of what he was going to say to his fellow plantation owners. It seemed like forever getting back to the Reid plantation and Big House. He was slowly regretting the fact that he was the one who had to have audience with his Eminence. He thought to himself, 'what did these men think that he was their salvation, their righteous conscious to speak on their behalf.' It was an undertaking he truly didn't relish. As a task of this serious matter to again befall him. Having to be the voice of reason for the other plantation owners. He could already in vision the conversation, that was about to be had and heard by the council upon his return. This did not in fact help him to decide how he was about to proceed, in his earnest efforts to convince the other plantation owners of the Archbishop and the Archdioceses, decision to help them with their pleas and convictions with the Yellow Fever.

"Aye Barder Reid, did you and his Eminence have a grand chat or a wee bit of a chat on our behalf?" asks McDonald who has the most to lose.

"Aye McDonald, I have and his Eminence says that it is up to the Archdiocese, and the church to decide on how to proceed with this proposal that I have discussed with Him in length," says Barder Reid as he slowly gives a look of disdain towards McDonald's direction.

"Well now I would say it was worth a definite try on Reid's part, and I would like to think that we are grateful he stood in your place and asked for audience with the Archbishop Himself," says McLeod who is so relieved that he did not have to go and face his Eminence. This went on until John Jr. Reid stood up and looked around at these men and said, "I have been listening to you all go back and forth over and over the same things. So now we have to wait and see if the church and the Archdioceses want to help us with this Yellow Fever problem."

"Aye that is all well and said for you young John, but do you really know about the plantation business, and are you prepared to help in any way," says McDonald with the most to lose and is desperate.

"Hold on there a minute McDonald, I do not like the tone you be taking with my son. As for his say in this matter it concerns his future and the taking over of the plantation," says Old Man Reid as he looks over at McDonald waiting for him to challenge his words.

"Now, now gents let us have a decent conversation and try to find a solution to this Yellow Fever epidemic that we are now facing," says McLeod hoping that they will listen to him for once.

"Aye you may be right because as it stands we are having a tough time finding a doctor of any kind to help us. The disease is killing more slaves and servants as the days go by," says the Old Man as he ponders what his colleague has said.

"So, for now let us put aside our petty differences and concentrate on how we can as a group of intelligence can find a solution to this devastating problem at hand," says McLeod as the voice of reason.

"Aye I am inclined to agree with McLeod here, but let us hope with that we can help each other and find a solution that will stop our slaves and servants from dying at an alarming rate," says McDonald trying to sound positive too.

As they deliberate into the parlor to have a drink of whiskey and par take of a cigar. They all wonder in their own heads if they can come up with a solution to the Yellow Fever problem, and how it will affect the other surrounding plantations as well. This mixed in with the waiting of the church and the Archbishop's decision on the matter of the Yellow Fever. It was becoming somewhat of an issue for the other surrounding plantation owners as well. But until the church and the Archbishop gave their final decision on the matter, everyone involved had to wait and wait.

This was not a strong suit of Old Man Reid, and his son John Jr. hoped that his father could just hold on and not explode, before they had a chance to hear out the church and Archbishop had to say on the matter. It would be a long wait and the plantation owners were becoming more and more agitated and impatient. Especially the Old Man Reid, this did not help him to be a nicer plantation owner, instead he became a tyrant of magnitude proportions.

This scared his son John Jr. and the slaves and servants that were still well enough to work. Everyone that believed in God prayed, and others just keep hoping and wishing for the church and Archbishop, to decide one way or another of how to proceed with the matter of obtaining a doctor of any caliber and hopefully one that will help heal the slaves and servants that are still able to be saved. It was a depressing time for all to be had and very scary time for those, not knowing what to expect from this disease called Yellow Fever and how it kills.

Now this was a grave concern for Agnes McLeod, as her husband did not want to engage in any or all subjects pertaining to the Yellow Fever epidemic. For the simple reason being that she as the Mistress of the Big House, she was losing servants as fast as her husband was losing slaves. This was a worry for both the McLeod's, and especially Angus McLeod as his plantation was not that big. With this being noted Agnes could not help wondering why the McDonald plantation was smaller in comparison and they lost more slaves and servants than the McLeod's themselves. Agnes decided that she would have Winifred McDonald over for "High Tea" with watercress sandwiches which Winifred likes.

She sent a servant to bring an invitation to the home of Agnes McLeod for "High Tea." This invitation got the curiosity of Winifred McDonald as she was wondering, why now after they have arrived for almost six months now? The High tea and watercress sandwiches is something they both acquired, while in England awaiting the ship that was to bring them to Jamaica, West Indies. So, Winifred decided that she would attend this afternoon tea party for two.

The trip to the McLeod plantation took about three hours to reach, it was a nice plantation and a beautiful Big

House. As Winifred starts to near the McLeod plantation she started to wonder why was Agnes having this High tea with just her, and not the other wives of the other plantation owners. As she reaches the front door she is greeted by the maid who takes her parasol and shawl as she motions her towards the parlor.

"Well hello dear Winifred, I am so glad that you have decided to accept my invite to High tea and watercress sandwiches. I do hope that my cook has made them to your liking," says Agnes as she starts to pour the tea and arrange the sandwiches on little plates.

"Well I must say that I was a little skeptical of your invitation, but then I remembered how you were by my side when I took ill coming over to this colony," says Winifred as she accepts the tea and sandwiches.

"Well hopefully after this High tea we can become better friends and maybe even close ones?" I know it has been awhile since our arrival and I am hopeful that we can achieve friendship," says Agnes as she tried to sound convincing and not ruthless.

"I hope we can be too Agnes after all we did have a time of it getting here from Scotland. It was a horrifying voyage to say the least. I was lucky enough, to have you to help me through the awful sea sickness that I had contracted coming to this Colony," says Winifred trying not to sound to suspicious and leery of her hostess.

The afternoon went along well as could be expected until Agnes could not contain herself anymore, she needed to know.

"Well how was the carriage ride over here and did you notice how the plantation is being kept, and my big beautiful home is almost in shambles," says Agnes with a little gloom in her voice.

"Well I was not really looking at the condition or state that your home or plantation are in, I merely came here to have High tea and enjoy your company again," says Winifred as she looks over at Agnes and tries to read her mind.

"Well if we knew what was said at the audience with Old Man Reid and the Archbishop, we would be able to understand more of what this Yellow Fever truly is and maybe be rid of it once and for all," says Agnes trying not to sound to conspicuous with her voice.

"I am sure that your husband has discussed the issue with you has he not? Most husbands and wives discuss matters that are serious, don't you agree?" asks Winifred as she continues to sip her tea.

"Aye Winnie, may I call you Winnie and you call me Aggie, our full names seem to formal for us, is that okay by you? Yes, Winnie you would think so but, the truth of the matter is that my husband the dear that he is, just thinks that all women are good for is keeping a house running. But

I think and know different and I was hoping you did too," says Aggie with hope in her voice trying to feel out Winnie.

"Well yes on calling me Winnie and why not, and as far as my beloved husband goes he too thinks that I am a fragile bird that needs to be treated with white gloves. He has no clue that I am stronger than anyone thinks. The voyage over been to this colony has made me a stronger woman for it. No I have not privileged to the discussion of the Archbishop and Old Man Reid as we call him," says Winnie showing her that she has a new-found confidence and she will use it if necessary.

"Aye my Winnie lass, I say bravo and do not let them take you down either, this Colony here has opened my eyes too. I see the slave and servant women toil right alongside the men in the fields and some in the mines and they do it with pride. I am amazed at their strong will to survive at any cost. You know we could learn a few things from them at surviving," says Aggie now almost convinced that Winnie is starting to understand what is at stake here for all the plantations concerned.

"Well this is true but do we really have to toil next to our men? Or do you mean become more involved in their affairs and not just keep house as they want?" asks Winnie trying to sound like she knows.

"Yes, Winnie and maybe we can find out on our own and see if we can do something in the mean time. Waiting for the Archbishop could take awhile," says Aggie as she tries to figure out if she is on board or not.

"Aye Aggie we must do something, the slaves and servants are dying almost every other day now it is serious," says Winnie now sounding a little frail again.

As the two women sit and sip tea and eat sandwiches they are wondering each in their own mind, what to do and how to do it without their husbands being mad. This was to be a problem for the women, it meant that they had to snoop around their husbands' study, and make sure they do not get caught.

In this endeavor of theirs' the women start to bond in a way, that was unfamiliar to either of them. They were also hoping that this new-found bond would help their cause.

As Winnie arrives home after her delightful afternoon of high teas with Aggie, her husband joins her in their parlor and sits down looking like he wants to chat with her. "So my sweet wife Winnie, how was the afternoon high tea and watercress sandwiches that you ladies had?" asks Andrew McDonald looking at his wife with curiosity in his eyes.

"Husband dearest, it was very delightful and Agnes is a very charming hostess I must say," replies Winnie hoping he won't continue with a barrage of questions.

Winnie my dear wife, I was just wondering if she is as brass as some people say that is all," says Andrew not wanting to upset his fragile wife.

"I am hoping that she invites me again, or maybe I can return the invitation and have her over here for high tea and watercress sandwiches," says Winnie hoping that her husband believes her.

He is always doubting her ability to think for herself, because he sees her a frail little bird. But boy is he wrong in all ways possible, because with her new-found friend Agnes McLeod she will become stronger and wiser of the ways of the world they know live in.

"Well I am sure she would enjoy an invite from you, it would be a lovely jester on your part my dear," says Andrew McDonald happy to see that his wife won't seem so lonely now after all.

'This was just the thing that Winnie needed,' thought Andrew, it would help him better concentrate on how to deal with the Yellow Fever dilemma that was plaguing the plantations, their slaves and some servants. It was believed that this disease could be transmitted too by clothing and blankets. This was to be a real concern for the slaves and servants as they exchanged blankets and clothing as hand me downs.

It was hard for the wives of the plantation owners as they had to have their servants healthy. So, for this to be possible they kept the servants and slaves that were not infected, in the mud shacks that they kept for supplies and things. This would prove to be a temporary fix to the Yellow Fever disease.

For the slaves that were infected, it would materialize as a rash then blistery pus like abrasions on the skin. Some of them even went into comas and never recovered. Others would seem like they were in remission then it would flare up again only this time more vengeful than the last.

This was becoming very hard and frustrating for slaves, servants and plantation owners as well. This disease attacked the blood, the veins and the motor skills. This would leave some of the infected with yellow looking eyes and blistering skin sores that were excruciating pain till they screamed with the agony that came with it.

The waiting for the church and Archbishop to ask or demand that a doctor of some sort, be sent to the plantations and help the poor infected slaves and servants before there were none left at all was taking forever.

Old Man Reid was wondering why the Archbishop was taking his time to come to a decision that could benefit everyone involved. It seemed to the council that this "audience" with the Archbishop and the church was a waste of their time, and that maybe Old Man Reid did not plead their case to his full potential qualities.

Yet this was just a theory that crossed the minds of the few plantation owners that made up the council. It would be a while yet before the church and Archbishop would come to an agreement of how to approach this Yellow Fever disease that was killing a lot of people especially their newly baptized Christians. This was something the church had to take into consideration because of how hard they pushed for the baptismal.

The plantation slaves and servants were dying at an almost alarming rate. This was proving to be a problem for the plantation owners as they were losing profits more and more as the days went by. They not hire the non-infected freed men and women to replace the dead slaves and servants, as the freed people did not want to come in contact with the plantation slaves and servants for fear of contacting this horrible disease.

It was with heavy heart that Granny was seeing her beloved friends and some family members being afflicted with this deadly disease. It was breaking her heart and she was getting sick and tired watching death claim it's victims on an almost daily basis. The badly infected slaves and servants were quarantined as best as possible, even the huts were disinfected and some clothes and blankets that were believed infected too. The slaves and servants that died were buried in the clothes and blankets they had on them at the time of their death.

Granny prayed every day and night to God asking Him to send a doctor, any doctor, to help her people with this death taking disease and making her heart cry. The church was God's House and his Archbishop and Missionaries should have some compassion, for the sick Christians that were baptized and made a bid deal about it. It would not change anything as far as Granny was concerned, she still believed that God was His Own Person and would help them through pray and faith.

"Louisa this is getting very serious now. You must ask John Jr. to help us if he can, maybe he can persuade his father to hurry up the decision to get a doctor here as soon and as fast as possible. Please Child," asks Granny with such urgency in her voice almost like she is pleading.

"Oh Granny, you know that I would ask John Jr., but he and his father are at odds now over my being his Concubine," says Louisa not looking at Granny to see the already hurt in her eyes.

"Well just ask him child maybe he will do it for you, and I will try and ask his father when I catch him in a good mood," says Granny knowing full well that catching Old Man Reid in a good mood there was a slim chance of that happening.

"Oh, okay Granny, I will try and ask John Jr. but I promise nothing he may want to then again he may not," says Louisa with an uncertainty in her voice.

"Well I have been praying that my grand babies, your children do not get infected. So far God has answered my prayers but, for how long can they stay non-infected to this death taking disease," says Granny as she studies her daughter's face for some sign of what she is really thinking of doing about asking John Jr.

This was to go on for a few more weeks till Granny is at her wits end. Again, she asks her daughter of when she intends to ask John Jr., about what his father's plans are in regard to the disease that is killing their family and friends, and the many graves that have been dug in the past few months that this disease has made possible.

It was heart breaking and gut wrenching to see these poor infected slaves and servants trying to stay healthy, but fighting a losing battle at best. It was a plague of mass proportions and made it hard to be able to tend to the sick and do their chores. Some of the not so sick slaves, and servants would at times must help with the weaker and sick ones which in turn could and would make some of them infected too.

What a vicious cycle for one nation to endure. To watch your family, friends and neighbors die. Not a living soul wanting or wishing to help, not even the church, who made them baptized Christians just to leave them to rot and die.

It would be something that was making Granny angrier and angrier every day, watching her people dying. Not even a doctor with their medicine to help even the slaves and servants that are not so badly infected by this horrible life-threatening disease. It was becoming harder to maintain a level of containing the sick from the not so sick as they were soon to find out. It had levels of remission only to come back again harder. It made the infected people look cured only to return again with a level of major symptoms.

This was a real concern for Granny and the plantation owners. How where they going to defeat this monster illness that has plagued, and taken countless lives to graves that were not foreseen. It was a very disturbing situation for everyone concerned; owners, slaves and servants alike.

It would prove to be the deadliest of diseases for that era and time. It was a disease that made the sick have black vomit, bleed internally, bleed from eyes, nose and ears and in some the internal organs would shutdown. This illness was taking everyone by storm and leaving almost no survivors in its reign of terror.

The more they died, the more Granny prayed and asked in His heavenly wisdom to help her sick and dying people to regain health and to stop the disease from spreading anymore. This was from Granny's lips to God's ears hopefully he is watching and listening to all that Granny has witnessed and prayed for.

It will still be awhile yet till anyone hears from the Scottish Mission Church and the Archbishop's decision on how to proceed with getting a doctor that would go and help the plantation slaves and servants who are afflicted and are in dire need of medical assistance. The days and weeks would drag on as they await the news and decision of the church and Archbishop. As they wait, the disease just keeps claiming poor lives that could and should be tended to with proper medicine by a proper doctor.

The Scottish Mission Church was surely dragging their heels with this decision they had to make. It was also because a few doctors that were learned in this field of medicine were not and would not want to help the plantation slaves and servants for fear of contacting this deadly disease and dying themselves. It was a coward's way of telling the church and Archbishop that they did not want to go at any cost to them whatsoever.

This infuriated the plantation owners. Some even went as far as sending letters of disdain for the church and Archbishop, on where they stand in helping the plantation owners and the Yellow Fever epidemic and how all parties involved were to handle this menacing matter.

It would still be awhile before the church or Archbishop came to an agreement with the medical doctors and even veterinarian doctors too, in the help to stop this deadly disease from spreading and claiming lives as it did. It was a very scary and unimaginable time to watch and hear your people in total agony.

The smell of dying bodies and decay was appalling and unstoppable without the aid of a doctor, even a Veterinarian. Even though it was a state of emergency it still was not enough to make the church and Archbishop hurry their decision of getting any medical aide whatsoever. The long wait was taking a toll on the sick slaves and servants, since there was a shortage of servants it was hard to keep up. It was proving to take longer at deciding on how to proceed with the doctor issue, then it took to decide on the baptismal of the slaves and servants. This infuriated Granny and the slaves and servants too.

The huts that they lived in were used for the very sick almost dying slaves and servants. The ones that were likely to make it or be saved were put in a make shift shanty. They found a shanty built with wood and tin roof proved to be a better way to keep the sick from spreading the Yellow Fever any further.

The huts that housed the very sick slaves and servants were made of mud and the roofs were made of a tar like substance and palm leaves. These homes were not suitable to ward off any serious type of disease, as they held on to all sorts of disease infected virus that would spread around.

As these huts or homes as they called them, could not be disinfected as they had mud floors and was not an easy task to give out. Now they had another perilous obstacle to face, it was a matter of burying the dead. The reason being that they had a superstition that if they buried the infected dead in the ground, it would stop the crops of any kind from growing ever again. Granny remembered hearing from the vendors in the town markets saying that in some countries that they burn their dead. It was a way to ensure that whatever they died from would not come back for the healthy people. So, Granny thought that she would ask the others what they thought about burning their loved ones. She herself thought this to be a solution to the problem, and a way to keep the deadly virus from spreading.

Granny knew the slaves and servants that came out of remission would and could infect even more of the people on the plantations. The servants and slaves that were not infected were kept apart, from the sick to the very sick slaves and servants.

So, she was pondering a thought in her head, to do or not to do? She had a potion or herbal remedy if you will, that can help most ailments that occur on the plantation. Granny has never had to use her herbal medicine in such quantity for the sick.

It was also taking a toll on poor Granny. She tried to help everyone that she could. She was especially worried for her grandchildren praying to God that they did not become infected or even worse die. The tending slaves, servants and Granny were trying their hardest, to keep everyone as comfortable as possible, and all the while praying to God for a miracle.

The Yellow Fever was not only at the McLeod, McDonald and Reid plantations; it also spread out to the surrounding plantations. This death defying disease also meant very little work was to be done in the fields and mines. The plantations and mines were not bringing in the profits as they should, as the disease was killing too many slaves and some servants. The servants that lived in the servant's quarters behind the Big House, were spared the horror of contacting the Yellow Fever but, they were left to do double the work to make up for the fact, that there was a shortage of slaves and servants from the slave quarters where some servants lived too.

The plantation owners could not even pay or trade with the freed men to come and work the mine. The plantation owners knew better than to ask the freed men to work the cotton fields as it was considered an insult to the freed man and woman. The plantations were suffering from lack of working them, and the mines where being neglected from not having any man power.

The town markets and merchants were also feeling the downfall of this horrible disease that has plagued the whole Colony and its' inhabitants. The yellow fever was having its' way with all that it came in contact with. Everyone was in a panic over this disease and at the rate people were dying because of it. The church and Archbishop needed to decide quickly, before it is too late and the dead body count will outweigh the living body count.

The Archbishop was having a hard time too if truth be told, the church was not in favor of persuading anyone to do things against their will or religious beliefs. This was proving to be a thorn in the Archbishop's side, and he was about to take matters into his own hands if the church did not come to a decision soon. The whole economy is unbalanced and in dire need of regaining the trading and selling of merchandise for the colony to once again flourish and prosper as it once was before the Yellow Fever epidemic.

The plantation owners were slowly losing patience with the church and the Archbishop. They were about to ask for another audience but, they were told that the Archbishop was gone away on business, to the High Church of England and would be returning in a fortnight.

This was not good news for the plantation owners but, all they could do for now was wait and see what the Archbishop will bring back as a decision to their disease problem. Could they get a doctor of any kind to help their sick slaves and servants, and stop this deadly virus from spreading any further?

"Aye I am wondering if the Archbishop has the official capacity to be able to persuade the High Church of England that we need a doctor to help our sick slaves and servant. They are dying to fast and too many at a time," says McDonald as he has the least of any of them in terms of slaves and servants.

"You do well to be concerned lad. These are trying times and we need to know where the Archbishop and his church stand on our problem. What they intend to do about it and when?" says Old Man Reid getting a little flustered as he voices his opinion.

"Aye lads let us not be hasty in our approach to the church and Archbishop they are trying to help us as best as they can," says McLeod trying not to sound like a man truly afraid to lose his place in heaven.

"We all know only too well that you are a firm believer in the church, and all its' beliefs so no we do not hold the m in the same regard as you do," says McDonald, as he looks over towards McLeod and stares at him with sadness in his eyes.

"Now now lads, this is not helping or getting us anywhere so let's agree on one thing, we need the church's' and Archbishop's help, if we have any chance at all of getting a doctor of sorts to come out here to our plantations and heal our sick," says Old Man Reid as he has the most to lose of any of them.

The other two men looked at each other then back at the Old Man, wondering what he was thinking. What plan did he have in mind as a solution to their problem that could work? They knew that Old Man Reid had more to lose than any of them, and that the Old Man was not about to let his plantation and mines fall apart because of some decision making by the church and Archbishop.

Mean while Granny and Louisa do their best to help take care of the sick slaves and servants. It is a blessing that Granny and Louis are not infected with the disease. It is for a reason Granny has concocted an herbal tea potion and it is helping in getting rid of the virus. But one must take it before as a precaution or in the first stages of the Yellow Fever symptoms. It was just a trial testing for Granny and she did not want too many people finding out about this tea potion of hers just yet. What if it did not work on everybody? It would be disappointing to everyone concerned and Granny would feel bad for a long time.

It was hard for her to keep this a secret knowing it might be able to heal some of the sick ones, and maybe prevent others from contacting the virus too. It also was hard for Louisa not to tell anyone, especially her beloved John. he later drops the Jr. But it was Granny that made the rules when it came to what was best for the slaves and servants living in her quarters as she says so many times.

"Louisa what am I to do child? This is getting so hard to bear and the dying around me is making my heart break," says Granny with tears in her aging brown eyes.

"Well Granny all I can say is that why not use your potion tea, and see if it can at least heal the sick. It would be some kind of start towards a new direction of healing the sick," says Louisa hoping her mother heard what she was trying to say.

"Louisa child have I not taught you anything? What if I was to do what you say right now and if it did not work, and few slaves and servants we have left up and died? The Old Man Reid would make an example with me right then and there for all to see," says Granny secretly wishing she could help all the sick people get better fast.

"And Louisa whatever you do please, please promise me you will not tell John about my potion tea and its healing powers okay child?" says Granny with a serious tone to her voice.

"Oh Granny, do not fear; I never tell John everything. Just what he needs to know and this he need not know alright now," says Louisa with a little smile on her lips.

Granny was happy for now with that answer so she did not pursue the matter any further. She was more worried about what to do in the meantime. Waiting for the Archbishop to return with a decision was proving to be life threatening as each day passed by. More bodies were being cremated by the dozens and it was making Granny angry and sick about the situation both at the same time.

Granny was Christian way before the church came to baptize the plantation slaves and servants. She was starting to question her faith a little. Was the God she always prayed to a kind and loving God? So why was He leaving such a decision of great importance in the hands of an Archbishop and church that does not care for the slaves and servants on the plantations. It was hard trying to keep the faith and hope without showing her own doubts and weakness towards the sick and dying people in her quarters.

Despite her current lack of faith Granny kept on praying and hoping that the Archbishop would return with great news and there would be no more sick or dying plantation slaves and servants by the disease known as the Yellow Fever. It was time for something or someone to help these poor people.

This was something that Granny was not comfortable with by a long shot, she knew that there was no way she could have a say in any of it. This was the new burial ritual from now on and everyone had to abide by it or else. It was hard for Granny to see how her people were being burnt, and not even a proper burial at that. The more they burnt the more Granny became infuriated, she would bite her tongue for fear of saying something and getting others in trouble.

This was not easy for Granny as she was a woman of spiteful character, and she was always ready to fight the good fight no matter the cause. This was a time that was hard for everyone involved to bear. It was hard to watch love ones die or become ill again, just so see them feeling better for awhile and be sick all over again.

There were piles of dead bodies piled up everywhere and they were all wrapped in the sheet or blanket they died in waiting to be burnt. This was a very horrifying look to the slave and servant quarters' and very scary for the children to witness too. The plantation owners were getting scared of the fact that their crops, and some mines were not being tended to as they should be. The surrounding plantation also had the same issue to cremate their dying slaves and servants. This could be seen from miles around when there was cremation happening, the sky lights up with the colors of the flames and the souls would ascend to Heaven.

Meanwhile John is wondering if Louisa and her children and God forbid poor Granny, should ever get the Yellow Fever what would he do. That night he decides that he will have a chat with Louisa, to ask her about what she plans to do if her children or Granny contact the virus? As John approaches the "Concubine huts" he slowly re-enacts the whole conversation in his head.

Louisa is there waiting as usual and now seeing the look on John's face, and wondering what he wants to say or ask her now. Louisa knew that look and knew what it meant or could mean, she was sure he had something on his mind and she was about to find out what it was.

Being John Jr. Reid's concubine was more than most of the slaves and servants had or knew, she was more than that she was his mate and she loved him with every fiber in her being. John also cared a lot for Louisa and in a strange way for the children and for Granny.

It was a hard knock life. Others either traded things, stole things or sold things and people. Some thought that being a slave or servant was a good life. While the freed men and women thought that being free and your own boss was the way to live. Two very different ways of thinking back then. How people think whether you are a slave or servant or a freed man. With this being the case for most it was still a scary time for all to be had. This Yellow Fever disease was a virus that took over the Jamaican people by a storm they did not see coming It was especially hard to contain in the slave and servant quarters on the plantations,

Although some plantations had their own form of doctor they called the healing doctor. These were not licensed doctors and were not recognized as such. They were more considered "Voodoo Doctors," Granny was one of these healing doctors as the slaves and servants of the Reid Plantation called her. These healing doctors had to keep their healing ways to themselves, for fear of being found out and being beaten or whipped! Granny and the other healing doctors kept their healing herbs and potions to themselves for now, especially Granny who could lose all the privileges her and the family have and make it harder for Louisa's relationship with John and her too.

John has now reached the concubine hut where he and Louisa share a home of sorts, he opens the door and as he steps inside to see her.

"Louisa my lass, there is something we must discuss and it is of grave importance," says John as he takes off his coat and boots.

"John whatever it is can it wait? I am a little tired tonight and need to rest. I have been helping Granny tend to the sick she is alone. No one to help but me," says Louisa hardly able to stand and help John remove his boots.

"I see that my sweet Louisa is tired but this is very important and needs to be addressed as soon as possible," says John with urgency in his voice.

"Oh alright then we can have a quick chat, I must say this is the first time you ever wanted to talk to me. I must say I am flattered to say the least," says Louisa with a puzzling look in her eyes.

"It is about the Yellow Fever here in the quarters and how are you not infected? How is that you and Granny help these poor sick people, and never get even a little hint of the virus or have any symptoms," says John with bewilderment in his voice.

"I guess it is all the good food Granny has been feeding me throughout the years and they have made me healthy. As for Granny, well, she ate the same food as us and we are healthy because of it," says Louisa hoping she sounded convincing enough for John.

"Well that may be the case but I think there is something more to this, and you are afraid to say anything at all," says John hoping she would give in and tell him.

"John I am sorry to say that all the rumors you heard about healing doctors is all false and please do not insult my mother with that please," says Louisa with a hint of doubt in her voice.

"Louisa my dear, that was never my intention to insult anyone and surely not Granny," says John trying to sound humble as he looks at Louisa.

"I hope you are not the type of man that listens to slaves and servants gossip and little stories," says Louisa looking at John trying to see a sign that he believes her.

"Well then that's me being told, I was wondering that is all not asking if was true or not?" says John feeling a little misunderstood and sad.

"I am sorry John for not trusting in you and believing your reasons for asking," says Louisa trying to smooth over the conversation.

"I understand Louisa my dearest, but you know that I would never bring any harm to you and Granny and the children not ever they mean too much to you," says John with sincerity in his voice and truth in eyes.

"I know that John, but still these kinds of rumors can get people hurt or worse killed," says Louisa with grave concern in her voice trying to sound not afraid.

This made for a long day and everyone was sick and tired, of watching everyone else become sick and die. This was grating on poor Granny's nerves and her health was taking a hard hit too. This was not what the God intended for the baptismal slaves and servants when they became Christians of the Church.

The conversation between John and Louisa got to the ears of Old Man Reid and he wanted to know exactly what was going on in the slave quarters on his plantation. He decided that as soon as he saw his son he would ask him about the later, they managed to keep some tongues from wagging and telling tales out of school.

The wait for the Archbishop and the church to decide on how to proceed with the doctor matter, and find one that will try and help the sick and healthy to stay healthy. The slaves were dying quickly and servants were not too far behind. The freed woman would work in the Big Houses, for wages and then go home and do their chores. Some freed men would work the cotton fields and some mines, only if they paid wages and if they were not to infected with Yellow fever.

This proved to be a very hard time for people to manage their lives and not think only of themselves. WE ARE ALL DYING!! The slaves and servants were saying to each other. So now everyone is still waiting for the answer, from the Archbishop and the Scottish Mission Church to make a decision quick as possible.

Meanwhile Granny and Louisa do their darnedest, to not get caught at healing the sick ones that they can. It was a risk they were willing to take; it was risky because anyone could say something and then it would be all over. With that in their minds at all times Louisa and Granny made sure they were not caught. There were times they came close to getting caught, but then they got out safe and sound.

They wanted to be able to help all the slaves and servants on all the plantations. But sadly, this was not meant to be and every man was for himself. They waited and waited for the verdict from the Scottish Mission Church decision. It was a decision that was taking a long time to be voted Yea or Nay. The plantation owners were getting angrier by the day and their patience was being worn thin. Also, this did not fare well either with the sick slaves and servants, they were all huddled in a few huts or shacks that were available to them. This meant that there was very little lodging for the ones that were not sick, and the housing situation was limited at best. This too was a factor of how easy the Yellow Fever virus could spread; they were living atop of each other like animals in a barn. That mixed with the fact that all the slaves also mixed and mated with the other surrounding plantation slaves as well. It was a contributing factor such as these that made it hard to cure the Yellow Fever virus themselves.

    The need for a doctor was great as they did not have the means or access, to any Antibiotics or other medicines that would cure this disease. Granny kept up her healing ways but was very careful to who and why she would help cure them if possible. It was such a dangerous way to help and heal the sick slaves and servants. Granny's biggest fear was that if the Old Man Reid ever found out, it would be the end to the privileges for her and Louisa and the children. She had to keep it a secret, and hope and pray that no one gets the idea to tell the Old Man Reid and have his wrath upon her. But that was not to be the case as the Old Man had a spy, who would bring clean sheets and blankets and other supplies as needed. This is how he knew that Louisa and his son had a conversation about Granny, but it was still undetermined what the conversation was pertaining to. This annoyed the Old Man and he wanted to know exactly what was going on his plantation with his sick slaves and servants. He sees John coming up the road taking the path towards the Big House, John pauses and looks up towards the sky and just stares for a second. He finally continues up the path and sees his father standing at a big bay window off the parlor veranda. John walks up to the door and enters in the foyer as he takes off his hat and coat for the butler to take, as the butler leaves with John's things, his father greets him with a puzzling look. Thinking to himself and wondering if his son is going to reveal all that he said or just what he wants his father to know. As John sees his father approach him, he sees that all too familiar look in his eyes.

John knows only too well what that looks means his father is about to try and pry, all information that his son can provide for him. This is not sitting to well with John, as he does not want the confrontation that is awaiting him. As a polite son, would do he joins his father in the parlor for a scotch and cigar, with the knowledge that he will soon be under his father's watchful eye. John tried to take this all-in stride but when dealing with his father, whom he respects most of the time and has had call to rebut and refuse his ideas on many a matter before.

"Aye John my lad I hear that you and that concubine of yours Louisa, have had a chat about the cure for the virus Yellow Fever?" asks the Old Man with a suspicious tone to his voice.

"Aye father that I have and it was a rumor and gossip not even worth talking about or even thinking of either," says John hoping his father will not press for more information.

"John that is not what I heard when the story was told to me, and I am sure you are not being forth right in your answers to me," says his father with a tinge of sadness to his voice.

"I am so sorry father that you were told such unfounded stories and lies. It is with true heart and mind that there was no talking of a cure or remedy that could cure this deadly disease," says John hoping to sound convincing enough so his father will not pursue this conversation any longer.

"Well I am sorry to hear that son; I was really hoping the Granny and the other elders may have come up with an herbal tea of some kind to heal the slaves and servants from this virus," says the Old Man hoping that his son is telling the truth.

Old Man Reid leaves the conversation as is for now; he will ask his son again about the disease matter later. But for now, he must see his spy and ask him or her what they heard and who said what. In the mean time John had to be careful when talking with Louisa, he knew that there were jealous slaves and servants that were very willing to say anything to discredit Louis and her family. Only this was not going to happen John would make damn sure, it was not going to be that way for any of them. He thought of them as his surrogate family and he was growing fonder of them as time went by. This would prove to be hard for John as he starts to make a civil friendship with some of the slaves. It would be hard when he loses Moses, his favorite of all and just a child at that he was about Alfred's age. When it starts to hit the children the slaves and servants start to worry and carry on with their wailing and crying all day and night. It was hard time for Granny having to cremate the children, as she helped bring most of them into the world. This would prove to be a trying and weary time for Granny, but not as heart wrenching as the experience she is about to encounter soon enough. It would still be some time before the decision is meet, and still more slaves and servants are dying. Until the plantation owners protest and demand that the Scottish Mission Church and the Archbishop come to an agreement very soon and to stop their dawdling over this issue. The slaves and servants are dying at alarming rates, and the economy is suffering too. It has gone on long enough it is for the plantation owners to act and demand that the church and Archbishop come to terms as soon as possible, lives are at stake and need help.

    The disease kept coming and the Archbishop and church still did not give an answer to their problem. It was clear to Granny that this was not going to be resolved anytime soon, and that she had to do something as quickly as possible. It was becoming very clear and necessary to start her healing potion. Her deciding factor was that her grandchildren were getting sick. It was because her family now was infected, and she did not care what wrath the Old Man Reid had in store for her. It could not be any worse that watching your own grandchildren die and not helping them when you know you can.

So, Granny's mind was made up, she would make more healing potion and cure her grandchildren. Louisa at this point was very frantic and could not stop from crying, worrying that she would lose all her children and be motherless.

Granny took her aside and told her about her plan to help Louisa's children. She was especially worried about Alfred as he had the disease worse than his siblings. So now Granny had to make sure no one saw her giving her healing potion to her grandchildren. If anyone did they would turn her in to the Old Man Reid for healing the sick. Granny's grandchildren were sick with the disease except for Melvina; she seemed to have the immune system like that of her mother and grandmother. But the three boys were not as lucky John the 3rd) he was named for his father and grandfather, and James for Jamaica and Alfred because it was a name Louisa always loved. The three boys had mild symptoms and Granny was afraid they would get worse. John the 3rd was not so bad and James was not so well himself and Alfred well he seemed to have it the worse. It was becoming a grave concern for Granny and

Louisa. They needed to talk and figure out what their plan of action was to be, it would have to be very secretive and very soon. This was a task that would be very hard to keep quite from the other slaves and servants, as some were jealous of Louisa being the "Concubine" of John Reid the plantation owner's son. As Granny thought more about she was convinced that she would take the risk, and the Old Man Reid could go to Hell and never come back. Granny went looking for Louisa tell her of her plan and how they were to proceed, and how they would try not to get caught ant any risk to them...

"Louisa, I have been searching all around the quarters for you where have you been? I need help with these children and they are getting sick too you know, and it is hard by myself. Melvina has to help to tend to the sick children, and she is a blessing with those poor sick babies," says Granny as she wipes her tired brow and attempts to sit on a poor saggy bed.

"Mama, you know I was trying to you to help, but John was asking all kinds of silly questions about your healing potion so he thinks. He was asking on the behalf of his father, that Old Man Reid is a pain in my side and butt. He makes me want to just whip him or hit him like he does to my son Alfred. That man is pure mean in my eyes and John knows as much, I told him so," says Louisa who is distraught and at her wits end with the children getting sick.

"Well that is well and good child, but if John gets wind of anything, do not for a minute think that he won't tell his father. Remember blood is thicker than water and always will be. Yes, you share children with John, but Old Man Reid is his blood not your children with him. Those children will never be recognized as his blood in this life or any other life either," says Granny as she continues to wipe her brow with sweat, and looks sadly at her daughter.

"Oh Mama, I know that it is true he does not see us as a family, but in my heart, I yearn and hope he will someday. And until then well I guess this is my life for now and we all can benefit from it okay my dear sweet Granny," says Louisa as she sits by her mother and stares far off as if she is thinking of other things.

'Well Louisa, if this is alright by you then it is alright by me too, but remember my daughter that this will never be the big love and romance you desire from him," says Granny as she looks at her daughter with sorrow in her heart for her.

"Granny, Granny come quick! There seems to be something wrong with my brothers, they are not feeling too well right now and they are vomiting like crazy," says Melvina with tears streaming down her cheeks.

"My child what is wrong now and why are you crying so much?" asks Granny getting nervous now.

"It is my brothers Granny, John and James have a very high fever and Alfred is vomiting, it looks like blood, but I am not too sure. It is hard for me to tell what is happening with my brothers," says poor Melvina with tears still streaming down her cheeks.

Now child, it is not your fault this is happening to our people, it is because someone caught a virus and brought it here to Jamaica and now we must fight it okay," says Granny now that she sees it is all up to her and Louisa to heal these poor sick people of theirs.

"I see now Mama that \I must help you and never mind John and his father for now. Just tell me what to do that my children are ill, I need to be there for them and not worry about John so much," says Louisa as she is sensing that she will need all her wits about her, to fight this horrible plaguing disease called Yellow Fever.

"Well we can start by seeing what and how we can heal your sons, and then maybe we can heal the others. But Louisa, Melvina you must promise me that this stays between us okay, no one in the quarters must know we cannot trust anyone at all. For there are jealous people here in the quarters so be careful," says a tired Granny.

"We understand and hear you loud and clear Granny, but it will be sort of hard, as some of the slaves and servants are helping us with the tending of the sick," says Louisa as she looks at her mother with questioning eyes.

"I know that too, but this is why I am so worried that you or Melvina might get caught and then you both would get in trouble or worse beaten," says Granny as she is still not very sure.

"Granny I am not afraid or even a bit worried about getting caught, if I do well then that is a chance I am will to take and not regret either," says Melvina as she stands straight and tall to show her courage.

"Now child that is all well and good but we must consider the outcome of all this, and what we are willing to sacrifice and who will be hurt by our plans of actions," says Granny trying to figure out if the three of them could pull it off.

"Whatever needs doing I am in no matter the risk or the beatings. I want to help heal my brothers and maybe others while I can," says brave little Melvina.

"We are so grateful already that you want to do this Melvina, but I could not in good conscience ask you to risk your precious young life for this. But keep tending and help as you are doing that will help enough for us you will see," says Granny as she looks lovingly at her granddaughter, with a big smile of kindness.

"Yes Melvina, I agree with Granny you should continue as you are doing now, and leave the rest to us and we will make sure your brothers get better and others too if we can," says her mother Louisa as she looks proudly at her daughter her first born.

The women decided that Melvina would only help with the children, and to leave the risk taking to Granny and her mother. The women started to collect and find any herbs that could help make the potion, which will heal their family first and then maybe others too. It was a labor of love to find and mix and hope and pray that this healing potion would be their answer to the long-awaited decision of the church and Archbishop. The way it was going it was taking too long for the Clergy to act on their behalf. It would take a miracle for this potion to work, Granny was known for her potion and healing herbs but this was totally different than any healing potion she ever made. She hoped and prayed it would heal all the sick and especially her grandchildren. But it was still strange to her that Melvina, Louisa and herself where not getting sick. Then it became crystal clear to her it was because she once made them a healing potion from goat's milk, and ever since then they have been very healthy. Therefore, also the reason that the babies are immune to a certain age from this disease it was the goat milk they drank. Yes, that was it a secret blending of herbs and goats' milk, her African healing powers were going to be put to use, and yes it was going to be a healing cure for everyone.

This was a cure Granny's great African grandmother used to heal all ailments back in Africa. She was afraid of using this for fear that she would be punished or even beaten for "doctoring" as they called it. This was an African healing potion that had many healing properties and was known to work every time. This Yellow Fever was spreading now like wild fire and every slave, servant and even plantation owners were getting fearful that they would have it too. This was becoming a very fearful and hard to bear disease, but everyone that showed mild to moderate symptoms could be saved by Granny's goat healing potion. Granny kept asking God for a sign to know if she should take a risk, and makes her healing potion even if it meant she r could be punished. But when the sign came it was in the form of Alfred getting very sick with the Yellow Fever. He was not getting any better and this worried his mother as well as Granny. So now she had her sign and her decision was made, she was making that goat potion and be damned with the consequences. This was going to be a sure-fire healing potion.

"Granny please help me I am so sick, and I cannot play with my friends and go rock candy hunting with my sister," says Alfred as he lays there with sweat pouring down his brow and face."

"There is help on the way and hopefully it will make you better and everyone else too. But we must keep it a secret for no one must find out. It is very important you understand, okay Alfred?" says Granny hoping that Alfred understood her.

"Yes Granny I understand and will tell no one not even Melvina and she knows all my secrets."

"Well then, I will go and fetch your sister Melvina and ask her if she will sit with you for a while. Is that alright with you Alfred?" says Granny. As she is anxious to start on the healing potion as quick as possible.

"That would be great Granny. She is a great big sister and I love her to bits. She is also my best friend and she finds the best sugar to make rock candy," says Alfred as his voice is starting to become shallow.

"Okay then it is settled, I will fetch Melvina and you will rest until she gets here, so that is what I want you to do and I will go and make the wonderful healing potion," says Granny as she hurries out to start on her healing potion. She finds Melvina and asks her if she will stay with her brother.

"Oh Granny for sure I will sit with Alfred he and I have the most fun of all. It is not like when I take care of the other two brothers, John 3rd and James they are little devils and very mean to Alfred. I would be very happy to sit with Alfred," says Melvina as she is happy that Granny did not ask her to sit with the little devils.

"Well thank you Melvina this will make my task a lot easier and not so worrisome." Granny thanks God for giving her a very kind and thoughtful granddaughter.

So now Granny sets about to make her African healing potion that will cure her grand babies and maybe some others as well. These slaves and servants she has lived with all their lives some she even midwife for. This was a labor of love for her family and the plantation family she has come to know and love. This was her home her family. Her husband was buried on this land and she raised her daughter on this land.

It was up to her to heal these people as she had received a sign from God Himself. She was not about to defy God and all his Angels and Saints. She knew in heart what was to be done and she had to move fast. For Alfred was not getting any better and she could not lose him. The other two brothers were not as sick as Alfred and made a good recovery. As Melvina call them "the little devils", this may be why they healed faster than Alfred or maybe they did not have the virus in them so bad.

Granny now has her ingredients to make the healing potion but she needs her daughter Louisa to help her and assist in giving the potion. She sees Louisa and calls out to her to come and see her mother and help her with her task at hand.

"Yes Mama what can I help you with and what have you decided to do about the African healing potion of yours?" asks Louisa as she looks inquiringly at her mother.

"Louisa it is like this, God gave me a sign and I am going to do it. I am going to make the potion and hopefully it will cure all our people," says Granny with happiness in her voice and reassurance in her eyes.

"Well then mama what are we waiting for let's get to it and soon as possible. Lots of lives are depending on this healing potion especially my dear sweet Alfred," says Louisa as she desperately looks at her mother hoping she saw her desperation.

"No worries my child, I will make this potion and it will make Alfred and many more better. We must try and keep it a secret for it could come back and hurt us terribly. I do not want to think of how this could end if word got out," says Granny as she hopes no one finds out and her plan stays safe long enough to help.

"I understand your worries but this is my child, my first-born son he must live despite the way the Old Man Reid treats him. He is our blood and we need him with us forever. I will not give up faith on my son not now not ever," says Louisa as she starts to cry uncontrollable.

"Please my dear daughter I won't let any of your children die and especially not our Alfred. He has suffered the most of all of them," says Granny.

It was settled, the healing potion was to be made and the sooner the better. She ran to the parts of the fields and woods were she always knew that one day she would need these herbs one day. She had ever confidence that this African healing potion would work, the only obstacle was getting goat's milk. She was sure that some of the servants had access to the goats but, which ones could be trusted and which one to ask? Then it came to Granny she would ask the young servant boy named Moses, who just so happens to like Melvina a lot. Could he be trusted she thought to herself, and if so, will he do it? So many questions and no answers. This was a real task, but it had to be done to many people were dying. It was making Granny very sick and mad to see how her people and family were being treated. She went off to find Moses and hoped to God that he would help get the goat's milk and save some lives as well. It did not take too long for Moses was never too far from Melvina. Moses is a light coffee colour and has a skinny physique, but he just loves Melvina and does almost whatever she wants. Granny knowing this goes to Melvina hoping that she will ask the young Moses for his help, and bravery too.

"Melvina dear, I hate to ask this of you but do you think that young Moses can be trusted, and would he help us get the goat's milk?" ask Granny as she looks at her with desperation in her eyes.

"Why Granny do you ask this of me now, I am taking care of Alfred as you asked me too," says Melvina with a questioning tone to her voice.

'Remember that secret healing potion I told you about well it needs goat's milk to be added to it, with the milk and herbs mixed together just right it makes a wonderful healing potion," says Granny with her heritage pride in her voice.

"Well then Granny if it will heal my brothers especially Alfred and others, then stay with Alfred and I will fetch Mosses and tell him we need goat's milk. It should not be so hard to find him he is always nearby me. Says Melvina with a little smile on her lips.

"Alright then child but be quick please, lives are depending on this healing potion and we need to make some fast if we want to save lives," says Granny trying to sound confident and cool.

"Well give a bit of time please I will be as fast as I can, and we will return with the goat's milk I promise," says Melvina as she turns and hurries out the hut to find Moses and ask him for his help. She runs to find Mosses and hoping she will find him, in time for the healing potion to be made and given to everyone that is sick.

"Oh Moses I am so happy to find you. I really need your help and you must not ask any questions please on our friendship," says Melvina. Hoping that he won't ask too many questions she cannot answer or want to answer either. He looks at her before he answers, because she has never asked him for anything so why now? As he is about to speak he asks himself should he help or not it was hard.

"Well Melvina you were looking for me, and what do you want with me and why? says Moses as he looks at her with questioning eyes.

"I need a real big favor. You see, being a servant's child as you, could you please, please get me some goat's milk? But you know what would be even better a goat so we can have our own milk," says Melvina trying to turn on the charm and hoping it will work, on the servant's young son Moses.

"Why do you need goat's milk for a healing potion that may or may not work? Why should I help you, for you never really talk to me to much now do you?" says Moses thinking he has the control over the conversation.

"Well this is a matter of life and death and it also is about Alfred. He is very sick and this is the only healing potion that will cure him and others too. Can you help us or not? Please do not waste my time with foolishness right now. We can talk of other things later, right now it is about saving my brothers and others too," says Melvina with such urgency in her voice, that Moses stops making light of the situation.

"Alright then Melvina I will do this favor for you and Granny and my little friend Alfred. For you see Alfred is one of the best marble players and I have yet to beat him," says Moses knowing what is asked of him is a little bit dangerous.

With the Yellow Fever, almost everywhere it was hard for everything to be accounted for and logged. But still he felt it was his duty to help and he wanted to be in the good graces of Melvina Reid, and he was going to do his best to help.

He had to wait until night fall and hoped that no one was around to see him steal a goat. The easy part was finding the goat; the hard part was taking the goat to the slave and servant quarters. He was lucky, for he found a sheet the same kind as they cremated the dead in. So, he wrapped the goat in the sheet and carried it down to the quarters. There he was meet by Granny and Melvina. She was very happy that he came through for her this was a good deed in his favor.

Now Granny could make all the healing potion she wanted. But there was something else she had to consider. Where was, she going to hide the goat and how to keep a secret from the others? It was going to hard be to hide a goat but Granny knew of a place and the goat would like it too.

Granny said a silent prayer to God in giving thanks for his help in her hour of need. And how this will help her to cure these poor sick people and her family. The fact that she could be caught was still a risk factor. Was she prepared for the outcome of all this? Yes, she was and the more she asked herself that question, the more she fell it is the right thing to do. As she kept thanking God she went about to make the potion.

It was a kind thing that Moses did and he never gave away the secret. His parents, Henry and Pearl were house servants. Pearl worked in the kitchen and Henry worked the sugar fields and sometimes the bauxite mines. Since Pearl worked in the Big House kitchen she had access to the barn animals. This is why Moses could get a goat for the milk to make the healing potion that Granny needed.

He hopes this will put him in good standing with Melvina and Granny too. He also hopes that his mother does not notice that there is one goat missing, or that she finds out it is Moses who stole it from the Big House barn. He was so afraid that this would happen that he made himself scarce from his mother's watchful eye.

In the mean time Granny went about making her famous healing potion with goat's milk. She had Louisa and some other trustworthy slaves help her find and pick the wild herbs and roots that were needed. All the while Granny was mixing this potion of hers, she was praying to

God that this healing remedy of hers will work and help make the sick slaves and servants better. Granny knew in her heart that only time and praying will help, so she waited and prayed fiercely all the while keeping her faith in God.

Alfred was getting more feverish and this scared his mother Louisa and sister Melvina. Granny was finally ready to try her healing potion, so she gave some to Alfred to see his reaction to it.

In all the fray of getting a goat and making a healing potion, Granny was not aware that Old Man Reid had got wind of what was happening in the quarters and was about to investigate for himself. The Old Man told his son John of his wanting to investigate the quarters and why. John knew better. His father wanted to see if Alfred was as sick as everyone says he is. John warns Granny and Louisa, about his father's plan to come and see for himself the degree of sickness that has the quarters almost quarantined. This was not something he envisioned at all and now that he saw with his own eyes he was getting worried now.

"Well John, I went to the quarters today and saw for myself the degree of sickness that has some of the quarters quarantined. This was not at all what I was expecting and it is going to ruin my plantation. But now your bastard child is sick too, he will not make it from what I have seen. I had a coffin fitted for him and the sooner the better, so we can bury him with the others," says Old Man Reid with no remorse of any kind of feeling at all.

"Father I would say you are a cynical man and have no regrets at all for your actions of having a coffin fit for Alfred. And I find this appalling behavior even for a man of your high standing." says John as he looks at his father with disgust in his eyes.

"Well my lad, I would not expect you would understand as you are in adornment of Louisa and therefore cannot be objective to this whole ordeal at hand," says the Old Man Reid with a look of disdain in his eyes as he waits for his son to answer him.

"Father, I understand that a young boy lays in a cot fighting for his life and you want to bury him like right now. Even for you father that is the meanest side of you I have ever witnessed and it is ugly and scary. I do not care to be around right now and so I take my leave and depart from your house for awhile, and then maybe you will come to your senses hopefully?" says John as he turns to leave the room and start his packing. All the while hoping his father will see reason.

"And where do you think you can go and live my son, and who will take you in?" says his father as he studies his son's face for an answer to his question.

"Father as you know I have had a lovely little house built for Louisa and I and her family. But we had to put

Alfred in the sick hut with the other sick ones, and so there is more room now for the rest of us," says John with an air of cockiness in his voice.

"Well fine as that maybe it will not last forever, and we all know that she is just a concubine that bore you children. It is no big mystery of any kind to me," says Old Man Reid as he looks dead straight at his son John to see his reaction.

"Well I am so sorry father that you feel this way but my mind is made up, and as for the coffin making for Alfred, I find it appalling even by your standards," says John with hurt and shame in his voice and feeling sorry for his father also.

"Well then my son, if you feel this strongly about my actions then maybe you should leave, and find your own fortune. It is about time now do you not think so?" says Old Man Reid hoping that his son will change his mind and stay with him.

"Oh father you cannot see the big picture can you, it is not just about Louisa and I. It is also about her family that she loves and cherishes so very much. You see, this is why you and I are at odds over this Louisa and I union. You could never understand the unity of family and how it can keep a family together forever," says John with a sentiment in his voice that his father has never heard before from him.

"Well my dear son John, since you feel that way about the situation then who am I to stand in your way? Go and follow your dreams my son, but always remember that you have a home with me forever," says his father with sadness in his voice.

"I thank you father and hope that all will turn out well for Louisa and I. That we find a cure for the sick slaves and servants so we can continue working our sugar fields and bauxite mines," says his son as he walks towards the door with suitcase in hand. He takes a long look around the foyer and then he turns, looks at his father as he turns the door handle to leave the Big House for his little one.

As John makes his way to the little house he shares with Louisa and family, he is hoping that this will not ruin his relationship with his father. It has only been the two of them since his mother died when John was a small boy. It was hard for John to leave his father just like that. But his father crossed the line when he had a coffin made for sick Alfred, and this made Louisa and Granny furious to no end.

So now John had to go and smooth over what his father had done. John was also aware that Granny with her African background knew "Voodoo." It was an African ritual that has been passed down through the ages. But John was sure that Granny would not put a spell on his father, and if she did it would not be lethal.

Louisa told John he had nothing to fear as Granny was too busy to even worry about the Old Man Reid at this point. She was too busy making her healing goat milk potion and did not want the extra attention, making a fuss about the coffin for Alfred would bring.

For now, Old Man Reid was safe and John could breathe little more easily. But little did anyone know that the said "coffin" was to be a bad thing turned into a good thing. It was to be the greatest good thing to ever happen to Louisa and Granny's family.

But for now, Granny had to concentrate on her healing portion to help all her sick slaves and servants. But most of all to help cure her grandchildren and her beloved Alfred. This was a labor of love for Granny and with each stir of the big copper pot she prayed and asked God and all the angels in heaven to help make the best healing potion that she has ever made in her life time.

She needed this potion to work its magic and heal these people of hers. It was so frustrating waiting and wondering if this is the cure they all have been waiting for. Since there was still no news from the Archbishop or the church, what other choice did they have? So now it was up to Granny and Louisa to take matters into their own hands and make the healing cure for all the people in their quarters. They both know it is a big risk they are taking, but it will be so worth it if they can save a few lives. The more they thought about it, the more they were convinced, that no matter the consequences they were prepared to face them head on.

With that in mind once and for all they set about making this wonderful potion. Hopeful that will make the sick slaves, servants and her grandchildren much better and well.

The goat that Moses procured was a great find. This goat was just the perfect kind to give its milk for such a worthy cause. Granny was so thankful that she falls to her knees and thanks God multiple times over and over again. This was to be a test of human strength and kindness and the want to help others live.

Granny and Louisa had their work cut out for them. They had to make sure everyone that was sick, did not tell how they managed to get better. It was a chance Louisa and Granny were willing to take to make sure no more people were getting sick or dying. As the days and nights wore on it was a miracle they would pray for, and hoped God and all the Angels in Heaven hear their prayers and help them to achieve their goal of saving their family and friends.

As fate, would have it, Alfred becomes worse with a bad fever. So now Granny was forced to put her worries aside and give poor ailing Alfred the goat healing potion. She went about making the potion and Alfred was the first to try it. Alfred was so sick with fever he did not even know what was being given to him, but he took it anyway and he seemed quite fine about the whole ordeal.

It was a very touch and go process waiting for the potion to do its magic and heal Alfred. For this would be the only way Granny could judge if it worked or not. She did this to see if God heard her and was about to answer her prayers. Yes, this was a risky part on Granny's side, but she was desperate and needed to take a big risk for all concerned. It was settled Alfred would be the first, and then they waited for the results of the healing potion.

During this waiting process the Old Man Reid went on one of his drinking binges again. This time the Old Man want to see if Alfred was as near death as everyone claimed he was. He made his way down to the quarters but being very careful as not to be near the "sick huts" as they were called.

The Old Man was very fearful of getting the Yellow Fever himself. He took every precaution he could think of, as the white doctors would not want to administer healing for fear that they might encounter the virus. He made himself a mask of sorts, from some old tattered cloth made of strong cotton that he tied around his mouth with a shoestring. This he hoped would be enough to ward off the virus and keep him from getting sick too.

Yet he was still a mean drunk of a man who still wanted to abuse and torture a sick child. This he made very clear as he bellowed throughout the quarters. It was hard to make out his slurred words with his new-found mask on. But this was to be a new-found factor to the whole Yellow Fever ordeal. It would come about as a fluke idea but a "blessing of faith" further down the road. Granny would believe it to be another sign from God and all his angels in heaven hearing her and Louisa's prayers. But it would still be awhile for them to come to that conclusion as it was a sign that came from Old Man Reid and they were skeptic at best concerning him altogether.

The Old Man Reid bellowed his way through the quarters yelling, "WHERE IS THAT SO CALLLED SICK BLACK SAMBO? WHY IS HE NOT DEAD YET? HOW LONG WILL IT TAKE TO BURY HIS LITTLE BLACK SAMBO ASS?"

This made Granny so damn mad that she almost bellowed back but instead she kept her calm and said, "Listen Old Man, I know you want to see this child dead, but you see I pray to God and he listens and he will not let any children die anymore," says Granny. Trying very hard not to lose her composure with this drunken infuriating old specimen of a man that was himself lost, confused, and scared. She felt pity for him and almost understood his pain.

It was scary for Alfred to hear his so-called grandfather as he felt for sure that he was coming to finish him off. But as always when she could Melvina stopped the Old Man Reid in his tracks, and hoped he would be in a better mood with her. She was hoping he would leave Alfred alone and let him heal in peace and comfort.

"Well, well Melvina so you are the one taking care of the sick black Sambo? Why is he still breathing and not dead yet?" asks the drunken Old Man Reid as he looks to Melvina, and then towards Alfred laying there covered in sweat.

"Well it is because we have been praying for him to get better and now it is up to God and all his Angels in Heaven," says Melvina. With a heavy heart and tears falling down her face as she looks fondly at her brother hoping the Angels and God hear her prayers and those of Granny and her mother Louisa too.

"Lass that should be enough you would think but I do not believe that God will save a Sambo like your brother Alfred," says Old Man Reid using Alfred's name for the first time. It was strange sounding even to the Old Man Reid.

"Say what you will, I believe God and the angels in heaven will save my brother Alfred, and all the other slaves and servants that are sick. You see the power of pray is just that powerful," says Melvina sure of her faith and love of God the Almighty.

"Aye lass you might have your prayers and faith but it still comes down to this, he will die just like the rest of the slaves and servants here," says Old Man Reid as he sneers with sarcasm and vile venom in his voice. He gloats at poor sick Alfred, as he says his poisoning words for all to hear.

But Granny had other plans, and all she needed was for poor sick Alfred to get better. Then she could put her plan in place but, it could only work if he gets better and stronger. It was another risky plan that had to go just right or it was dooms day for Granny as well as Alfred. This plan that Granny had in her mind was the only way she knew how to save Alfred and maybe many other s as well.

The only obstacle in her way was Old Man Reid. His drunken bursts of bellowing and cursing all the poor sick people in the quarters. He would parade about the quarters with his homemade mask and mock all the sick slaves and servants, especially Alfred the grandchild he wishes were dead.

All this made it harder for Granny to make her healing potion. For she feared that the slaves would get scared and tell Old Man Reid about her healing potion and all would come to an end and many lives would be lost.

Granny and Louisa had to move fast and make as much of the potion as they could before the Old Man got wind of it. They worked all through the day and night, in hopes it would be enough for the all the sick people of the quarters. Thanks to Moses, they could get the goat's milk that was so badly needed. They said a silent prayer for him and the goat.

This was a true labor of love by any standards and they never tired at all. This was something that Granny just had to try and even if it did not work at least she and Louisa gave it their all. But Granny being the believer she is was not giving up just yet on God and His angels up in heaven. She was a strong believer also in prayer and she knew the power of praying all too well. For awhile there they prayed and made healing potions. All with the belief that God and His angels were watching down on them and hearing their prayers of hope and faith. This would be enough for Granny and Louisa to soldier on in hopes of making the best healing potion there ever was and God help them it would be.

It was still a waiting game to see if Alfred's body would take or reject the goat's milk healing potion. This was taking days and nights and the wear and tear from exhaustion was taking its toll too. But even with this depleting energy Granny and Louisa stayed diligent to the healing potion. It was not only a labor of love but a way for lives to be saved, and not just buried or cremated. Granny knew it was not going to be an easy task to do but she had to, it was her duty as a grandmother and the eldest of her people to help them.

Her African grandmother and mother taught Granny many healing herbs and potions; it was always needed back in Africa for one sickness or another. She now thanked her mother and grandmother for their medicinal teachings, and God for making it all possible.

It was a long and scary wait to see if Alfred would get better or worse. He would vomit a lot and his fever was the same. This was also very hard on his mother and Melvina his sister. Melvina would stay by his side and wipe his feverish brow and give him sips of Granny's potion. The family prayed and prayed for Alfred's recovery and that he would come back as the same sweet boy that he is.

But this was not going to do for Old Man Reid he wanted poor little Alfred dead, the sooner the better. That is why he had a coffin built just for him and it was made to measure. This was the last straw for Granny and his mother and sister. Granny prayed that if Alfred made it through this disease she would free him of this abusive man that was his grandfather, a drunk and tyrant man.

The days turned into nights and nights into days. It was just a vicious cycle of waiting time. But Granny had a plan and she was going to need some outside help, and she knew who could help her with this plan. But she had to wait on the condition of Alfred's recovery and how it will turn out for him.

It was a rainy night and a bit of fog was rising from the ocean. Melvina comes running out of the sick hut and starts shouting for everyone to hear with tears in her eyes.

"ALFED'S FEVER IS BROKEN AND HE HAS STOPPED VOMITING FOR HALF A DAY NOW AND I AM SURE HE IS CURED FOR REAL."

"Melvina child, why are you shouting so loud and what is this about Alfred and his fever?" says Granny almost out of breath from running.

"Granny its Alfred, he stopped vomiting and his fever is almost gone too," says Melvina still crying and trying not to shout.

"Calm down child and let us go and see what this all about and what is really going on with Alfred."

"Alright Granny but I think he is getting better and you will see it for yourself too," says Melvina with more control of her voice decibels and emotions.

They go to the sick hut and to Granny's surprise there is Alfred half sitting and half laying down, propped by his elbow. He looks at Granny and then his sister with a weak but loving smile. They both smile back at him and see that he is doing much better than they expected. This was a big relief for mother, sister and Granny.

"Alfred from where I am standing I can see that you are getting better now. This is what I have prayed for," says Granny with tears in her eyes and love in her heart.

"I am thirsty now may I have some water please and something to eat please?" says Alfred with more strength in his voice than the weeks before.

"Oh yes my dear boy you may have whatever you want, and I am very pleased to see that you are getting better," says his grandmother as she looks at him fondly. Tears falling from her weary eyes. She also knew what she had to do now, she had to fulfill the decision she had made with God and his angels. She would help to cure the other people in the quarters that are sick, and hope that they will react as Alfred did and get better.

It was going to be more long days and nights waiting to see results and hoping for more miracles. She would need Melvina's help this time as well as Louisa's. It was going to take a lot of goat's milk, herbs and prayers this time around and a lot of faith in God too.

But she also had another problem to fix, it was hiding the fact that Alfred was getting better and that the Old Man Reid wanted him dead. But Granny was not having any of this; she was going to put her plan in action. She was going to make believe to the others but not to Melvina or Louisa, that Alfred was dead and put him in his readymade coffin and smuggle aboard a ship that her friend Harry worked on. She was silently hoping that the ship Harry worked on was cleaned and able to ship off from Jamaica. It was a long shot but she had no other choice. If the Old Man Reid found out, he would probably kill poor Alfred himself just to be spiteful and very cruel. So now all she had to do was wait for an opportune moment and then she would escape with Alfred in his readymade coffin. As luck would have it a forth night goes by and Alfred gets stronger by the day. This very night it rained like it has not rained in ages, and the fog was a little heavy too. But Granny did not falter she went in search of Harry to see if his ship was ready for sailing. She knew she had to go to the nearest salon to find Harry, he liked to drink a bit and look at pretty ladies. Granny and Harry go way back, they came to Jamaica as small children with their parents. Granny was happy to find Harry after the second local she found. He was still a bit coherent and recognized Granny right away. He always fond of her and her fond of him.

"Well my dear, dear friend Harry, how are you? And tell me now are you still working on the ships these days?" asks Granny as she sizes him up and down seeing that he still looks like Harry.

My, my look who just came in here to see little old Harry and I am so glad," says Harry with a hint of teasing in his voice as he looks at Granny with a smile.

"Yes, Harry it is me Mabel and I have come to ask you a favor if possible?" says Granny with an air of pride in her voice. As she is a proud woman and hates to ask for help.

"Well ask away and if I can help my old and dearest friend than I shall. And please let me help in any way I can," says Harry not so teasing now and more focused.

"Well it is about my grandson Alfred the one that keeps getting hit and abused by his so-called grandfather Old Man Reid," says Granny with disgust in her voice.

"Well yes the ship I work on is ready to ship out soon in about three to four days," says Harry as he is wondering why now and why all the questions to him?

"It is because I want to smuggle my grandson in his coffin made for him. To get him away from that awful terrifying Old Mad Man and save his life. He had the coffin made when he thought Alfred was dying," says Granny now crying her heart out and praying that Harry can help her and Alfred.

"Well first you must stop crying, and let me help you with smuggling your grandson on to the ship before we set sail," says Harry wanting to be a comfort to her.

This was what Granny needed to hear she could now get Alfred away in time. So now all that was left was for her to put her plan in motion, and hoped it would work to save Alfred from his monstrous grandfather Old Man Reid. It was another great risk for Granny to take also this time, she was not too sure of who she could trust outside of the family. She had to be very sure that whatever was said about her smuggling Alfred had to be kept a sacred secret. It would be a little while yet before she could execute her plan of departure from the quarters. In the mean time, she and Louisa had to pretend that Alfred was still very sick and near death. If Old Man Reid ever found out about it, he would probably try and kill poor Alfred himself just by abusing and torturing him for days. This was an image that Granny had in her head and it was something, she was never going to let it happen ever. As time went by she still made her healing goat's milk potion, and it was helping a lot of the sick slaves and servants. It was also helping to make Alfred stronger everyday too, but this was hard for she had to make believe that Alfred was feeling very poorly. She would give a little less potion as he got better so as the healing process would seem slow acting.

It seemed like forever waiting for the Norwegian ship that Harry was sailing on. It was a ship from Norway, but most of the crewmen were from mostly America and some not so rich British too. Everyone mostly spoke broken English. Finally, the day for shipping out had arrived and it was a glorious day for Granny and Louisa, this meant that Alfred was to be freed from the horror known as Old Man Reid. It was a very tricky and risky chance to take, but what other choice was there to make but this one. And it was an opportunity that presented itself and it made perfect sense too. It was still going to be hard to bring a coffin aboard a ship, but Harry had a plan for that. The hardest part was leaving the plantation with poor Alfred still breathing inside. They had to devise a way for Alfred to breath in the coffin and still appear dead. Granny had a cure for that, she would give him an herbal tea and he would seem dead, but just deeply sleeping and would awake after a few hours. Hopeful if she could get her plan in motion as quick as possible this just might make the ship in time to sail away from Jamaica. Knowing this made Granny, Louisa and Melvina very sad for they knew in their heart of hearts they were never, ever going to see their precious Alfred again in life. This was mostly hard on Granny as she practically raised Alfred all by herself but the thought of him having to live in constant fear everyday of his life was more that she could humanly bear and her wanting him to stay would be selfish on her part.

    She would wait till night fall and hope she would be able to sneak out of the quarters with a small coffin, unseen by anyone especially the jealous ones and spies for the Old Man Reid. She knew she needed a strong man or boy to carry the coffin. Even though Alfred did not weight a lot now it was a lot for Granny to carry on her own. She asked Moses one last time for help and he said yes he would be very happy to help once again. Poor Moses, he was still in love with Melvina, hoping she would return the feeling if he helped her family. So now Granny had everyone she needed for her plan to work. Louisa and Melvina would be the lookouts for anyone suspicious in anyway. Granny and Moses would carry the coffin. Now there was just one more thing to consider, it was John Jr. Reid, after all he did like

Alfred and he would want to know about his condition. Granny thought about it and then considered it would be better for John Jr., to tell his father that Alfred has died. Louisa and Melvina also agreed that it was a better solution all around for everyone concerned.

It was settled it was to take place tonight and it was to work or else they would know a wrath like no other. Granny and Moses make their way through the fields and woods until they reached the harbor's edge. There they wait a bit for Harry to arrive as he must smuggle Alfred aboard. As they see Harry approaching they feel and hear Alfred starting to wake up. So now Granny must explain to Harry about the herbal sedative tea she gave Alfred, and to Alfred why he was leaving Jamaica for good. It was going to break her heart and soul.

"Harry my friend, I am really grateful for all your help and I will never, never forget what you are doing for my family," says Granny as she chokes back a hard sob and big wet tears streaming down her face as she looks at Harry with a smile.

"My dearest friend Mabel you are my oldest and dearest friend and it is my pleasure to help you and your family in any way I can," says Harry with pride in his voice.

"I know this is a lot to ask of you my dearest friend but I have no one else to turn to. I know the risk you are taking also and it is very kind and loving of you to do so. But please if by any chance we get caught, please let me take all the blame and no one gets punished. They will not hurt me as much as they could you and the rest of you all," says Granny this time crying and trying to be brave as always.

"Well dear Mabel you are not alone in this, you have people you can trust and that will help in any way we can," says Harry sounding more positive than before.

"Yes, Granny you do and, I AM NOT AFRAID I WILL STAND AND FIGHT," shouts out little Moses who has been listening all the while the elders talked.

"My how you are so brave Moses. Bravery is a good quality in a man and very noble too," says Granny as she beams at him with pride and love.

"Thank you Granny I hope that I will live to up to these manly ways," says Moses proudly as he looks at Granny and Harry with watery eyes.

"Well, let us move on then before it becomes daylight and we are seen smuggling a coffin aboard a Norwegian cargo ship leaving Jamaica for parts unknown," says Harry, as he looks around to make sure they are not seen or heard, smuggling little Alfred in a coffin aboard the ship. It took them a little while to make it aboard and just in time too for Alfred was awake now and hollering at the top of his lungs.

"WHY AM I IN HERE AND WHY AM I BURIED? I AM NOT DEAD. I AM NOT DEAD," shouts Alfred as he awakens inside the closed coffin aboard the ship.

"Stop you screaming and be quiet, we know you are not dead and you will not die in there either," says Granny with her sternest voice she could muster up.

"Well then why am I in a coffin and why am I not dead?" asks Alfred as he does not understand at all. It is making him get scared and worried. Just then Granny and Harry pry open the coffin lid and let poor scared Alfred out to explain to him what was about to happen and why.

My dear sweet boy Alfred, you are not dead, and this is not heaven either. You were brought here for a reason, to protect you from the Old Man Reid and his brutality towards you," says Granny trying not to cry too much in front of Alfred.

"But why Granny, am I really that bad do you all hate me and want me gone and never see me again?" says poor Alfred scared and starting to cry.

"No, no that is not the reason Alfred it is because your mother your sister and I, feel it is for the best and hope you understand why we have to do this," says Granny with a heavy heart and soul herself trying not to cry either.

"Where is mother and sister and why are they not her to say good bye? Do they want me gone too or is it just my brothers everyone likes now? Says Alfred not understanding at all and hoping this is all a terrible joke.

"They had to stay behind and make sure no one followed us here. It was for your protection and safety," says poor Granny trying very hard to answer Alfred's questions and be brave at the same time. It was very hard for her to bear all this but she knew it was her duty and that was that for now.

"So alright then I will try and understand as I truly hate to be hurt again by Old Man Reid and not see his face ever again. But not to see my mother and my sister and you Granny and all my friends? Never to see you all again, it hurts me and makes me very sad," says Alfred trying to be brave and not act so much like a child.

"I will tell them how you feel and you know in their hearts and your heart they will always remember you, as you will always remember them and your homeland Jamaica," says Granny with pride and courage that will carry her til her dying day.

She would come to mourn poor Alfred in silence til the day she died. His mother would lie to John Jr. and his father about Alfred's passing and how they cremated him and poured his ashes into the sea. It would be a heavy secret that Granny, Louisa and Melvina also Moses, who still loves Melvina, had to keep. It was a secret that would bond them all together for years to come.

Harry also came through as he promised, but Granny could not help wondering if he would get the "walk of the plank" or the two of them thrown overboard or even worse. It was a great loss for them and they all were happy for

Alfred but they suffered with the lost of him too. But for now, she had to believe that Alfred was safe with her long-time friend Harry and all was well aboard the ship for Alfred. Hopefully it would be better than being tortured by Old Man Reid with his crazy ranting too.

    She would move on and deal with life at hand as best as she could under the circumstances as they were. She set about making more potions and healing as many sick slaves and servants as possible. The decision for a doctor of any kind to come and tend to the sick people of the plantations was not being settled at all. It was as if they wanted the slaves and servants to die. This disease was brought here thought Granny, so why the Jamaican people should suffer a disease in their own country and receive no help. So, as her defense she made her healing potion and waited for the results. It was also a way for her not to dwell on the departure of her dear grandson. Everyone thought she and her family were in mourning and in a way, they were, so the crying and the mourning was real not for the dead but for the living far away. The Old Man Reid was kind of sad that Alfred died to his knowledge, but it was only because he had no one to torture anymore thought Granny and she was right. So now Alfred was free of him and she was happy about that. But she silently cursed the Old Man Reid ever breathing day that she was to have, for making her send her grandson almost alone to fend for himself and deprived them of him in their lives. It was a hate that Louisa and Granny and even Melvina would have for the Old Man Reid. They knew that when he died his Old Man soul would end up where it belongs in HELL. Unfortunately, the Old Man Reid would live for another ten years yet, but that did not stop Alfred's family from loathing the Old Man Reid until his death. Meanwhile no doctors came and Granny continued with her healing potion healed most of the slaves and servants that were not too sick or still savable. This potion of Granny's was going to be the talk of the surrounding plantations. She would be sought out by many plantation owners who needed her assistance. Seeing as there was a need for Granny's healing potion the Old Man Reid decided he would charge for her services, and tries to recuperate some of his losses that the Yellow Fever incurred him. But Granny being wise as she was, would also salt away a bit of the money charged for healing potion and the Old Man Reid was never the wiser. It was her way of getting back at him for making her fake Alfred's death and sending him away forever. She could not in all her Christian teachings forget or forgive the Old Man Reid, if they both shall live in this life or any other they would share. Granny's heart was broken as well as Louisa's and Melvina's too. It was a very hard decision to make regarding the smuggling of Alfred. As time went by they all acted as if he was dead, the way they were mourning made it seem even more real. This was to be a good thing because it helped them, to continue hiding the truth about Alfred living.

It was not so easy though for Alfred's family and friends as they missed him terribly. Some of his friends would talk amongst themselves, about the great times they all had together playing marbles and eating sugar rock candy. These were the times that Granny would miss Alfred the most, when his friends were talking about the great times they had with him. But as always time passes and it becomes a little easier to bear. But for Granny it would haunt her to her grave. Lying awake at night wondering, if he will ever remember his family and if he will become a good man and have a happy life. These questions would always be in the back of Granny's mind and consuming her every thought.

As for Louisa, his mother she could not go and say good bye to her first born it was too heart breaking. But the more she thought of it the more she wished she had gone now and said good bye. But she did say her goodbyes before he left but it was not the same, for she now felt it was the last time she would ever see her son again.

For Melvina she did say her goodbyes a few times to her brother and she was very sad and quiet about her brother's fake death. Eventually everyone mourned Alfred and then they went on with their lives. She prayed to God and asked him to take this evilness from her heart and make her have faith again in humanity.

This was also sad for Moses as he also felt the loss of Alfred but true to his word he never gave away the secret, not even when his father and mother threatened him with a whipping for stealing a goat. Everyone involved that night with the smuggling of Alfred all mourned him very differently from the others. As they knew the truth and that he was not coming back, it was as if he were dead. It was a time that a little light skinned brown boy had to live his home and every loved one he ever knew.

The only person that did not mourn Alfred was the Old Man Reid, in fact he celebrated by getting more drunk than usual. But John Jr. mourned him a little and he was sad to see how devastating it was for Louisa, Melvina and poor dear old Granny.

As time went by Granny could not help wondering why when Old Man Reid came down to the quarter to see how much of his property was he losing he always had a clean piece of cotton around his mouth and held up by strings on each side. One-day Granny went to the Big House and went to find Moses' mother and asked her why the Old Man showed no signs of Yellow Fever at all. She told Granny it was because his friend McLeod said his wife Agnes said that when she was coming to Jamaica by boat, they had a virus scare and they made first class passengers wear these things called mouth protectors it was to keep from contacting any virus. She thanked Moses' mother and returned to the quarters. It would surely help keep the not so sick ones from getting any sicker, and maybe to help the ones that are in remission also. Granny set out to find as many clean sheets as she could and had Melvina cut them up to fit their mouth and made ties to hold them in place. It was another risky plan to take on but she had more reason now than ever to help her people and maybe plenty others. It would take time as always but she was more confident now that she had "mouth protectors" it was another God send. She went about doing her healing and praying that sick person that was left would get better.

 She still mourned her beloved grandson Alfred and she tried to hide it but it was hard at times. Just like the other day when she treated one of his school mates that he would play hookey with. It was also very hard for Louisa and Melvina just knowing that they will never, see his face or hear his laugh or watch him grow up to be a man. Yes, it would be hard but when they would stop and think about the life Alfred had on the plantation with the Old Man Reid's reign of terror; it was worth the heartache and almost made the pain bearable. The three women would bury their sorrow and put all their energy into helping save the lives of others. This was to be their lives for now til this crazy disease was stopped. But thankfully Granny had her healing potion and mouth protectors and it would prove to be a big help in the long run. on as usual for some others would mourn their loss ones too.

As time went by the Yellow Fever passed and more were getting less infected with the disease. The doctor finally came out to the plantations after they had heard that, Granny had a "healing potion and mouth protectors" that was giving the disease a run for its money. The Archbishop and church wanted to save face so they finally decided to send a doctor out to the plantations. It was thanks to Granny that they finally sent a doctor to help the slaves and servants on the surrounding plantations and the plantation she lived on with her people. Granny would soon come to find out that the Old Man Reid paid a priest of the church not to press the matter of finding a doctor for the plantations. He did not his little enterprise to be compromised so he decided to bribe a priest instead. He felt very sad to see his little sideline business going away, but he felt no sadness at all for his loss of slaves and servants. He was a heartless and cold man and showed no empathy except for his son John Jr. It was a hard for everyone to bounce back from the horrible disease called Yellow Fever and it also took its toll on Granny and Louisa even more. Melvina felt it too.

The Old Man Reid never knew even on his dying bed, that Alfred never died and still lived somewhere on earth. It was a comfort of sorts for Granny and Louisa and Melvina to know that Alfred would go on living and the Old Man Reid would never know, not even when he died. The only close person that mourned the Old Man was his son John Jr., and his friends McLeod and McDonald who came with their wives to pay their respects to the family. His body was sent to Scotland to be buried near his beloved wife. After the estate was read John Jr., stayed on the plantation and Louisa remained his concubine til their death. As for Granny, she died with a broken heart for the loss of her sweet grandson Alfred. Melvina married Moses when he became a freed man and they went to live their own lives away from the Reid Plantation. As for the other slaves and servants, they had a choice of staying as freed people or leave for better places.

In 1910 the Jamaican people were tired of being slaves and servants so that decide no more slavery on the plantations ever again. But this was something Granny and the Old Man Reid would never witness as this law came about after their deaths. Louisa and Melvina thought it was a shame that Granny did not live to see this and even more regretting that the Old Man Reid missed out on the joyous occasion too. The many family and friends now gone either through mating or dying, it was not like before. The quarters were now shanty towns and the plantation owners had to pay wages to the once slaves and servants they had on their plantations. Yes, and that Alfred could escape his abuser and tormentor forever to live the life he should to grow up and be a good man.

The Norwegian Ship

Harry had to try and hide Alfred till he could talk with the Captain. He was hidden away for a week or so before the Captain even noticed he was aboard the ship. He knew it was going to be a bit hard to communicate with him, because the Captain's English was very limited at best. Poor Alfred, he was confused and felt very lost and almost abandoned from his home. But in his childlike mind and heart he knew it was the only way for him to survive the Old Man Reid's reign of terror. Harry also knew he was doing a good thing. It may not have the greatest idea as far as ideas go, but at least the child would be safe for now and away from his mean spiteful grandfather.

So now all Harry had to do was convince the Captain to keep Alfred aboard as a cabin boy for him. It would take some convincing on Harry's part too for he and the Captain were good friends but they had a big communication problem. But this was true of all the crewman on the boat for they were from different parts of the world. It was like a melting pot. Different nationalities and not all meshed together either. Some were prejudice and others just did not care either way, so it was hard to tell at times who the enemies were as Alfred would soon learn once he was aboard the ship for awhile. Harry helped as much as he could but some things are just self taught. But as luck would have it the Captain takes a liking to Alfred and agrees he can become his cabin boy. Alfred was not sure how to react to this decision made for him but under the circumstances what choice did he have? There he was again being told what to do. But the Captain was a fair man and that is why he always had a full crew to work for him. One more crew member was not going to be a problem at all.

Alfred was officially the Captain's cabin boy and he started out doing menial jobs, such as empty out spittoon buckets as well as urine and feces ones too. It was a terrible chore to do. Alfred also had to swab the deck and help the crew men at times. But Harry would help him out and show him the ropes and how to survive aboard a cargo ship headed for the high seas as sometimes it can get very scary out there.

This was to be Alfred's new life and he would adapt to it seeing it as an adventure to see the rest of the world. Something perhaps he would have never done if he had stayed in Jamaica all his life. Some would say this was a learning experience for young Alfred and he could benefit from it a lot. But to Alfred it was a way to escape the reign of terror at the hands of Old Man Reid. Even Harry had to agree with that logic, it was the only way for Alfred to be free of the horrible grandfather in a way. This ship life would prove to be another learning experience into the journey his life was about to take. He was going to see and do things he never knew existed. He was going to make his own way in life. But it was not an easy road as it was thought to be. He would again face adversaries and at time endure things beyond his control. He would of course have Harry, Granny's friend to watch and protect him. Then things would happen, and he would wonder if his Granny and mother made the right choice for him. Harry was always so kind to him and made sure when he could that Alfred was protected from any harm or danger. But when the Captain said that he would make Alfred, his "Personal Cabin Boy" at least he did not ask him to, "walk the Plank." This was a good thing as Alfred would later come to know and understand. He would do what the Captain would tell him to and he had to learn from the bottom and work his way up. It was hard work at first for Alfred but the Captain was amazed, at how quickly he picked up the work of the cabin boy. At times Harry, would help and show him how certain things were done aboard a cargo ship and how to stay away of jealous crew men that were just plain mean. This at times would prove to be a problem and the men in question were mean and nasty. They would come back from shore leave and be very drunk and verbally abusive to Alfred. Alfred thought here we damn well go again. They would come back to the ship drunk and looking to pick on Alfred. They would urinate on him and vomit on him and say that he did it to himself. Because they would never do it in front of Harry or the Captain. This would only happen when the Captain and Harry would join them on shore leave and return drunker than the abusive crew men. Alfred would try and explain it to the Captain but the Captain spoke broken English. He went to speak to Harry and ask him if he would help him with his crew men problem. Harry said he would try and be helpful but that he had not better go with the men on shore leave to stay sober and see what happens. Alfred was sure that his friend Harry would help him out. Harry also tried to explain to the Captain but he also had a hard time understanding Harry too. The accent and language barrier was enough to make the conversation difficult at best. Alfred kept trying to make the Captain understand the best he and Harry could under the circumstances. It was something that over time would manifest into a friendship and admiration for these three men, Alfred and Harry and the Captain of the Norwegian cargo ship. They would have a certain bond that made some crewmen jealous.

There were only a few crewmen that Harry sort of trusted; there were four men in total. They were; Johnny a somewhat fair-skinned Jamaican that knew Harry from their younger days. Harry got him the job on the ship when Johnny became a freed man back in Jamaica; he is about thirty years old. Then there was Neville, he too was from

Jamaica a dark-skinned man forty years old who meet Harry awhile ago as they worked on the ship together. There was Henry who came from either Calcutta or Bombay India. Henry was a man of brown skin and smaller features than his Jamaican fellow seamen. Henry was never sure where he came from as he was sold into slavery as a child and managed to escape as a young man. He was now forty-five years old. Then we have Mr. Pike known only as Pike. He was the original Norwegian crewman on that ship. He was a white skinned man with blondish hair turning gray as he was only fifty years old. The other Norwegian crewmen died of scurvy and some other crewmen also from other countries.

Let us not forget the Captain Sven, he was a good Captain but spoke broken English. Even with this barrier he and Harry did communicate and Pike would translate when needed. The Captain was also a white skinned man and he was fifty-five years old and a little weary at times. His gray hair showed signs that once he was a very blonde haired man. Harry only had a few somewhat close friends on the ship and these men were it. Harry was more inclined to be closer to the Captain Sven than any other crewman on the ship. But he also knew that if he had to depend on someone it would be either, Captain Sven or Johnny whom he knew from their homeland Jamaica.

Alfred was seeing the world as he never knew existed. He saw different ports from different countries and learned about different cultures too. But this was not an easy time for Alfred either as he had to learn about the ship from the bottom up. He was not thrilled about his duties but he had no choice really. This was to be his new life for the next few years. Little did Alfred and Harry and the Captain Sven know that their lives would intertwine with each other and they would build a bond over time. This will be hard, for as people will be people, and the green-eyed monster called jealousy will rear its head. Little did Alfred know that he was to know a different kind of abuse and torture, but this would not last long and he would eventually be able to defend himself like never before. This was to be an awakening for young Alfred and his friend and mentor the Captain Sven and his best friend Harry, whom he has come to depend upon and like so much for saving him. The only thing that Alfred missed was his mother Louisa, his siblings and his precious Granny whom he adored. Now all gone from him and in his heart, he knew that he would never see them again. This was a burden that Alfred would carry throughout his life time. But as hard as it seemed he was determined to make a better life for himself. As his dear Granny said before leaving him with Harry, that Alfred must mind Harry and try and keep himself safe, and to be the best man he could ever want to be. Alfred kept those words in his mind and he swore that he would do just that and make his family proud.

It was hard for Alfred to always be working on the ship, as he was use to running in the sugar fields and eating rock candy and playing marbles with his friends. This work on the ship was totally different and strange to a young boy still in short pants. Yet he was determined to do as he was told by Harry and Captain Sven. They would guide him and help Alfred to adjust to his new life on the ship as a "Cabin Boy" this was how a seaman starts off learning the trades of a seaman's life. It would prove to be challenging for young Alfred and he would find it hard but he still soldiered on and learned the ropes.

This cargo ship at one time carried dead bodies to be buried from various countries. But this proved not to be such a lucrative cargo as cargo goes. It was for the main fact that the ship itself, was not outfitted with a cooling system such as a refrigerator or "cooling box" as they called it back then. And because of this it was hard to keep diseases at bay with dead bodies on board. This was a poor ship by the standards of the times, and Captain Sven was trying to make money so he could outfit his ship and have a cooling box too. The money in those days came from shipping spices, tea, rum and dry ice. It was the rage of Europe, but, as it turned out there were not enough ships to supply the demand. And this was what Captain Sven was trying to do and in the process, make some decent money he hoped. It had been a long time since Captain Sven had a good stroke of luck concerning his cargo trips. He wanted to retire with some money so he could live the rest of his life by the seashore, for the sea was in his blood but, now he wanted to see the sea not live for it anymore. But before this could be true, he had to make money now, and then get himself a "cooling box" and make enough money to pay his crewmen and live by the seaside when he retires.

It was a hard life as he had been at sea and some days were good, like back in the old days now it was harder. He lost too many men at sea when he was shipping dead bodies to be buried. Now he was shipping teas, spices and rum also the occasional male passenger looking for passage on the boat to get to the next harbor. This was still going to take a while yet so Captain Sven thought to himself, "yes it may take longer but I am ready and willing to meet the challenge ahead".

Alfred was still too small to fix any mast that help sail the ship, these needed mending very often as the high winds and rain storms were very damaging to the ships sails. For now, poor Alfred had to do the jobs he was asked to do. This was hard for a young boy who was use to running in the sugar cane fields and play marbles with his friends. He would soon learn that this was a way for him to become a man and learn about life. He would also learn that grieving is a part of growing up and this would be the hardest lesson of life for him. Leaving his home so young and never being able to go back this was something a young lad will have trouble understanding. He must overcome obstacles and hardships and the most awful of all "loneliness," for the family he would never ever see again in his life. This would hurt Alfred's heart for years to come and he would always wonder how his family was doing without him. Even thought the Captain Sven and Harry tried to make his transition easy as they could. To a young boy leaving his homeland, never to return there again was devastating for even Alfred to bear. His life on the ship would make him sometimes forget but he still had a nagging feeling of never belonging anywhere in his life. He would travel the world some and see sights and new things he only saw in books. This was an adventure that would take him from a boy and make him a young man that would always be thankful to Harry and Captain Sven for saving him giving him a place to call home for now.

Granny did a great thing by taking him to Harry and leaving Alfred with him. It was her only option and having Alfred grow up on the plantation was not an option anymore. So now that was settled and Alfred was told to mind Harry and listen to him. Alfred asks Harry, "Why did my Granny and mother Louisa agree to have me smuggled aboard this ship with you after I got better?"

Harry replies in kind: "Well young lad, your grandmother and mother Louisa decided that if you got better and stayed on the plantation, your life would be nothing but misery, abuse and torture. They just couldn't stand to see that happen to you anymore. It was too hard for them to bear witness to ever again."

"Harry thank you so much for being honest at least and letting me know why I was leaving my home in the middle of the night and smuggled onto a ship in a coffin fit to my size," says Alfred still wondering how it all happen and when.

"There is something else young lad I would like to discuss with you and maybe be helpful too," says Harry as he tries to find the words to explain to a young boy.

"What is it that you want to tell me Harry, it is something I did or did not do?" asks Alfred a little worried now and is a little nervous at this point too.

Harry looks at Alfred all nervous and worried he says to Alfred, "Now do not worry your head at all it is not bad, I just want to give you a piece of advice from my own experience at sea. You have to be careful who you make friends with and trust you talk to and most of all tell all your secrets to."

"Well then I had better do a good job and keep my head down and listen to what I am told. May I ask you Harry is that why you have only a few crewmen that you deal with and talk too?" says Alfred with a quizzing look in his eyes.

Harry replies in kind: "During my time on the big sea and sailing the ships and big cargo boats I have learned a lesson or two. You must always be aware of your surroundings and watch everything around you that moves or doesn't move."

"I am listening to you and taking your advice. It sounds very true to me, it is like almost having to live on the plantation and being aware of your enemies," says Alfred trying to understand that this is his life now and there are new rules to it.

"I am sure you will get the hang of things as you go along. It is not easy as crewmen's life and it is hard and lonely and tiresome too. But you learn to survive and move on with your life," says Harry trying not to sound too morbid and harsh.

Alfred says "I will also do a very good job for Captain Sven, as he let me stay on as cabin boy to earn my keep. I am also grateful to you too Harry for helping me and my family smuggle aboard this ship of yours and Captain Sven."

Harry looks at Alfred fondly, "Well dear lad I hope I didn't scare you and make you afraid before you even really started?"

"Well, no not really, but I am worried about the crewmen you do not talk to, are they dangerous or mean or just not happy?"

"All that and more I suspect, but who can say for sure, I have to work alongside and some I give orders to, but that is as far as I care to go with them," says Harry. From Harry's way of talking it was a hint to stop now and talk about his chores. Alfred made sure that he did what he was told to do, such as swab the deck from port to stern, also clean all latrines of feces and urine matter. He did make a promise to Granny and his mother, to listen and learn everything he can from Harry and Captain Sven. He also gave thought to what Harry had said about keeping his head down, his eyes open and mouth shut. He also stayed clear of the other mixed "Motley Crewmen" his first aboard the ship. This was to be an adventure so Alfred thought but the truth was that, he would work for his passage fare and logging aboard the ship as the Captain's cabin boy. This was okay for now to Alfred he also caught a bit of luck as it turned out, he got to stay in the Captain's quarters on a cot put there for him as he was the Captain's personal cabin boy and "scabby" meaning the lowest member to join the crew ship. This was how all the crewmen started apparently and they had to work their way up in ranks as all the older ones did. He was hoping too that one day he would get to hoist the sail and maybe even steer the ship. But that would not be for awhile yet as he still had to learn a lot more about the ship and what it entailed. This was to be an education of sorts for young Alfred as he had no school to go to anymore, and now well this would be his school and the sea and crew his books and mentors. He would see places and learn of cultures and languages of different countries. He would marvel at the new wonders he never knew existed, and at times be amazed at how people can be different and yet all the same. Life at sea was not at all like his life on the plantation in Jamaica or being with family and friends. Those days were long gone and never to return. He resigned himself to this life for now. One day he knew when he would become a man himself his life would change again and bring about new adventures and more stories to tell.

Harry was a great mentor to him and helped in any way he could he also showed Alfred how to make "sailor knots." It was a way that the crewmen made knots in the rope to hold steed fast and not break to much against the high sea winds and rain storms. The high winds and rain storms could ruin ships and the ship could lose some of its crew to either sickness or just dying from the storms themselves. Therefore, a crewmen's life aboard a ship is not long he either dies from illness, lost at sea or just too damn old.

As time went on Alfred adjusted to his new life and did not complain too much, as he did not want to come across as a snitch or rat. Being a snitch was frowned upon by the crewmen and they hated any snitches no matter who they were. Alfred saw things and had to be quite about it, he even was questioned at times to see if he could be trusted. That would be okay for awhile until the night that the some of the crewmen and the Captain and Harry went ashore. They were docked in Venezuela and they went looking for rum and women, Alfred had to stay behind as he was not of age yet and could not go drinking with them. It was not until they returned that night that hell broke loose. The crewmen were drunk but not as drunk as Harry and the Captain Sven, when it all started. The men knew that with Harry and the Captain Sven very drunk and passed out, they could now abuse Alfred to their hearts content. It started with them pissing on him and vomiting on him. Some would even throw feces at him from the latrines. It was hard for Alfred to bear as he knew it was an abuse he did not know, but was familiar to other kinds of abuse. In other words he knew about abuse and now he was about to learn of a different kind of abuse. But in time he would be able to avenge himself, but for now he did not snitch or make any trouble for himself. He would just stay out of their way as he did with the Old Man Reid, and hoped that would be enough. Even though the Captain and Harry had doubts about what was going on until they had proof or Alfred came forward nothing could be done. This was becoming frustrating for Alfred because this would go on for a few years and with each day Alfred grew taller and stronger and was developing his own muscles and strength. Yet he still was not strong enough to fight against the motley crewmen that would abuse and hurt his feelings.

Alfred learned at an early age that not everyone was in his corner, or would come to his rescue or help him in anyway. Except of course, his beloved Granny and his mother Louisa and his sister Melvina, whom he adored so much. These were the only people in his life that ever cared for him and now he was on his own and had to take care of himself.

Harry and Captain Sven also became fond of Alfred and tried to help him whenever they could. And as far as the motley crewmen abusing Alfred does not last for long, as Harry and Alfred are not aware that they have an ally that all will be good friends. He will come and help them without any fuss or attention seeking either. Their ally will be of sound and honest stock, a person of truth and justice for all mankind. He will put this abuse to an end once and for all and no one will object to the methods that the ally will use to bring justice once and for all. It will be a revelation for all to witness as this ally will be someone that no one even thought would take a stand and fight for a good cause and win in the end doing this good deed. It will be a surprise for all to see. It will be someone that not even Alfred would consider a friend, but then it is hard to tell when you have friends or not aboard a ship, especially when you are just a cabin boy. But Alfred and Harry will be very surprised to see that even when you think that you can't trust anyone, out of the blue here comes a friend to the rescue. It will also come as a surprise to for the motley crewmen and they won't believe their eyes and ears. Yes, it was a revelation of some kind and hopefully a lesson to be learned in human kindness towards your fellowman. Even poor Alfred will be amazed at how some are not what they seem to be and others are just what they seem. He will learn also that you pick and judge wisely, who are your friends and who can be trusted in life with your life. The learning of the ship and how it is sailed and how it is to live at sea, but also how to be with other people of different walks of life and mannerism and cultures and traditions. Alfred would also learn how to be a good seaman and how to be a good man also that knows how to defend himself when needed and how to be good to others when needed and warranted too.

  Alfred had a guardian angel and it was about to reveal itself and help the Captain Sven and Harry see what the motley crewmen were up to and that they were the one responsible for the abuse of Alfred. The reason for this was because these abuses would only happen when they were on shore leave or drinking heavily in the galley. They always thought that they were smart for getting Harry and the Captain Sven almost blind stinking drink. They would come back from shore leave and want to urinate and throw feces and vomit all over Alfred. But this one night after many times of this recurring abuse and humiliation, someone stood up and took a stand and defended poor Alfred. It was not easy nor a pretty sight either but it was warranted and long overdue. This person could no longer stand aside and watch how these so-called crewmen, abuse and humiliate a young boy for no reason other than because they could. This person was getting sicker and sicker by the many times he had witnessed this abusive behavior Alfred endured. He was wrong to wait but he was hoping that Alfred would get fed up and say something himself. But to his surprise and admiration Alfred took it like a man and did not wimp out like a baby. While keeping his honor and dignity intact. This person also knew what being abused felt like for he was a slave once upon a time himself. He was not about to let this go on any longer, he had to intervene and say or do something or both. First he gathered proof and then he decided that he would show Harry and Captain Sven his findings. Hopefully they will agree with him and take into consideration what has been happening to poor Alfred and how were they going to deal with this matter at hand. It was a hard one at best to decide what course of action to take against the accused. But the Captain believing himself to be an honest man waited to speak with Alfred and then make his decision. But Harry just wanted revenge right away, he knew that whatever the person said it was true. It was true to Harry because Harry knew the person to be an honest one, and they had no reason to lie or gain anything by it or for it. Neville comes forward and tells Harry and the Captain Sven that Alfred is being abused by his motley crewmen. They ask how does he know this and he tells them it is one night he heard them talking, about it and how they like to get the Captain and Harry stinking drunk so they can abuse Alfred. They knew Alfred would not talk for they threatened to throw him over board one rainy stormy night. He just bides his time until he could defend himself, but this was taking too long and Neville was hating every second that he hesitated and waited on Alfred to declare his abuse and abusers. He also knew that his would alienate him from the motley crewmen, and he was fine with that.

It's hard for someone that has lived in slavery most of their lives and know not to complain. But then you are freed of that slavery life, just to be introduced to another kind of slavery. Not a slaver put in chains, but a slave where you are not quite free as a person. This is what Neville saw when he witnessed the abuse and meanness

Alfred endured, at the hands of the horrible motley crewmen.

    The Captain asks Harry his opinion and Harry is not having it at all, he wants revenge and blood and guts if he can get them too. It was hard for him to hear what Alfred had to endure on top of being threatened by a bad bunch of thugs. Harry promised that he would take good care of Alfred and make sure that he would be safe. He felt that he had let down Granny, Alfred, and his mother Louisa too. Harry knew that he had to make it right by Alfred and he knew that Neville was by his side too. This was going to be bad, a lot of bad blood could be spilled or spared depending on the outcome of the situation that has presented itself. Harry knew deep down that the Captain always has the last word, and if he thought that the Captain was going to step aside for this one was not a chance. This was going to be a very tough situation to prove without a doubt. Neville had brought evidence that proves it happened and Alfred was the one receiving the abuse and humiliation of it all. Of course, the "motley crewmen" denied all the accusations that were made against them. Their spokesperson for them was a crewman named Turk he was of Turkish parents but born in Norway. He spoke a bit of Norwegian and English and he also was a troublemaker. He like to cause havoc wherever he went. He would not last long as a big shot because when the truth comes and it will, some crewmen must pay for their actions and suffer the consequences ahead. Now this was a matter for the Captain to decide but the Captain only spoke broken English so he had to have Harry translate for him. In the hopes that it will be civilized as much as possible. These days the moral of the ship has not been of the greatest of moods. But little did the parties involved know that now they all had a better understanding of English and some Norwegian so maybe they would be able to have a somewhat civilized conversation among themselves hopefully.

"Well looky here, if it ain't the Captain's "Lap Dog" doing everything Captain says. And here he is thinking is better than the rest of us," says Turk who hates Harry and his little circle of friends.

"I help him talk Norwegian a little bit," says the Captain as well as he can in English.

"Well I know what I saw and heard you men say. That it was funny to have gotten the Captain and Harry so stinky drunk each time. They could not remember any of those nights," says Neville finally standing up to Turk who has been quiet this whole time.

"Alfred what have you to say about the bullies?" asks the Captain with concern in his eyes.

"Well Captain I do not like to be a snitch but yes, some of these men did abuse me by urinating on me and vomiting too. Hey they think it is a big joke but I find no humor in this at all Captain, at all. Also, since you are well informed, the man called Turk threatened me and a few others if we talked," says Alfred as he feels a weight being lifted. He was not sure how the Captain would react to his words.

"We must take an action and see why these crewmen did this horrible thing and why," says the Captain as he looks around the ship at the men in question with suspicious eyes. Wondering if they will confess or lie their way out of it as usual.

"Well now Captain are you going believe the words of a pica-ninny boy and his "black angel" or that of your loyal and hardworking crewman?" asks Turk who is wondering if his ragtag gang will back him up or sell him down the river?

"Ya I believe young Alfred for you see, I have doubts but no proof. But what you know understand about me or even know, as young boy back home in Norway my father a big scary and brutal man. He beat me and my mama and my brother, even the dog sometimes. So, you see Mr. Turk I believe Alfred I see fear in his eyes, the same fear I had when I was being hurt and tortured by my father," says the Captain with a very heavy heart. He turns to Alfred and says, "My dear boy I so sorry for not seeing before but now I pay more attention okay and make sure no more hurting anybody."

"Captain I guess this is the best you can do, but I would like Turk and his motley crewmen to say sorry or at least say they will never hurt Alfred or anyone again," says Harry as he is waiting for Turk or one of his ragtag gang to throw the first punch. But Turk and his gang are at lost for words so they say nothing.

Turk and his boys managed to stay quiet for awhile but they were not to be trusted and so Harry, Neville and the Captain all kept an eye out for Alfred as best they could. As time went by Alfred grew stronger and older and could now help with the loading and unloading of cargo. These times were not often as Alfred was still under age to be a full-time crewman. For now, he would be happy just loading and unloading certain cargo aboard the ship.

During this time, the Captain could buy a cooling box, so that families could have their dead shipped back home to be buried properly. With the "cooling boxes" which at the time was like a fridge, they could carry more ice which in turn would keep the corpse from decomposing before arriving at their destination. This was what the Captain and his crew were waiting for even if it meant more hard and longer hours to keep. If the men were honest with themselves too they were also in it for the money. This was to be a good business venture for the men aboard and they would all have a better pay wage. Alfred also was interested in how the "cooling box" worked. He would study it all the time. He liked the mechanics of the "cooling box." As time went on the ship would transport dead corpses or dry ice whatever cargo that needed a "cooling box." This was making the crewmen happier for now and they were just concentrating on the bigger pay wage they were getting. It was a good moral booster for now and it is keeping Turk and his boys at bay.

The crewmen had no time to argue and fight as they were too exhausted by day's end to squabble at all. This would be the normal for a little while until another tragedy erupts and everything goes crazy and no one cares.

The Captain still watches and Harry and ragtag gang still patrol the areas around the boat. But Turk and his gang are being extra careful too as they do not want to be left behind on the money making. They stay quiet biding their time and waiting for when to strike again. Young Alfred continues to be a cabin boy and learn what the life of a seaman is. He learns very quickly for a young lad that only had grade four education. But Alfred knew what was to be done and how he would watch in silence as the other men went about their duties. The longer Alfred stayed the more he got to see and learn for himself. But the learning experience he was having was about to be used and it would be a challenge that Alfred would rise and prevail. It would be a challenge like he had never known for this would be where Alfred becomes the young man he was meant to be and like for himself.

    The days tuned into nights and then weeks and months and eventually years. The time went by fast as Alfred started to get a hang of things. He started to see his life on the ship as a learning adventure about the world. This was something he only ever heard about from other people on the plantation. It was an adventure that Alfred could never have dreamed possible, he was still very sad about leaving his home and family. But not of being away from Old Man Reid and his torture that was the only thing poor Alfred did not miss at all. The life of a boy or man on a cargo ship was not one of glory. It was a life of hard work little pay at times and if they were lucky, they got to see land it usually meant there was a harbor nearby. This could mean at times shore leave and maybe a few small kegs of rum, if their wages would permit. Then there were the days that could be at sea for days on end and see no land at all. Those were the hardest times of all for Alfred not seeing any land anywhere as he was use to seeing land all the time. His homeland had rivers and lakes but he and his family did not live on the ocean or the sea. As time goes by and Alfred starts to become a young man, he builds muscles and gets taller and a little broader too. This is good for Alfred for now he does not feel like a child anymore. He starts to feel like a man and wants to be treated with respect, but as

Harry says respect is earned not just given lightly. Alfred decides that this is how he would earn respect and give it in return. As the ship sails for days, weeks, months and years, this year of all years was not a good one. Nineteen hundred and fifteen March, it was the first time that young Alfred saw with his own eyes, a massive storm that turned into a raging storm from Hell. It hailed and rained big hail pellets felt like little pebbles that were being hurled at them. It rocked the boat back and forth not gently like you would a baby, but like you were trying to push something off a ledge. It was something for Alfred to witness he was not quite sure of what to make of his first hail storm. It was something to see and live. It made every crew member on board take stock, and man there posts without hesitation of any kind. Alfred's duties were to make sure that the water buckets were always emptied and ready to fill with the heavy rain that was attaching itself to the ship. Harry was yelling orders, Turk translating to a few men for him. The Captain trying to maintain order and have the ship run smoothly. This was not an easy task and it meant a lot of hard work from every crewman aboard the ship. They had to pull together and put arguments and bad feelings aside and do all that they can to save the ship and themselves. It was a crazy storm that lasted for our hours which in sea talk was not too much, but the way the storm started was. The sky was blue and then it turned almost black in minutes. It seemed like it was just a normal rain storm for that time of year. But it was not it was a hail storm mixed in with rain and boy did it rain. This was something that Alfred would remember for the rest of his life. The storm finally ended and the crewmen were not too badly hurt or tired from working so hard to save the ship.

The damage to the boat was quite extensive. The sails were damaged with big holes and some water damage to the starboard part of the ship. This meant all hands-on deck working day and night if need be. The ship was in the middle of the ocean not the sea and the big tidal waves just banged the ship all up. Patches here and there also boarded up parts of the ship too. And the galley was all upside down and to be re-fixed all over again, with the cook being very upset and not pleased at the mess before him.

Also, the "cooling box that the Captain had purchased was not usable as before, it worked but not to its full capacities. It kept things cool but not cold as it was supposed to do, it was a big loss for the ship and the Captain's ship budget too. Captain Sven wondered how long it would last before dying all together, since they were at sea it was hard to find someone with the skill to repair it. Then it dawned on the Captain he could set course for to go see his brother Lars and his wife Hilda and his niece Nelda, whom they call Nelly. Lars is repairman for cooling boxes and other mechanical things of various kinds. But the problem remains will "cooling box" stay working long enough for ship to reach Nova Scotia, Canada. By the Captain's calculations the ship would dock in Nova Scotia in about one to one and half months give or take a few days. He explained as best as he could, but Harry and Turk were translating just fine and working together for once. The crewmen knew that the "cooling box" brought in a lot of money and more wages too. It was what they all agreed upon, and so they set sail towards the Atlantic sea and head for Nova Scotia, Canada. The ship's course was not as brutal this time as it was when they encountered the raging storm from Hades. It seemed like for not seeing land for such a long time.

By now Alfred is eighteen almost nineteen and is getting stronger by the day. But this has not made Turk afraid of Alfred he still harbors a grudge against him, for those years back when he was made a fool of. So now after all this time Turk has been waiting and bidding time to plot his revenge. One night after all the ship's mending was done the crewmen go into the last three kegs of rum left. They proceeded to get stinking drunk all except Alfred who hated alcohol because of the taste. Harry drank with them but was watchful of everyone especially Turk, he did not trust that man at all and now even more so. Harry sees Turk try to seek away unnoticed so he can go find Alfred, and finish he left off so many years ago. But Turk was in for a surprise as he found Alfred alone by himself, Turk approached Alfred and was looking for a fight. This was not going too easy as it was those many years ago. Turk went to punch Alfred in his face but Alfred blocked the punch, and counteracted with a punch of his own. This knocked Turk clear out of his boots and down on his butt. It was to be the last time Turk would ever try and hurt Alfred again, it stopped here and now. The word got around that now Alfred landed Turk on his "butt" everyone knew for sure now that Alfred would fight back. He no longer was a lackey for anyone he was a cabin boy working his way to be a seaman like the rest of them aboard the ship. Alfred knew that even with him defending himself that he still had to watch his back. It was a little easier now that Turk and his motley crew backed off for now. But as time went on the sea became a better friend to the ship than before with the outrageous storm. They sailed somewhat peacefully along the waters and gentle waves. But it was still a long way from being out of the woods yet. The mast and the port of the ship got hit the worse, it was a heavy task to repair these items again. But with all hands-on deck working together it all worked out not to bad. But they did not think that the storm was over, most these seamen have seen storms like this before. And they have been known to return with a vengeance so bad it could capsize the ship entirely. But then again, this calm sea could be on the level and everything is just fine for now. The only real big problem now is how long is the cooling box going to stay working, hopefully until they reach New Brunswick? It is a very tricky situation and the Captain and the crewmen need to pray, for a solution the cooling box to keep working till they reach their destination. The repairs they did to the ship were holding very well and this was a good sign. Alfred tried to learn all he could and this pleased Harry and the Captain Sven. But as luck would have it the cook comes down with a croup and is too sick to cook, he asks Alfred to step in. Alfred accepts and the cook tells Alfred what to do behind a closed door and with a megaphone of sorts, on how to cook and prepare meals and how to put it all to good use. The Cook wishes he could see Alfred and what he is doing to see if he is following the Cook's instructions to. He enjoyed being by himself for a few hours a day and starting to like cooking too. Alfred like the few hours of solitude that bought about the having to deal with Turk and his gang. It was God send in a way that Alfred got to be in the ship's galley. He hoped that the Cook would get better soon and show him around the kitchen the proper way and how to cook more meals. The crewmen were not happy to have a cabin boy cook all their meals, even if the cook was coaching him from the sidelines. It was hard in the beginning of his kitchen training, but the crewmen soon learned to like Alfred's way of cooking and eat it without too many complaints. He was getting better and the better he got the less the crewmen complained. The Captain and the Cook were happy too as the Cook was still under quarantine and would be for awhile yet. So now Alfred was taught how to cook another life lesson to be learned. He would embrace this learning experience for as he gets better he finds that he does enjoy cooking. It is also good for the men aboard the ship for they do not take to not having good meals lightly. The transition becomes a success and all is well again for now. The ship sails along safely and the Captain is having good feelings about reaching New Brunswick in time before the cooling box stops working all together and dies.

    The Captain was trying to stay optimistic about the "cooling box", this was a big deal for the whole crew of the ship. The reason being was that this meant more cargo to be shipped and more money to be made in the process. It would make a big dent in the money situation if the "cooling box" decides to conk out before reaching Nova Scotia, Canada. Even though the voyage to New Brunswick from Nova Scotia was not a very long one, considering the times they were having trying to reach that port. These times were promising for the Captain Sven was on his way to get a new cooling box in Nova Scotia, Canada and at the same time see his brother Lars and his wife Ingrid. They had a daughter who is the Captain's niece Nelgrid but everyone called her Nelly. The Captain and his crewmen were to pick up a cooling box in Nova Scotia, say hello to his family and take his niece to New Brunswick, Canada. The Captain's niece was going to New Brunswick to attend a school for nursing and secretarial studies. They were to reach Nova Scotia port in a fortnight, and the Captain would have either a new "cooling box" or fix the old one they had. Captain Sven was also very happy about the fact that he was going to see his family. The Captain and his brother Lars had not seen each other in many years about six or seven to be exact, and his niece Nelly was all grown up now. And times have changed too she was a woman going to Nursing/Secretarial School for Women. This was a big honor for the family that Nelly was attending a very prestigious school for those times. Nelly unlike her family spoke very good English, because she came to Canada at the age of 4 so she learns to speak English quite quickly. When you are a young child like that you absorb things like a sponge. But then things change and we see life different as it would be for Nelly. She will encounter a whole new way of life aboard the ship as she sails with her uncle to New Brunswick for her schooling. She meets all the crewmen and she sees Alfred, and all the other crewmen were a blur to her. Of course, Turk being the King Pin as he proclaimed himself to be, tries to win the affections of Nelly so he would be in good standing with Captain Sven.

But that does not work out for him and this is another reason for him to hate Alfred as he now has the Nelly swooning for him and Turk. But Alfred does not do anything to encourage Nelly in anyway, for he knows from his homeland that Whites and Blacks do not mix.... But the European people the ones that were not small minded accepted the Black and Brown skinned people, but the lighter skinned black and brown people had no problem really. Alfred was a very light skinned man they called back home either a "High Yellow Skin" or "Redbone Skin." This made Turk even madder at Alfred, for the Captain's niece wanted Alfred and certainly not Turk with his brutish ways and heavy drinking. Whereas Alfred did not drink and was not a brutish man either. So now there was another storm a brewing and it was not coming from the sea or ocean, it was one man's hatred for another and what was to come.

    Captain Sven's niece was a fair haired young, with a pretty smile and blue eyes. Also, she was a well learned young girl as well, she also was a very healthy and buxom. The women and girls in Europe were all or most were healthy and buxom. Thus, was the only thing that Turk saw in Nelly and she was quite aware that he was a true brute. Her father Lars was a bigger man than his brother Sven and very protective of his wife and daughter. He would tear Turk apart if he knew what his intentions were towards his daughter Nelly. But now her mother on the other hand was a more Christian like woman compared to her husband Lars healthy and buxom just a little more older and rounder than her daughter Nelly. It was hard for Nelly's parents to let her leave them for schooling so far away. But thanks to the fact that her "favorite uncle" happen to be a ship's Captain, she could travel and go to the school of her choice. It was a longer ship ride than she thought, and Turk was always trying to find ways to get next to Nelly. She was not interested that Turk man at all, he was a drunken brute in her eyes and that was that. She only had eyes for Alfred for as she took stock of all the crewmen and decided that there was a few her age, but it was Alfred that caught her eye. He was a strapping young man with wavy light brown hair, gray eyes and a physic that would shame Adonis. His skin was lightly tanned and working out on the ship, in hot sunny days the sun would bleach his hair to a golden brown and his shin to a caramel color. This was a young man that Nelly found very enchanting and oh so different, from the other crewmen aboard the ship and from her fellow countrymen too... Nelly would watch and try to get Alfred's attention but that at timers proved to be hard. Alfred was concentrating his duties and he was also warned from Harry that she was the Captain's niece. But that as it may be did not stop young Nelly from getting Alfred to notice her anyway... This went for a long-time week almost half the trip to New Brunswick, Canada. She would try everything she could to get him to notice her and it was making Alfred very nervous. He knew that she was the Captain's niece and after the way he saw the Captain tell Turk to lay off, he was not about to be told off like Turk and be made fun of. Nelly was almost to the point of being relentless and this was scaring Alfred, he did not want the Captain to make him walk the plank either. Alfred tried to avoid Nelly, but she was always spoiled as a child and given everything she wanted no matter the cost. This was new Nelly not getting her way and being catered too, she was not sure how or what to do so she just waited and bide her time. She had confidence that Alfred would eventually come around to her way of thinking and she will have him for herself. This was a challenge that Nelly had never encountered before and she found it a bit amusing too. Alfred on the other hand was not aware of what was in store for him at all. He would find this anything but amusing, and he will not be easily intimidated by a spoiled girl.

 Seeing that Nelly found his shyness amusing, Alfred thought her to be a very spoiled and not amusing at all little girl. But one would think that this would put off Nelly but not in the least bit. She was more determined than ever now to be with Alfred and cure him of his shyness. But Alfred was not shy he was just being cautious, no to offend the Captain Sven as this is his niece and he was very fond of her. She was a spoiled and relentless young girl and did as she pleased. The pursuit for Alfred continued and she was hoping he would in turn court her. Harry told Alfred many times that he should stay away from Nelly, but Harry saw the way she would hound poor Alfred every day. Then one day happened Alfred had about enough and tried to tell her in so many words.

"Alfred what do you think of my new frock my parents bought for me to come on this trip and see the world before I start my studies in New Brunswick, Canada," says Nelly in hopes that Alfred will respond in kind.

Alfred looks up at her from his swabbing the deck and says. "Well, Miss Nelly I have a lot of work to do, and your pretty frock is to pretty for a ship."

"Well I never have been so talked down to in my life," says Nelly with an air of sarcasm in her voice.

"I hope I did not offend you Miss Nelly, but this a ship and it is dirty and a lot of crazy men aboard this ship, you have not seen any women but yourself for a long while," says Alfred hoping she won't go and tell the Captain her uncle.

"I see then, well I guess you could be right and I do see the way some of the men look at me. But you Alfred do not look at me that way. Why do you not see me as a woman?" asks Nelly desperately hoping Alfred will say yes.

"I see very well thank you Miss Nelly, but the reason is that I look at you, like I am doing now an d in hopes that your uncle my Captain does not make me walk the plank," says Alfred in hopes that she will understand his position on this ship.

"Okay I will let you work but under one condition, you come and have dinner with my uncle and me in his cabin. I will not accept no as an answer either," says Nelly with her air of arrogance and sureness about her, making it hard to say no to her.

"Alright then I will attend the supper tonight, but you must all so meet my conditions too. No making eyes at me or trying to get close to me, because if the Captain your uncle finds out, I am walking the plank for sure and this does not interest me at all." says Alfred wishing he had not accepted her invitation now.

Alfred waits impatiently as Nelly goes to tell her uncle Sven that Alfred, joining them for dinner and her Uncle Sven has or will not disagree with her. This was a big step for Alfred and the Captain, as he was not aware of what his darling little niece was up to. This supper was to be a revelation for all parties concerned and the outcome was yet to be seen. Alfred was n good standing with Captain Sven, and he did not want to ruin that in anyway. But the talk aboard the ship was that Nelly was the Captain's only niece and he doted on her and her every whim. So now

Alfred knew that he had to attend this supper and be on his best behavior and mind his manners. He could hear the words that his beloved Granny always said, "Alfred no matters where you go be a gentleman and polite and the world will be kind to you." These words stayed with Alfred although his life. So as not to offend the Captain Sven or his niece, Alfred decided that he would be on his best behavior and be a gentleman always regardless of the outcome ahead.

This would prove to be an evening of wonderment and questions that were to be asked. This could be the supper that would tell it all, now the only other thing that Alfred had to worry about was having a proper pants and shirt to attend the supper in. Harry who has been a great friend and mentor to Alfred let him his best shirt and pants. It was amazing to Harry to see that how much Alfred has grown since his escape from Jamaica, he fit almost perfectly into Harry's clothes.

The next question was where would get a pair of nice boots also. Low and behold Neville his native Jamaican friend lent Alfred his boots. So now Alfred was all set to go to the supper in the Captain and his niece Nelly in the Captain's cabin. This was also a privilege as only a very few got an invitation. But Nelly being the Captain's favorite niece it was all together different and no one could complain about it either. So, when the day finally came

Alfred took a bath something and combed his lovely wavy hair, and spit polished Neville's boots till they shine like diamonds. Alfred was very nervous and did not know exactly what to say or not say. Harry and Neville tried to help him as much as they could, Alfred never had any training in these matters but he was a quick learner, and listened to what the men had to say and watched and did as they did. In the end Alfred was still nervous but very willing to try, and see what the whole fuss was about and why. It would be an experience that young Alfred now a young man, no longer a little skinny boy that was smuggled those years ago. He was becoming a man of his vision and doing, he also respected those who respected him. He had come along way and now he was ready to go even further in life, with the hopes of one day returning to his homeland JAMAICA. Yes, Alfred was on a journey of life and where it was going to take him was still a mystery to him. He had to get over his shyness and nervousness to show Captain Sven that he respected him and his niece Nelly. And that he had no intentions of doing any harm to his favorite niece that he so much adored. This was what Alfred intended on saying to the Captain Sven if the question should arise. In the meantime, he kept up his work and kept his head down. As to not give anyone just cause to give him grief because Nelly chose him, instead of any other man on the ship to have supper with her uncle the Captain. Alfred was on pins and needles thinking about this supper he was to have with Nelly and her uncle the "Captain." He was nervous and all the crewmen could see it especially Harry. Harry helped him with his table manners because eating in the galley was not the same as eating in the Captain's cabin. Alfred found this to be a real chore and did not understand the fuss of it all. He was happy to eat just in the galley with the rest of the crewmen, but this invitation could not and should not be refused at any cost. So, Harry convinced Alfred that this would be in his best interest, and it could lead to better things for him in the future. As the invitation was soon approaching Alfred had to suck up his fear and be a man for this is what real men do, they accept a lady's invitation to supper and show up. It was all settled and a done deal Alfred got himself ready he wore the waistcoat that Harry lent him, and a nice white crisp and the polished boots from Neville. Alfred thought he looked a little odd, but then the more he looked at himself the more he saw the man he was becoming to be. He liked the look after all and decided that he looked good enough to make an impression on the Captain. Of course, Nelly would notice this too and be very happy that he decided to accept the invitation to the supper. But then Alfred was wondering who was going to do the cooking as he was helping more and more in galley. He was hoping that the supper would not be disappointing to the Captain and his niece. He was starting to feel a little anxious as the supper was finally here and he was still uncertain why his presence was asked to attend this supper. Deep down he was wondering if this was the doing of Miss Nelly and her way of getting him alone to some degree. But then he thought what harm could she do her uncle would be there and she had to behave as well as Alfred had to behave. This was weighing on his mind and he had to be clear headed to be able to answer and be honest with the Captain about his niece Nelly. But as Alfred was to find out that Miss Nelly who has an adoring uncle that gives her everything she wants, and if Alfred was what she wanted she was going to have him and that was that!! Poor Alfred he felt like he was going into an ambush and had no way to defend himself, this Nelly had a big crush on him and she was not about to let him slip away. She knew that if her uncle was on her side she and would eventually have Alfred, had he would have to succumb to her and she would be victorious. But this matter of the hearts was not what Alfred had in mind he was there to work and save his pays, so he could one day go back to Jamaica and see his mother Louisa, Granny and his siblings especially his sister Melvina. He longed to see his homeland again. But he was sure if he saw the Old Man Reid again he would not take his abuse and torture no more. He was a man now and he was not that little boy that was smuggled so many years ago. He missed his family very much and often thought about them and how they were and if Granny was still alive and if his mother ever found happiness and his sister any joy in life.

The supper with Captain Sven and Nelly has arrived and Alfred is all decked out in his bib and tucker looking quite dapper and very handsome and smelling wonderful. Harry made him pull out all the stops so to insure the Captain Sven that he was respectable to him and his niece Nelly. But Miss Nelly had other things in mind as she was such a willful young woman and spoiled beyond any boundaries that she came across. Nelly was determined beyond any reasonable doubt that she wanted Alfred and would whatever it took to get him. But she was forgetting one thing that Alfred had a mind of his own and was not so easily swayed. She was a spoiled young woman that was always handed everything she wanted and more. This was not going to settle well with Alfred he was not very fond of Nelly in that way. But this was a challenge for Nelly and she was sure she would win having her uncle Sven on her side to give in to her every whim. Nelly was very sure of herself and she was sure that her uncle would persuade Alfred to be her beau and maybe even marriage some day. Little did Miss Spoil Nelly did not know of Alfred's background and how he came about to be on the ship in the first place. She did not think things out as she was always use to getting her own way and this always proved to be a problem in her past. When Nelly did not get what, she wanted she could be a right difficult woman to deal with. She could be a handful at times and other times very sweet but only if she gets what she wants. This was not going to be easy for Alfred to endure he did not want to offend the Captain Sven and Nelly in anyway. But now he is plagued with the thought that if he does not succumb to the desires and wants of Nelly, the Captain will be offended and that could lead to Alfred being put off the ship or worse "Walk the Plank." Either way Alfred was not amused with any of these decisions that could occur. To hurt someone's feelings was not what Alfred was about he knew firsthand that hurting people was not right or kind. But then he thought to himself how could he break it to Nelly and the Captain Sven that he did not want to hurt anyone's feelings, and hopefully they would understand and be grateful for his honesty. But then again this Miss Nelly was a real piece of work, and she was out to get Alfred at any cost and she would use her uncle Sven to do it. Now this would put poor Alfred in a bid and he had to think about what he was going to say about all this. Even if Nelly is a spoiled young lady she still had to be told the truth and deal with it. This was the hard part and Alfred had to choose his battle ground very wise and carefully. For this poor Alfred was dealing with a tiger of woman and she was determined at any cost to get her hooks into him. So now before heading to the

Captain's cabin Alfred seeks out Harry and Neville to ask about how to approach this situation that has arise, and how is the best way to deal with it and to spare anyone's feelings in the process. Alfred was concerned with not wanting to hurt the Captain or Nelly and he did not want to hurt himself.

So now Alfred had a plan he would answer the Captain's questions with as much honesty as possible. The only disaster he could foresee was that Nelly being the Captain's favorite niece was the hard part because if she wanted, she could turn this whole supper around to her advantage. This was a problem that Alfred was not eager to enter lightly. Nelly wanted what she wanted when she so desired to have it, Alfred had witnessed this behavior first hand. Miss Nelly had the Captain Sven her uncle wrapped tightly around her finger, she just had to pretend that she would be devastated. At the thought of not getting what she wanted she would burst into tears and her uncle caved in. This was very alarming to Alfred he was not use to seeing a woman let alone a young girl get her own way from a man. But all in all, she did have a somewhat nice side to her that did not portray a spoiled brat. At times, she could be nice in an odd way these times were when she would strike up a conversation with Alfred. It was very clear to every crewman on the ship she had eyes only for Alfred, this made Turk even madder at Alfred than before. Turk was still under the impression that if he could just have a little conversation with Nelly, she would change her mind and see that Turk was the better man for her, and not some young buck that did not know women at all.

This was not going to impress Miss Nelly at all for she had her mind made up, and she was out to get her Alfred and be damn with the rest of them. The Captain s first was not totally blind either to his niece's whims, yes he gave in at times but it because he had no wife or children and she was his heart. When she was born, he gave her the nickname Nelly and he is also her Godfather as well as her uncle. Because of all this the Captain was weak in telling his nice Nelly "NO". Nelly at times would exploit her uncle's good nature and act like the real spoiled brat that she is. Another day to go and the supper party will be upon us thought Alfred. He was not looking forward to this, but the Captain has been very kind to him since his first night on the ship.

He promised Harry that he would be on his best behavior and mind his manners as well. He was troubled because he still could not for the life of him figure out why Nelly was so smitten with him. It was sure making Turk crazy with jealousy and hate. Alfred was aware of this hatred and jealousy coming from Turk, he watched his back a lot around Turk.

The day has finally arrived and Alfred will be dining with the Captain Sven and his niece Miss Nelly. But oh, what a supper it will be for the food will be great and the company very entertaining to say the least. Nelly was going to make her play for Alfred in front of her uncle hoping this will make Alfred once and for all, say what he feels and if he is not interested to tell her why. This was not the way Nelly wanted it to be but under the circumstances she did not have any choice. Nelly was a willful young woman and she always got what she wanted or else she demanded it anyways. It was an honor to be invited to supper with the Captain even if his niece did not join them. Alfred felt very special to be invited and to eat the same food as the Captain does. Eating in the galley was not the same as dining with the Captain in his stateroom. The Captain ate fine delicious foods and drank the best ale too. The galley food compared to the Captain's was not so great, so for Alfred to get an invitation was a feast he would enjoy despite the spoiled Nelly. He was determined not to let her ruin this night for him and try to ignore her when possible. Alfred was looking forward to eating the wonderful food he saw night after night being prepared for the Captain that his mouth would water. But tonight, it was water no more he would taste but the wonderful meals he always saw being prepared.

But Miss Nelly also was making plans for poor unsuspecting Alfred, on how to corner Alfred in front of her uncle the Captain. She was sure it would work it is her uncle's ship and she is his favorite niece and Goddaughter. She was so sure that her plan would work and she did not care about anything else. She was not only spoiled but self-centered to no end. This was infuriating to Alfred as he never could understand why she had her own way always. She was a young lady that needed to have her desires meet always. It drove Alfred crazy, he thought she was acting very childish.

In the shadows lurked Turk waiting for his opportune moment to take Nelly away from Alfred. Turk overheard the Captain telling Harry that if he had stayed in his country and help run the family business, he too would be well off like his brother Lars. So now Turk had an interest to start courting Miss Nelly and make her love him so they can marry very quickly... Turk would take this information and make it his mission to get Nelly to love him so they can get married. Turk did not know that Nelly found him repulsive and uncouth, he was not a hygienically clean man either. This was important to Nelly she loved to bathe whenever she could, this was something they had in common, they both loved to bathe and be clean about their appearance. But this was not going to stop Turk he saw Nelly as his meal ticket out of cargo shipping forever. He wanted to stop sailing everywhere and settle somewhere he could call home. He was tired of the ships since he was a wee lad he worked starting at the docks, and working his way up to crewman. Yes, it was hard but he did it now he was getting tired and needed a break from it all. If his plan worked, he could retire and live very nicely off the money Nelly's parents have. He had it all figured out, hopefully the plan does not back fire his face.

Nelly was not at all interested in Turk and made it clear to him on many occasions. But tonight, Nelly was saving all her energy for her capturing the heart of Alfred Reid and all that it entailed. Nelly was hoping that her uncle would be her ally as well in all of this, but the Captain for some strange reason was not looking forward to helping or giving in to Nelly at all. The Captain secretly hoped that he would be able to say no to Nelly at dinner. This saying no to Nelly would be a first for the Captain, because he knew that young Alfred was not about to give into Nelly as he always did. Nelly would get furious at the sound of hearing the word "no." She was so spoiled that she thought she was better than others, but this did not impress young Alfred Reid in the least bit. As Alfred makes his way from the galley to the Captain's cabin for supper and an evening of Miss Nelly, he tries very hard to be enthusiastic about the whole ordeal. As Alfred gets closer he tries not to seem too nervous as this could and might give Nelly girl the wrong idea. Alfred reaches the Captain's cabin he knocks but just before entering he hears only a female voice and now he is wondering what is going on here...

"Please do come in and make yourself comfortable, supper will be ready soon," says Nelly as she opens the cabin door.

"Oh, hello and how are you and the Captain this evening?" says Alfred as he looks around the cabin for the Captain who is not present in his own cabin.

"We are quite fine, thank you for asking, my uncle will be back soon he has gone to his private cellar for some wine," says Nelly with a twinkle in her eye as she gazes upon Alfred. How handsome he looks in some smart coat and long trousers with shiny black shoes, looking very clean and dapper just the way she liked her man.

"Well that will be fine then we can wait for him if that is alright with you Miss Nelly," says Alfred trying to stall Nelly in any way he can and hopefully it works.

"That is perfectly acceptable by me and Alfred please call me Nelly. I am not an old spinster yet I hope," says Nelly hoping that Alfred will get grasp the hint.

Just as Nelly was about to put her plan into action her uncle Sven opens his cabin door and sees that Alfred, has already arrived is sitting at the table like a real gentleman. He looks fondly at his niece knowing in his heart that she is up to something and he is not going to like it at all.

"Hello uncle and did you find the wine you were searching for in your wine cellar?" asks Nelly trying to keep things light for now.

"Oh yes I did and I am glad to report that there are a few more too," says her uncle Sven.

Alfred gets up from his seat and greets the Captain, "How are you this fine evening good wine, Captain Sven?" In a way, this evening had a good point to it; Nelly could translate for the Captain this evening for the language barrier it would be e got challenging. After all the greeting were said and done they decided to sit and eat the wonderful meal and drink the good wine that the Captain graciously picked from his personal wine cellar. So far the meal and wine wonderful and the conversation good. But by now Alfred was starting to worry again he got saved the first time when Captain returned with the wine. How was he going to dodge Nelly advances with her uncle right in front of them? The food was good just as Alfred had imagined it would be, he made sure he watched the preparation from start to finish. Alfred also noticed that seeing food being prepared then cooked into a delicious meal was something he liked and watched intensely. They ate the meal in a little bit of silence, and stopped to talk in between mouth full's and sips of wine. Seeing as Alfred and Nelly were young adults the Captain had no worries about offering them a bit of wine. But by now Nelly was getting anxious and wanted to resolve the matter of Alfred and her feelings. Her uncle could tell that his precious niece Nelly was getting bored and wanted to start something to her advantage as always. And this was the dreaded time that her uncle was trying to so hard to avoid for their sake as well. This was going to be a disaster if he must tell her no, and if Alfred does not reciprocate her feelings either. Just as the Captain thought that the supper was going along nicely, Nelly decides she has waited long enough and she wants answers and wants then now! Her poor uncle Sven sees that she is in battle mode and is about to do battle if she is turned down.

"So Alfred have you decided what you are going to do once you are finished working on the ships for my uncle?" asks Nelly trying to put her plan in action.

"Nelly I am not quite sure yet and still have a few things that I would like to try," says Alfred trying to keep the conversation on a light tone.

"Well you could always come and work for my father in Nova Scotia, Canada he has a very big factory there. He makes steel and aluminum siding for doors," says Nelly hoping it could convince Alfred into thinking about it at least.

"Thank you so much for offer Nelly but I am still very happy working on the ship for your uncle the Captain Sven," says Alfred with pride and joy in his voice.

This did not sit too well with Miss Nelly and she was starting to fume. The Captain noticing this tried to steer the conversation in another direction. He was just about to tell a joke when there was a knock at the cabin door. As the Captain gets up to answer it there was another knock only this time more urgent than he last one.

"CAPTAIN, CAPTAIN COME QIICK THE COOLING BOX JUST BUSTED AND WATER ALL OVER THE GALLEY NOW," bellows out Harry from behind a closed door. The Captain says his apologies and runs out quickly to see the mess.

Nelly saw this as an opportunity to find out how Alfred felt about her. But this time the fate was on Alfred and the Captain's sides. Only she was about to find out and she would not be happy. This was a "no" moment waiting to happen for real.

"Oh Nelly, I am so very, very sorry but my place is beside my Captain and the crewmen I work with. I have no choice but to go and join them. Please try and understand this is my job and I must do it no matter the circumstances," says Alfred silently thanking God for answering his prayers. With that he saw her there with a look of disdain and bewilderment all in one. This has never happened to her Nelly, the Queen of the Ball never ever happened to her.

"Well then you must leave must leave I must understand then also. But never you fear Alfred we will resume this conversation again at some point," she says as he turns from the door and looks at her without saying anymore words.

As Alfred approaches the top deck he notices that two out of three cooling boxes have exploded and water is gushing from them molten lava. All the crewmen were on hand to help every man pulling together for a common good. He was happy in a way that his happened for the simple reason being, that it made it possible for him to avoid any of Nelly's questions without hurting her feelings. She was very persistent kind of girl and that made Alfred very nervous. The two busted cooling boxes were gushing out water the crewmen had to fill and empty buckets of water at a time. This was something new for Alfred, still it was not as bad as the storm awhile back that they had to endure on high wind seas. The crewmen emptied and filled up more buckets it seemed as if it would never come to an end. The cooling boxes just kept gushing water and seemed like it was forever. But then after about three to four hours of filling and emptying water buckets, the crewmen took a break again they saved the ship to sail another day. This pleased the Captain very much and hoped he could repay his crewmen for their loyalty to him one day. But for now, he must get to New Brunswick and quick for this left him with one cooling box for the rest of the trip. Thankfully the cooling box that did not burst was the biggest one and it could hold a lot more than the ones that burst. If the Captain's calculations were right they would be able to make to New Brunswick, Canada Nelly who has never been away so long from her parents, the school she was attending has the best Nursing skills. She was lucky to have parents that can afford such prestigious school that offer good education and strict rules. In a way, she was looking forward to this it would be an adventure for her. She already met a young man that she fancies and she hopes he fancies her too. But for now, she must wait and see what and how she can make another excuse to be with Alfred.

All the while Alfred and the crewmen were bailing water from the ship, he was thinking how he had a narrow escape from the clutches of "Miss Spoiled Nelly." He wondered how he was ever going to get away again from Nelly and her desires. But now he had the job of mopping up the rest of the remaining water left which was not enough to bail out. This would take Alfred a few hours seeing as the ship was a long one to mop. Nelly knew she had to be patient this was something new she had to learn. It is very hard for a person that has always had what they wanted when they wanted it. Then suddenly your life changes and you find yourself, learning emotions and comprising things that you never knew existed before. It was a life shocker for Nelly when she realized for the first time in her life, she had to learn "patience" a word she never liked before. She was growing up a little thought her uncle Sven, but it was mostly wishful thinking on his part. Nelly's being "patient" seemed like an act to him. Down deep in his heart he hoped his beloved niece Nelly, would someday not be so selfish and try to think of others and not just herself. Her uncle Sven hoped that he would live long enough to see her change and be happier than she is now. In the mean time Captain Sven had to fix out how to get to New Brunswick, Canada before he loses his only remaining cooling box before it decides to gush out water too. The days wear on and the biggest cooling box is still running good. The crewmen are all looking forwards to docking in New Brunswick, Canada. He crewmen have heard from other crewmen that New Brunswick has more to offer for crewmen and sailors than Nova Scotia. They were already planning their shore leave and where to go. It had been awhile since the crewmen had any shore leave and the Captain knew that deserved some time off and relax for a bit. Also, Nelly was looking forward to two things one going to her Nursing School, and two getting Alfred on dry land where she could put plan two into operation. Everyone had plans for docking in New Brunswick everyone but Alfred, he was just happy to be seeing dry land again even for a little while. Alfred liked the sea but his homeland is on dry ground not wet. He would be home sick for his Jamaica always wondering how is family were doing, and if they missed him and if he would ever see them again. He was also excited to see New Brunswick, Canada a place he only knew by name but soon a place he will know period. The whole ship was looking forward to being in New Brunswick, and all the good things they heard about now they will see for themselves. It would be an adventure for some and others a new way of life. Either way it would be a life changing experience for some and others just a change of scenery. But for Alfred it could be a life changing experience that he could never believe would happen to him at all. It would be new and exciting and pleasant; it would change his life forever more and the better. But there will be obstacles in his way through out.

But there were to be obstacles in his new life to be had. It was all the excitement of going to New Brunswick, Canada and seeing the wonderful land that everyone was talking about. How it was a great place for raising livestock and farming. But the crewmen were not interested in that stuff, they were more interested the dance halls and the ladies there and the great whiskey they would serve. When seamen are at sea for too long they tend to get antsy and restless for land. They need to feel the earth under their feet from time to time, they loved the sea life but needed land life too. Alfred was looking forward to seeing New

Brunswick also he would hear how the others would describe it, and he found himself becoming curious about this place each time the crewmen would talk about it. And of course, Nelly talked all the time about her Nursing School she was attending there, she describes it from a scholar point of view. Either way Alfred found himself wanting to see this New Brunswick, Canada. He was seeing the world and all it had to offer. They sailed for a forth night finally reaching their destination. It was almost dawn when they docked. Nothing was opened yet. They were able to find lodging and food but had to wait for the local taverns and dance halls to open. In the meantime, the crewmen got their lodging and food and decided they would rest till later that evening. So, they would be nice and rested and fresh for the "dance hall ladies" and the great whiskey they sell too. But Alfred who by now was a grown man and had worked his way up to first mate in the galley, that's why he knew what the Captain always liked to eat and what they were given. Even though Harry and his friends would invite Alfred to join them he would always decline and say he had something to do. All the crewmen and Alfred and the Captain were under the impression that they were to stay in New Brunswick for just a week, but then they found out that they were staying longer than they thought. It turns out that the cooling boxes were so badly damaged that they could not be fixed in the time allotted.

So now the crewmen had to stay or they could work on other ship if it took too much time. The Captain Sven goes to see the man that his brother Lars who is Nelly's father told him about. Captain Sven finds this man named Mr. Wilson and he can apparently fix all makes of "cooling boxes." Captain Sven by this time is hopeful they will be fixed in time to sail.

"Hello Sir, are you Mr. Wilson, and do you fix cooling boxes?" asks Captain Sven. "Yes I am he. And whom may you be sir, and how did you hear of me and my trade?" asks Mr. Wilson a portly sort of man with a handlebar mustache.

"I am Captain Sven and my brother Lars Mendel from Nova Scotia, his daughter is attending the Nursing School her name is Nelly. She will be staying with the Morgan's until her school starts. I think you know of them maybe?" says Captain Sven hoping he is talking to the right person and seeming foolish with his accent.

"Oh yes, I know the Morgan's they live nearby my home, and they did mention his daughter attending school here and staying with them. You have come to the right place Mr. Mendel," says Mr. Wilson now that he knows who he is.

"I am so glad because my English not so good and I have trouble sometimes with the words," says Captain Sven with a sigh of relief on his face.

"Now that we have that out of the way, let us talk business and see what I can help you with today. And please do not worry about your English or they way you speak. It is all the same to me I am here to help you not to judge okay?" says Mr. Wilson glad for the work and hopefully repeat business and a satisfied customer.

"Mr. Wilson, I have three cooling boxes and two broke down on me while the ship was at sea. So now they just gush out the water no keep water like ice anymore," says Captain Sven hoping Mr. Wilson understands his problem. "Well Sven may I call you Sven, you may call me Michael I understand your dilemma and I assure you there is a way to fix your cooling boxes. But I am afraid it will take some time as I must order the parts required to fix them and make sure they run smoothly," says Mr. Wilson hoping that Sven will say yes and stay to have them fixed before he has to leave with his ship and crewmen.

"Yes, please call me Sven. Michael and I am very sure that you can fix them, but now my question to you is how long I wait and how much to fix both? asks Sven hoping that Michael will be a decent man and not charge a high price.

"Well let's see there are two of them and they have to be able to stand the rough seas and the everyday usage of them also. With this in consideration it could take between two and six months depending on how long the parts take to arrive here. And the price all included parts and labor about one hundred and fifty dollars," says Michael hoping he too did not sound too harsh in his pricing of his work.

"Well the price is fine and reasonable but the timing is too long, my crewmen have to work and their wages are not that of a rich man. Is there any way we can fix my cooling boxes in less time and still be workable to take to use at sea," asks Sven?

"You could get used parts but then your cooling boxes would just burst and gush water and make no ice. It is up to you Sven it is your decision I am here to help only. You think about it and get back to me in a day or two alright Sven?" asks Michael trying his best to sound fair as he can be and hopefully Sven sees that to.

Michael, I am hearing what you say and hope in a day or two as you say, we can figure out something else. And if not well then we will go with what you said about the two to six months' wait, but let us hope that we will not have to okay?" says Sven secretly hoping on his end that a miracle will happen so he and the crewmen will not have to wait so long to return to the sea once again. But as fate would have it the parts for the cooling boxes did not arrive in two months' time as hoped for. So now the Captain Sven was faced with the task of telling his crewmen that would have to stay longer. For some of the crewmen it was fine especially the single ones, but then there were the married ones with families. This worried the Captain Sven and he was not anxious in having to tell his crewmen the dilemma they were in. He mulled it over and over in his mind there was no way that this could be resolved without waiting for the parts needed. So finally, he decided to speak to his men. He gathered them up in the ship's galley and made sure every man was there before he started his speech. It was a speech he hated having to give knowing that this was a big setback for them all and for awhile yet.

"Men of my ship, I have asked you to come today to have a small feast and speak of the cooling boxes matter. Hoping you will understand why we need these cooling boxes fixed good so there is no more burst of water all over the ship," says Captain Sven secretly watching their faces hoping they understood him.

"Next question, how long do we wait and will we be paid for this time off unwanted?" says an almost angry Turk.

"You see men this is where it can be hard to understand. The parts for the cooling boxes are not arriving before another five months and we cannot sail till then," says the Captain wishing he had better answers than the ones he does have.

By now the men are talking and they are yelling and screaming about how they have families and feed. It was a bit of a commotion but then Harry stands up and sort of quiets down the crewmen, all eyes are on him waiting to hear what he says.

"MEN, MEN please settle down and listen to the Captain for a minute. He did not say he wanted this, he is saying that this is the situation and what can we do to fix it?" says Harry wishing now that he did not stand up and get evolved at all.

"Men listen to me please I have heard that local farmers are looking for field hands and they pay well and lodge like the ship," says Captain Sven.

This was good for some but others did not care for this plan at all not even for a little while. They took a vote and some voted to work on the farms, others opted to find work elsewhere on other boats. It was hard for the Captain to see his crewmen split up and not feel a little sad and responsible for them in a way. The crewmen voted and each went his way except for Alfred, he had saved his wages along and never spent any. He had lodging and food aboard the ship so he did not need to spend his money. He was saving to go back home to Jamaica one day. But for now, he needed a place to sleep and eat or he was no good to anyone. Alfred being young single man needed very little a bed to sleep and a table with chairs to sit and a cooling box for food, and a wood stove to cook and maybe a radio to listen to. This would be a good life for himself thought Alfred as he went looking for a rooming house. He was hoping to find a rooming house with furnished rooms for now till he decided what he was going to do. The furnished ones did not come cheap and if Alfred wanted to be broke for six months he had better find a job he thought. He took a few days off to look for his dream rooming house, the hotel was nice but getting expensive so Alfred was in a hurry to find a room. A few days had passed and Alfred found the perfect room for him and what he could afford too. He then set out to find a job that would allow him to stay in New Brunswick, Canada until the ship could sail the high seas again. He did not want to work on the farms it reminded him of the plantations when he was a child. He swore to himself the next soil or land he farms ever again will be his only. Time passed and eventually Alfred found himself a job it was working in the coal mines. There were a lot of immigrants like him but they hardly spoke any English. Even though Alfred spoke English with an accent himself it was more English sounding than the other immigrants. He was hired right away he enjoyed the work even though it was working with coal. He would be tired at night and by now Nelly had he were sort of sweethearts. It was not the passionate love affair she hoped for, Alfred courted but never made any real promises as far as marriage was concerned. It was not that he did not like Nelly. Her demanding and spoiled way about her, it made hard for him to warm up to her. But now with this job of his in the coal mines and Nelly's schooling, they saw very little of each other for periods of time. This made Nelly furious at times but as Alfred pointed out to her he needed to work and did not have a rich family to back him up. Nelly knew he was right but still being the spoiled and demanding girl, she is, she hated that Alfred never gave in to her whims of fancy. This drove her crazy and Alfred knew he was not about to be another of her "Yes Nelly" people in her life. And how dare she think that he could be bought. His grandfather Old Man Reid tried that many years ago and Alfred is still here! Yes, Alfred was becoming a man of honor and respect for himself and others too. It was another turning point for him as he sees this as a journey for him, and how he must follow this come along path wherever it may lead him. As he sits in his rented room he thinks to himself, "I have come a long way from being a snuggled child aboard a ship, and survived abuse on the ship and on the plantation and the violent stormy high seas."

Alfred now was wondering what would happen next. He knew this thing with Nelly was okay, but his heart was not totally hers and he felt bad for her and wish it was not so. But life goes on and people go along with it. Some of the men went to work for the local farmers, and some of the other crewmen looked for other ships to work on. The Captain was beside himself. He hated that his going out to sea depends on the cooling boxes and their repairable parts. He was invited to stay with the same family that is hosting his niece. He was still troubled over how this was affecting his crewmen and wondering if any of them will return to his ship and sail once again with him. But only time will tell and the arrival of the parts for the cooling boxes and all will be good again on the high seas.

    Mean while he was glad to see that Alfred and his niece Nelly were keeping company, going to the pictures and going on picnics when they had time to see each other. Sven hated that Alfred had to work long hours in the coal mines. Because his poor niece Nelly would whine all the time about how Alfred, works to many hours and they do not see enough of each other for her liking. Her poor uncle was at his wits end with her constant harping and whining when she did not have her own way. This was a shame because when Nelly was not harping or whining for something she could be almost like a normal young lady. But those times were few and far between and it was not something Nelly tried to practice. And these were the times that Nelly would be with Alfred and she would try her whining and harping act, and Alfred paid her no mind at all. Which in turn infuriated Nelly to no end but she did not let on and would bite her tongue to refrain from going any further in her whining and harping act. She knew that this was not the way to impress Alfred and make him take her seriously. But how he made her so very mad that she had to bite her tongue hard, so not to say or do any spoiled and demanding word or jesters. This was hard for Nelly had she was not use to being told no and or ignored during a tantrum... But Alfred was told by his Granny that people who act like the world owes then something is in for a very rude awakening. He tried to tell this to Nelly as nicely as he could but she was not having any of it. He stopped trying and left her to tantrums and demands, when she was not behaving as a spoiled brat he would go to see her. But this was also a reason why Alfred did not want to spend too much time with Nelly. But he also did not want to hurt the Captain Sven's feelings and Nelly's either. But he must be honesty and true and tell no lies. It was hard when he would try and tell Nelly about how he felt, she would look so as if she has lost her best friend her in the whole world. This also made Alfred feel bad for her and wishes he felt differently about her, but truth be told he disliked her tantrums and acts of fancy whenever she felt like it for attention. This did not sit well with Alfred and he was not about to love a young girl like that. The longer the Captain Sven and his few crewmen that were left stayed behind and wait for the cooling boxes parts, the more Nelly pursued Alfred in hopes of capturing his heart. Alfred was nice to Nelly and honest from the beginning, but even with him being honest she was still persistent in her goal to capture the heart of Alfred Reid. But it seemed to Alfred that at times Nelly acted as if this was her lifelong goal, to capture his heart as her sole possession. Alfred already knew about being imprisoned by choice or not, and he was not having any part of that in this life anymore. He was a little undetermined as to whether to stop seeing Nelly all together. But knowing that she would have a tantrum, and his not wanting to hurt the Captain Sven made his decision a little hard at best. But she was becoming impossible at times and her demands were becoming unbearable. He had some hard thinking and decision making ahead of him. He finally got to start to work at the coal mines, the coal mines were in Minto, New Brunswick, Canada which was just a small mining town about forty miles from Fredericton, New Brunswick. Alfred lived in Fredericton and worked in Minto, he would travel wanting all those miles twice every day. He sometimes had a lift with a co-worker or he would hitch hike a ride to his home. In Minto, it was a small community with just farming or mining those were your choices. It was a quiet community and mostly consisted of immigrants and some locals.

    Alfred did not mind working in the mines except for the coal dust part. He worked long hour's right along other men working just as hard. He would come home many a night tired and just to see his bed and sleep for hours.

Some weekends when he was not to tired he and Nelly would go to the picture shows at the local movie theater, or if weather were permitting they would go to the park for a picnic. Nelly was happy when she and Alfred were spending time together and having fun. She had a lot of school studies and homework. She found herself studying a great deal more than before, she was realizing that Nursing school was hard work and perseverance and a focused mind. It was a challenge that Nelly knew she could tackle and win, but she also knew that she had to be focused and pay attention more to her studies to succeed in her nursing career. But Nelly being Nelly did not want to think of this right now, her focus now was on Alfred and how to make him love her. She was almost at the point of obsessing over Alfred. This was alarming to poor Alfred he did not want to be her object of desire, he wanted to keep the friendship the way it already was. But then he thought to himself how can he tell her to slow down a bit without her taking a tantrum fit and being a spoiled brat as well. And then we must also consider the Captain Sven and how he would feel if his niece's heart is broken. This was a lot for young Alfred to take in and rationalize, he was at his wits end. He missed Harry at these times, Alfred over the years on the ship has looked at Harry as a surrogate father and highly respected his advice. He was not quite sure who else he could approach with this delicate matter. It was making him a bit crazy form all the sleepless nights agonizing over this Nelly problem. But unknown to Alfred the Captain Sven has been watching his niece when she interacts with Alfred she is demanding and spoiled. He knows in his heart that she this way because everyone has doted on her from birth. But even so it is not a good example that her family has taught her. She will be the one to pay later in life and it maybe too late to show her ways are not going to get her through life. He was also concerned that Alfred was staying with her out of some gratitude towards him. He hoped that his niece would change her ways before Alfred decides, to call it quits and she is left with a broken heart forever. It is also her first real crush and her uncle Sven is worried, that her first crush will not be the fairy tale she envisioned. Captain Sven knew he had to intervene and see where everybody's head and heart are at. Captain Sven he also very fond of Alfred he watched him grow from a boy to the young man he is today. But on the same hand he loves his niece and "blood is thicker than water." Still he felt very sad for them both he was hoping they could come to a compromise, but that would be very hard as Nelly never had to compromise in her life. This could be a shocking experience for her and she might not like the idea so well. Either way someone was going to get hurt here and it was not going to be an outcome that the Captain had envisioned. For now, he would observe and wait for the right opportune moment to make his plea. The mines were getting very busy now some men were getting promoted, which left other job positions to be filled. The mines were also recruiting new workers almost weekly, it was expanding so fast and people were using it for their stoves to heat and cook. Alfred was hoping for a promotion someday too but for now he had to wait and see what would be available to him. In the meantime, Alfred worked extra hard and kept his head down and be mindful to the boss. After all he had to be nice to the boss who gives him his wagers. Alfred was not new in a sense to the mines back in his homeland Jamaica, he saw how the men worked the bauxite mines. This was not so bad except of the black coal dust that was left on his skin and clothes at the end of the day. He would wash himself every night and day too, but sometimes the black was hard to remove. A co-worker of his told him in their best English of a soap, made of lye and chamomile base as to not burn the skin too much. It helped and the black coal dust eventually disappeared form is skin and some of his clothing. Seeing as this soap only worked on his skin he decided that his clothes already stained, with coal dust would be his work clothes and that way he did not have to stain all his clothes. Alfred like to maintain an air of cleanliness and he liked the clean shaven and combed hair, nicely dress too. This is what impressed Nelly for she liked a man that takes pride in his appearance. This pleased Nelly very much that

Alfred was like that. But as time went on the situation between Nelly and Alfred stayed the same. Of course, this did not sit very well with Nelly, as she always had to have her own way. But Alfred continued with his life and left Nelly to do the same if she so desired too. But Nelly had other plans and she was not going to let Alfred off that easy. She decided to try and plan another supper with her uncle present again, this time she must corner Alfred a little better. Hopefully it will be more rewarding than the last one on the ship. This time there is no ship to save from any disasters or broken cooling boxes. She was sure her plan would work this time and she was not accepting any "no's" as an answer either. She wanted to have him for herself, and how she would look at him with such longing in her eyes. But Alfred was not having any of that he was very nice and sweet to her, but not in a way that she wanted. It all goes back to the fact the Nelly is spoiled and demanding and is the Captain's niece favorite one at that. But even more so it is the fact that could she change her ways to be with Alfred. Now this was a question that both Alfred and Captain Sven have pondered during this whole courtship between Alfred and Nelly. But still for the time they already had together proved to be a question that would be left unanswered for now... But Alfred now was making friends and enjoying his work in the coal mines. He got promoted to supervisor and got to meet the men that worked in the coal mines with him. He got to meet to brothers who only one of the two spoke any English. His name was Jean-Babtisite Jacquart and his brother Jules, they had come over a few years before from Belgium a country in Europe. They were close to France and they spoke English also with an accent. But Alfred would see Jean-Babtisite and his brother Jules every week at the local market in Fredericton. They lived in a very small town where the coal mine is too. But there is no real market just a general store and they do not carry everything. Alfred would run into them every weekend while the brothers were getting the family supplies for the week. This would go on for about a few months seeing them at work and then on the weekends at market. Jean-Babtisite and his brother both noticed that Alfred always bought only fruits and vegetables very little meat. They went home and asked their parents if it was alright to invite their supervisor (to them it was like a Boss) to have Sunday dinner with them. They had to ask even though they were the biggest bread winners for the family. The two brothers came to New Brunswick first with their father whose brother helped them to come to Canada. Then later Jean-Batiste's parents sold everything they had. The bakery shop and the sewing and mending shop. His parents did this so his mother and five sisters and baby brother, could come to Canada and be a whole family again. Jean-Babtisite and Jules went home and asked their parents if they could invite Alfred to a Sunday dinner and introduce him to the family.

Meeting Anna

This was all for new to Alfred to be asked to a family Sunday dinner. He felt very pleased to be asked such and honor. It had been a long time since Alfred has any family resemblance of any kind in a long, long time. He was looking forward to a home cooked meal for once since his arrival to New Brunswick. It would also make a change from being cooped up in his little rooming house room. He liked it for the most part he had a clean place to sleep and wash and do the occasional cooking too. Now the only dilemma he foresaw was telling Nelly that he could not see her this coming Sunday. He knew beforehand that Nelly would kick off and start a scene for nothing. But Alfred was willing to take the chance because he wanted to go and have a good hot meal for once. But little did he know what was waiting for him at this wonderful Sunday dinner he was imagining. Nelly for sure was not having any of it, she wanted Alfred to decline and say he was sick or something. But Alfred told her no and she started to protest and it was not good in her favor. She should have just let it go but being who she is she couldn't let it go.

"Alfred, I see that I cannot change your mind and that you are going anyway? How could you do this to me knowing how I feel about you and that Sunday is the only day we can be together all day?" says Nelly trying not to be to outraged.

"You see Nelly, I am tired of eating the same thing every week because I have a small hotplate to cook on, and this is a good opportunity for me to get to know my worker men since I got promoted to Foreman. It will help me get to know the men better and get better work done with them too," says Alfred hoping she would understand and not make a scene of any kind, but that was not the case at all.

"ALFRED, I guess you have made up your mind and there is nothing that I can say or do that will change your mind, and make you stay with me instead?" asks Nelly trying not to sound to desperate and trying to hold back tears.

"I am sorry for you feeling this way Nelly, but I believe that if I have a good relationship with these men the work could be productive for everyone concerned," says Alfred without sounding to harsh and to the point, of hurting her.

"Well I see that you do have a point somewhere in your way of thinking. But still it is not what I want to do Sunday, your only whole day together."

"I know that Nelly but having good comradeship with the miners will be good for me. The big bosses will be happy to see that my men are very productive and better wages for everyone. I could even move into a two-room place and eat better too," says Alfred now becoming a little agitated with Nelly and her spoiled ways.

"I guess then your mind is really made up and I am not so sure that you will change it for me at all. I know you are ambitious but so am I. This feels like you and are heading in different directions and it hurts to feel this way," says Nelly hoping he will change his mind and give in to her and not be so stubborn.

Alfred more determined now than before was going to go, regardless of what Nelly said or felt. He was his own man now and he could decide for himself without having her to decide for him. As the Sunday slowly approached Alfred was getting ready for this family dinner. He had been looking forward to it all week. He hoped that even with the language barrier he would try and understand. He had docked a few years back in New Orleans, U.S.A. And picked up a bit of Creole. But this was not the French that Jean-Babtisite and his family spoke. It was called Walloon a dialect from Belgium also another dialect there was Flemish. But the Walloon language today would be considered French from Paris. He still hoped that he could fit in at least.

He liked Jean-Babtisite and his brother Jules, they were very hard workers and hardly ever complain about the work. It was a real treat for Alfred know he was going to be feed a wonderful and delicious home cooked meal. He was so happy about it that he went and got some flowers to give to the brothers' mother, Harry told him that it was a very nice gesture and showed he had manners too. He went there by horse hoping not to seem to show off, he did not want them to think he was a rich man. But as a man of little means like themselves for he too was an immigrant to this country. And knew all too well how strangers get accepted by the local people. Yes, they were white folks but white folks that spoke only French and so they were sort of outsiders too. But even so Alfred knew in his heart that he was more of an outsider than they were. He still did not let this in anyway change his mind about going to this Sunday dinner, at his new friends the Jacquart brothers' home. Oh, how he missed a good home cook meal it had been ages since he had one. He felt like this was a little piece of home and maybe the closest to it for now.

 He still felt a little sad for Nelly knowing she did not want Alfred attending this Sunday dinner at all. But he was looking forward to meeting the Jacquart family and the brothers' siblings. Alfred was told that the brothers had five sisters and a baby on the way, so counting the parents there was eleven people all together. This reminded Alfred of his home in Jamaica where he lived with his siblings and other relatives too. This was going to be a good day for him he thought to himself and he was hoping that he would not embarrass himself in front of these people he was about to meet.

As he was approaching the farm house he saw from afar a young girl bringing in pails of water. She was carrying them along her shoulders, with a long piece of wood and a pail hanging at each end. She entered the house just as Alfred rode up with the horse, he dismounted the horse and proceeded to the walk towards the farm house. As he was approaching nearer to the farm house, the two brothers Jean-batiste and Jules came to greet him but Alfred was searching around for the strawberry blonde girl carrying the pails of water. As he got nearer to the house he saw a vegetable garden that reminded him of his home and Granny in Jamaica. This made him think of home, back in time to his so-called childhood. But as quick as it came it left.

They lead him into the house to meet the rest of the family. First came Alena, then Irma, Anna, Olivia and Julia then the one younger brother Pierre and their mother Clementine who was with child. He was happy to meet them all but most of all he was happy to know the name of the "strawberry blonde haired" girl Anna.

He also detected smells and whiffs of some good cooking and maybe even hints of a pie. As he was asked to sit down he looked all around at this big farmhouse before him, and thought to himself how he wished he could be like this with his family too. He had an arduous like as a child and now it was getting a little easier. And finding friends like this was a bonus to him, he liked working with the Jacquart brothers Jean-Baptiste who he nicked named John only and Jules stayed the same way his only regret was that Anna did not speak any English or at least a bit of it.

As he sat down to eat this wonderful meal he looked around at this big family and thought that he too would have a big family and have a big Sunday dinner like this one. He ate a wonderful roast beef with boiled potatoes and garden vegetables and yes the whiff of pie was right on there was two pies apple and blueberry both of which Alfred liked a lot. He was enjoying his meal and the wonderful company of this lovely family that has invited him into their warm and pleasant home. He was also hoping that they would invite him again, it had been a long time since he ever remembered having such a wonderful meal.

"Nelly I am so happy that you accepted my invitation to afternoon tea. I thought it would be nice since it is a beautiful day outside," says Freddy hoping to get her in a good mood so there may not be any scenes since she was prone to having them.

"It is nice also to see that you have time for me, since you have made new friends and such," says Nelly trying to hold back her sarcasm for not liking his new-found friends.

"Well actually I have asked you here for another reason Nelly, and please hear me out before you give me answer. Here it goes I am not satisfied with our relationship and I think it would be wise to end it now. I am very interested in another young lady and would like to pursue her and hope she feels the same too," says Freddy holding his breath in anticipation that she might not take this well.

"So Freddy as you like to be called now, is that the new name your new friends gave you? And as for not seeing each other again fine but mark my words, do not think that when she says no that you will be welcome in my company anymore," says Nelly as she tries to walk away with her dignity and pose intact. But this was not the end she thought she was not letting any little snipe of a girl get her Freddy or Alfred from her ever.

"Well I must say you have taken this well considering the way I have presented it to you," says Freddy still waiting to see if she will kick off and make a scene that she is so famous for.

"Now I know why you have been avoiding me as of late. I was not truly certain but I found out that these new friends of yours, have five sisters could that be a reason for avoiding me Freddy?" asks Nelly trying very hard to contain the anger that was seething inside her terribly.

"Well now Nelly I do not know if that is really the cause but it could be a part of it. And as for the sisters of my friends well I hardly know them, I only know a little about them. As some speak broken English and others do not," says Freddy hoping to ease the tension that was building in the atmosphere around them.

"As I see it I am going to leave you now and bid you farewell. But mark my words Freddy Reid you will come back to me and maybe I won't want to you back," says Nelly as she turns and walks away without even a backward glance in his direction.

This was too easy thought Freddy and what was she up to? He knew that this was not the way she wanted things to be. He was afraid she might tell her uncle Captain Sven before he had a chance to speak to him. Freddy went looking for the Captain himself so he could hear the situation from Freddy's point of view. It took Freddy a few days to find Captain Sven and he went to him to explain why he ended his courtship with his niece Nelly.

"Oh, hello Captain Sven, am I ever glad to see you. I have something very important to tell you and hopefully you will not be to angry," says Freddy with bated breath awaiting the Captain's reaction.

"Well here it goes and please Captain hear me out first. I am ending my courtship with Nelly as you may or may not have heard. But it because I have fallen in love with another fair young lady and would like to be able to court her. But know this is not right to be courting two young ladies at the same time, so I am ending my courtship with your niece Nelly as to be fair to both young ladies," says Freddy hoping the Captain will understand and respect his feelings.

"I must say Alfred or Freddy is it now? You have come to me as a gentleman and as for my niece she is very spoiled and must have whatever she pleases. This is the families fault we give in to her whims and fancies, so do not worry I will handle my niece," says the Captain Sven.

This pleased Freddy very much as he knew the Captain would make her understand why Freddy had to end their courtship. So now it only left Freddy to ask the Jacquart brothers if he could court their sister Anna. But now there was another obstacle in his way Anna spoke very little English at best. He would need her brother John to translate all the time, but if he was smart as he knows he is, he will teach her to speak English in no time.

Freddy did not know that Anna was a very shy and timid young lady, and she was protected very much by her brothers and father. He would have to make a very good impression when he asks permission to court their sister and daughter Anna. Freddy already had a plan, he would wait and ask at the Christmas dinner. It was a time of giving and hopefully he would get their blessing.

Anna also had an eye for the handsome young man that her brothers had brought home to dinner one Sunday. And now there was talk he might come for Christmas dinner too.

She was hoping that the rumor was true. She also noticed that he watched her every move that Sunday. She noticed him that Sunday coming up the road towards the house. She made like she didn't because she was afraid to make eye contact and she would not know what to say if she did. So as not to embarrass herself she kept her eyes down. But this time if he should come to Christmas dinner and he looks at her she will look back. She was getting giddy just by the mere thought of him making an appearance again to her home. Now all that was left was for him to show up and let fate take its course.

By now it was getting cold and there was a lot of snow. Freddy had seen snow before but from afar while on the ships. But this was different he was walking in it and watching it pile up each day. He was glad that he had purchased warm long johns and sweaters to keep himself warm and cozy. But still he was not used to this cold weather and probably might never be either. He saw that sea and all water around them was frozen solid, so everyone who wanted to return to the ships had to wait for the water to thaw. This could take months said the local people who were used to the way the winters were in Fredericton.

By now the Christmas holiday was nearing and Freddy got an invitation to have Christmas dinner with the Jacquarts at their farm house. It was going to be a joyous occasion for Freddy because it had been a long time since he celebrated

Christmas or the New Year. Sure, he had celebrated on the ship but it was not the same as sitting down to a proper meal and a warm home to have it in. He was most happy to have been asked and he knew this feast was to be grand. The brothers Jacquart assured Freddy that their mother and sisters were cooking up a storm. They were making some traditional meals as well especially their native holiday meal which was made with veal and mutton. There was also to be this time pies and cakes and maybe even homemade beer and wine. Freddy was so looking forward to this meal that he almost forgot to ask Anna's brothers, if they would ask their parents' permission to let Freddy court their daughter Anna. He was feeling very nervous to ask this of them after all they did extend their home and friendship with him. But he was sure from the rapport he had with the brothers that they would not disapprove, but winning over the parents was another matter all together. Freddy had to approach this matter delicately and hope he wouldn't be misunderstood, seeing as the Jacquart's parents were limited in their English vocabulary. But fortunately for Freddy John and Jules between them had a pretty good knowledge of the English language. Especially the older brother John he had came to Canada with his father a year and half before the others, except for Jules he came about six months after John and their father. And the rest arrived almost two years after the father and two brothers, their parents had to wait to have enough money to bring the rest of the family over. Also, mother Jacquart refuse to leave Belgium without all her children in tow. So, they sold the bakery and her dress shop and made enough boat fares for her and the rest of her children.

It was hard for the family as first to adapt to the harsh winters and be isolated at times from other people. They made a garden and made preserves out of everything that they grew and stored it for the winter months that were ahead. The girls like to cook and bake and make preserves with their mother. Back then girls did not attend school to much only if you were rich like "Miss Nelly." But even thought they did not attend school their older brothers would teach them as much English as they knew themselves. It would take time but then again, they had all the time in the world, for this was their new home and they would have to try and fit in. But first they must conquer the language barrier and then go on from there. Anna being the shyest of them all was having a hard time to master the basic English language. She so wanted to be able to speak English like her brothers and have conversations with them. But hard as it was she was not going to give up anytime soon so she studied hard and paid extra attention.

In the mean time Freddy is trying to get his courage up and ask the brothers if they would speak on his behalf. He also hoped that it would not ruin their friendship by asking them this question. It was so mind boggling that he almost talked himself out of it and second thinking this to death. He just had to be brave and ask the brothers and see what happens from there. He knew there was only two answers yes or no, so it was a fifty, fifty draw, win or lose it was what is was. Freddy felt like this was a big step for him, he never felt this nervous when Captain Sven found out about him and Nelly. Nor was he as nervous when he told Nelly and the Captain that it was over between them.

But this was strange and good all at the same time. It was a feeling he had never experienced before not even with Nelly. He just had to muster up the courage and go and ask the brothers or he will lose his courage and lose a good opportunity in his life. So now Freddy had a decision to make and he had to make it before he was to attend the Jacquart family Christmas dinner. He was more concerned with how the family might react to him asking to court their daughter since his skin was a darker color than theirs'. This was a problem that Freddy had always faced from childhood and sometimes now in is adulthood too. But some countries he had visited while working on the ships were not prejudice against people of color or even language. But then Freddy thought for a moment and realized that the Jacquart family did have him in their home, and they did not make any references to his skin color at all. So maybe he had nothing to worry about at all. He just had to relax himself and ask the brothers to ask their parents for permission. Freddy was a little shy by nature but he knew he must be a real man and approach this situation as an adult and not as a young boy smitten by love. He knew this is what he had to do and the sooner the better before he lost all courage and hope. He thought it would be easier to ask the brothers to ask their parents because of the language barrier, and it would or might be better coming from their sons on Freddy's behalf. He thought he would ask them after work one day to see if they would be on board with the idea of him courting their sister. He finally confronts the brothers and asks them the question, will they speak on his behalf?

"Hello John, hello Jules how are you both feeling today? I have a huge favor to ask both of you and I am hoping you will say yes," says Freddy with anticipation hoping they will say yes to helping him.

"Okay then Freddy what is it you want to ask us," says John with a questioning look in his eyes. "Yeah the Freddy, as Jules likes to call him in his broken English. "what you want to say us?" with a questioning look also.

"I am not too sure how you both will react to my question and |I hope we still be friends? I would like for you to ask your mother and father if they would let me court your sister Anna if you both agree too," says Freddy with bated breath in hopes that they will say yes.

"Well then Freddy," says Jules as he tries to look serious, "I must ask John to ask because he is the oldest and me well I am younger."

"John will you ask them for me and I would be very grateful to you both," says Freddy sweating over this now.

"I will try and talk to my father and mother for you but I can talk for them, you must be there too so they know that you are serious about courting our sister Anna. You know Freddy she is my sister I love the most so please be sure or I will not talk to mama and papa," says John in his most serious voice.

"Well I hear what you are saying so I promise whatever questions your family have for me I will answer in all honesty and with truth too," says Freddy hoping to convince the brothers that he wanted to court their sister Anna for real.

"Then let us say we ask mama and papa when we have Christmas dinner at our house on the farm. It will be a festive time and papa is always happy at Christmas," says John hoping this will turn out good for Freddy as he really likes him and is happy he is his friend too. So now Freddy was a little less nervous knowing he had the Jacquart brothers on his side and hopefully they will be able to convince the parents too. Freddy must now wait for the Christmas dinner to find out for sure if he will be able to court the lovely and very pretty Anna Jacquart.

The Christmas day and dinner were finally here and so was the moment that Freddy would find out for sure if the Jacquart family were in willing and accepting of Freddy courting their lovely daughter and sister Anna. He was getting more nervous with each step as he got nearer to the farm house, he was anticipating the outcome. Back home his beloved Granny would say that Christmas was Jesus' birthday, and a day for all mankind to be kind to each other and a day for miracles. So here was Freddy praying for a miracle to his question in hopes of a good answer. A positive answer.

	As he approaches the front door he is greeted and greets the family, starting with the parents first and then the children in order of birth. It was this way last time too he remembers the brothers telling him, that this was the way in their country you would greet a guest to your home. He liked this custom for each time they would greet him he got to see Anna again, and not just a fast glimpse like at the mines when she brings lunch for her brothers. As he entered the house he smelt all kinds of delicious things. Freddy looked at the table it was huge and filled with food from every angle and it all smelled so darn delicious. He knew one thing for sure even if the Jacquart family declined his permission to court Anna at least he would have dined as a King this Christmas day. The Christmas table was set very nicely it had on it, a very large turkey, potatoes two kinds mashed and boiled, also the vegetables that were grown in their very own garden. And of course, the mouth watering pies and cakes. But there was a sausage like food there also but it was black instead of the usual sausage color. It was explained to Freddy that in their country, Belgium it was called "Blood Pudding" a form of sausage like substance made from the blood of a pig or cow. Freddy thought to himself that this was worth trying if he wanted to court Anna and he did so he must also adapt to their ways not just with food but everything. He was determined to show the Jacquart family that he was worthy of their daughter Anna.

He was so amazed at how this family with all the children were so happy. This was foreign to Freddy for he never saw happy families til now, and it made his heart feel warm. The father sat at one end of the table and the mother sat at the other. Freddy and John sat to the left of the father and Jules on his father's right side. The girls in order of birth sat around the mother on opposite sides of the big farm house table. Anna tried hard to sit across from Freddy but manage to sit almost in his line of vision. She liked Freddy and was hoping he liked her too, but she was unaware that he was going to ask her parents' permission to court her. As the dinner was coming to an end Freddy hoped he did not make a bad impression on the family. That they would not mind at all about him courting their daughter. But also, he did not know for sure if Anna felt the same way. They have never shared more than a friendly glance or a shy smile from Anna herself. Freddy was hopeful that Anna seemed to like him too even if they had a language barrier. Oh yes, he thought, the language barrier he would ask John and Jules to help him with that and he in turn would help them with English.

Freddy was hopeful and felt in his heart it was right. He never felt it was right with Nelly and he sort of felt bad for her too. But you can't help what the heart wants and his heart was telling him he wanted Anna. As dinner ended the girls cleared the dishes and removed all the plates and bowls. There was a lot left over as the Jacquart women cooked like they were going to feed an Army.

The father and brothers sat around the now cleared table. As the father Jacquart prepares his after-dinner pipe, awaiting his coffee, he feels like his sons have something to ask him. Being somewhat of a wise man he can only think of one thing. Yes, he is aware and not blind to the feelings between men and women, he has noticed on occasion that Anna and Freddy have exchanged shy looks towards each other. He was sure by the way that Freddy was a little nervous he wanted also to ask father Jacquart something too. Father Jacquart found this to be amusing and fun to watch how young g people fall in love, it would be entertaining too. For he knew how hard it was for a young man to ask to court someone's daughter, and if he should so desire to marry Anna one day it would be even harder to ask then.

"Papa may we speak with you man to man on behalf of our friend and guest Freddy, for as you know he cannot speak our language yet," asks John. Speaking for both he and his brother Jules who is very shy to ask their parents anything at all.

"Well my sons what is it you want to ask your dear papa? And by any chance does it have to do with one of your sisters Anna perhaps?" says papa Jacquart as he smiles at his sons who are in disbelief of how their papa knew of this matter.

"Papa how did you know and when, and for how long now? We were afraid to approach you before now we were not sure of your reaction to this matter we must ask you. We are also hoping that we speak for Freddy and we also approve of him as a suitor for our sister Anna. We hope you and mama and the rest of the family feel this too?" says John hoping he convinced his father who will convince their mother also.

"Well that is all well and good but what about asking your sister Anna, how she feels and if she is also wanting to be courted," says mama who has been listening all this time and waiting to answer on behalf of her daughter Anna.

"Well then it is settled we will ask Anna and then we can decide as a family how to tell Freddy yes or no," says papa as he sits back smoking his pipe and watching poor Freddy as he sits nervously waiting for an answer to his question.

"Freddy, we have spoken with our father as you have heard, my parents agree that we should speak with our sister Anna first. It would be better if she had a say as to what she wants to do also. She may be shy but she prefers to do her own thinking and talking for herself. You know what I mean right Freddy it is only fair," says John hoping that poor Freddy will not have a heart attack over night and not know for sure Anna's decision about her wanting to be courted by him or not.

"I must say you are men of your word and I am very happy that you spoke for me to your parents. Let us hope that your sister will listen to you both and maybe let me court her. I like your sister Anna very much and would like to know what she feels for me," says Freddy with hope and courage in his voice as he speaks with the brothers.

"It may have to wait until the New Year dinner. It will have given us time to talk with our sister and parents at the same time. Can you wait that long or will your heart burst before the New Year?" asks John as he is eldest and must protect his family.

"I am very sure I can wait till then it is only a week away. That will give me more time to practice your woolon language. And better to communicate my intentions to your family," says Freddy hoping all will go well in his favor for the following week.

"Well then, we will wait and see what our sister Anna decides to do and say on this matter and how best to handle it good or bad no matter the outcome," says John.

Freddy takes his leave and bids everyone a good night except for Anna, she was hiding in her room, listening all the while to what her brothers and parents were talking about. She knew by the sounds and some words they were saying it was about her and Freddy the new young man that worked with her brothers. He was handsome and very tall compared to her height. He also dressed very dapper and smelled like clean shaving soap. It was a change from smelling her brothers from the mines with their sweat, and he papa with his manure smell to him after feeding and tending to the farm animals. She had a week to think of what to decide and why her parents were not too sure of letting her be courted as she was still too young. But she was wise and could cook, clean and mend and even work the land. She was fearless in these ways but the ways of the world were still a mystery to her and she was about to learn that too soon.

Freddy waited patiently but wanted so much to ask the brothers how "the talk" was going. It would be weeks until Freddy got his answer but to him it felt like months. He was a little confused at times about his feelings because he never felt this way for any woman or girl before now. He was hopeful though because the brothers kept on being his friend and keep him up to date on Anna's well being. But as for telling him of their parents' and Anna's decision, the brothers were quite closed mouth. It was a little frustrating for Freddy but he knew that this was the way of Anna's family and he had to show respect and honor to Anna as well as her family.

Anna before coming to Canada two years prior had just made her first communion and so she was still a very naive young girl. Her parents and older brothers were not about to make any haste or drastic decisions concerning their little Anna. Freddy waited hoping the answer would come soon, and he would not be so nervous anymore he could relax and breathe again. Unfortunately, he still had to wait a little while longer as Anna's parents were not too keen about her being courted off yet. She still was a little girl in their eyes and they were not ready for her to grow up and be a young woman.

The fact of the matter was back then, young girls were considered a woman at the age of fifteen years old and Anna was thirteen soon to be fourteen so her parents knew that she would be looking for a suitor soon. Still it was a hard thing for them to think about.

They already went through this before with their other daughters; Alena, Irma, and Olivia. This left only Anna and Julia the two youngest daughters. As for the sons, Peter had just gotten married about six months before, and Jules was engaged to be married whereas John the eldest was undecided yet. Mrs. Jacquart was expecting very soon so this would make either another daughter or son.

So finally, Anna's parents asked her what she thought of Freddy from Fredericton, New Brunswick and would she like for him to court her? Anna asked her parents if she could think about it for a few days. she had heard her sisters talk of being courted and then married. She did not understand all of it but she could understand what she needed to know and how to give her parents an honest answer as well. Anna took her few days and finally sat her parents down together and proceeded to give them an honest answer. They were also very curious as to what Anna would say, and Anna was curious as to how her parents would react to her decision today.

"Mama and papa, I have to accept the courtship proposal from Freddy from Fredericton. I know I will like and eventually love him. I have been watching him now for awhile when he comes here for dinner, and almost every day when I bring my brothers their lunch buckets to the mines," says Anna. Hoping her parents will say yes too and they will see that she is very honest with her answer and she likes him also.

Her father clears his throat and says, "Well then Anna I can see by what you are saying and acting you are truly fond of this young man Freddy. He is a gentleman every time he comes here and from what your brothers say he is a good man who goes to church too. But the only question I keep asking myself is how will you both converse with each other, it will be hard no?

Her mother looking at her daughter and then her husband before answering, she wants to be very sure that this is what her Anna wants.

"Anna, I can see that you are truthful in your answers and you took the time, to think and reflect and see the positive and negative that could prove to obstacles. Like your father says the language barrier could complicate things for you both," says her mother Clementine. Hoping in her heart that her Anna has made the right choice to be happy.

"Mama and papa please be happy for me and give me your blessings. Both of you please. Also, my brother John who we all love and adore, will be there to chaperon and translate everything we say to each other, until the day I can speak for myself okay?" says their daughter Anna. Hoping they see she is very serious about wanting to get to know

Freddy better and they did not have to worry as John is there too.

As John walks into the parlor where his parents and sister are sitting, he looks at them before he attempts to answer on Anna and Freddy behalf's. He clears his throat a bit before speaking his mind on the matter at hand before him.

"Mama and papa, I see that Anna has made her decision and I hope that I can report back to my friend Freddy that he is getting the answer he wants and should have okay?" says John hoping he said enough but not too much to ruin Freddy's chances.

"Son we have all decided that your sister Anna can be courted by Freddy and that you will chaperon and translate for them also. Is that acceptable to you and hopefully you can tell Freddy that these are the terms for now, until Anna can speak for herself," says Mr. Jacquart as he stands up to walk over to his son and shake his hand, as to seal the decision that they had all just made.

He kissed Anna on her check to symbolize the same seal of the decision too. It was a good day in the Jacquart house for all was happy and good. John was happy to be reporting to Freddy the great news and he was happy too that he was making his sister and friend happy. It made his heart feel good that he could help Anna and Freddy be together even if he had to be present all the time.

He thought to himself he must also try and be discreet and not seem to be in their business too much. His parents hinted to the fact that he could also try and court a young lady. As his married sisters have single sister and cousin-in-laws that were very interested in finding nice single young men to court them. But John preferred to find a nice young lady on his own and in his own time as well. This is what would make John happy. He did not want to be hassled by his parents to find love and settle down. John believed that he was still young enough, twenty years old, and had a lot of time yet for all that. The irony of it all is that he would settle down and marry, if he could find the one true love he so desired and wanted secretly in his heart and mind too find. But for now, he must go and find his friend Freddy and tell him the good news and see what his reaction will be to the answer.

John asked Jules to go with him as Freddy asked them both to be his allies in this matter of the heart. Jules said yes and they both set out to go and find their friend Freddy from Fredericton and make his day that much better.

As they reached his rooming house they rang the bell and waited for the landlady to answer. When she came, and opened the door they asked for Freddy. She said he was at the corner restaurant having a meal. She bid them a good day and shut the door. She was not a very cheerful old lady.

The brothers turn around and went to seek out Freddy at the corner restaurant. As they approached the restaurant window they could see Freddy sitting in the back-booth drinking coffee. They crossed the street and as they got near the restaurant, Freddy sees them coming towards the restaurant and waves to them to join him. As the brothers get closer to Freddy they have a sober look on their faces, making poor Freddy think that bad news is coming his way.

They enter the restaurant and go to sit with Freddy and they order coffee as well. Freddy looks at them with anticipation and sweaty hands, hoping he will get the answer he has been waiting for and he will be happy. They sit down slowly not saying a word but all the while looking straight at Freddy. The suspense is getting to Freddy and he wishes they would say something, anything to ease his nerves and mind too.

"Freddy, our dear friend, we, my family and I do not know how to say this to you. We all have come to same answer even our sister Anna. We want you to know we think about this for long time and Anna too. So, we all say yes to you courting Anna and she says yes also. One thing you must say yes to or papa say no, I must be there so I can be protector of Anna and help her speak and understand English. Is that okay with you and will it make a difference?" says John.

Jules looks on to see any reaction from either man sitting down before him. He always lets John do the talking in these matters.

"I see then, if that is the way it must be then so be it, but one thing I ask of you John," says Freddy with a hint of teasing. "Will you promise to teach you sister Anna how to speak English better than you already speak yourself?"

John looks at him and with a wink says, "Well I cannot say for sure if my teaching of English to my sister will be quick, but for sure it will be enough hopefully for the two of you to understand and speak together. As for my chaperon of my sister that is my parents wishes and I will do as they ask, until they ask of me no more," says John this time no wink and more serious than before he wanted Freddy to understand him now.

"Well I would never ask you John or Jules, to go against your family for me that is not being a gentleman at all. To show I respect you and your family and Anna, I will let us be chaperon until your parents are sure of my intentions with your sister Anna," says Freddy hoping they will also understand him and respect his answer to their demands as well. It was hard to tell if they believed him.

Sitting there listening to all being asked and answered Jules looked and hoped they will also understand why he is speaking now too.

"I have always let you talk my brother John, but this time I want to speak too. You must give Freddy a chance also obeying our parents is good too. It is how mama and papa taught us to respect them and love our family. So please let him court our sister Anna and see what kind of man he is and if he can fit with our family."

"I guess my brother has a voice after all. I was getting to wonder if he lost his tongue, but God gave it back to him I see just in the time he needed it. My goodness I do believe God is with my brother Jules today amen," says John. Thinking that he is being outnumbered somehow and believing that his brother Jules may be right this time around.

It was finally decided upon they would have another dinner and invite Freddy, and then the whole family could make the announcement at the same time. It would be better this way and less embarrassing for Anna and Freddy. The first time officially courting it was going to be a great night for all.

Freddy was still worried about the dinner and the announcement to be made that night. He still had time to make a proper proposal himself, but he was not quite sure how or what to say. He surely did not want to offend Anna's family in any way possible. Freddy made very sure that when he arrived at the Jacquarts for dinner he would be prepared and gentleman like and respectful too.

As he sat in scrutiny of her two brothers he thought to himself these two gents are my friends but there are first and foremost Anna's brothers. Bearing this in mind he had to make sure he was right on point when he would address Anna's whole family that day.

All in all, it was going to be a great dinner and he was feeling positive now that he knew and got his answer, so this also would ease the tension and his nerves. Freddy thought to himself that life could not get any better than this moment and he was happy, truly happy.

For this happiness was almost like how he was happy as a child. Except for the torture and abuse by his grandfather Old Man Reid. He vowed to himself a long time ago that he would not dwell on this part of his life, since he was smuggled on the ship and never looked back. Yes, he was always homesick for Granny his mother and his siblings, and a few of his friends too.

But for the most part since he left Jamaica he had made a new life for himself. Being a man now he could make his own decisions be they good or bad. It seemed like a life time ago when he was running in the sugar cane fields and eating rock candy. Now he would make new memories and a new life maybe even get married and settle down here in Fredericton, but that was a long way off yet. He had to court Anna first and be sure that she wanted the same thing too.

So, in the meantime he will be happy with just courting for now. He had faith in himself and God and he knew that God would direct him down the right path. It is because even though Freddy seldom went to Sunday School back in Jamaica he still listened when Granny would preach the gospel so he knew about the power of praying. He knew that praying helped him many times when he was scared and lonely as a boy, and as a man helped him make the right choice. At times, it was hard for Freddy to do the right thing being a young boy, growing into a man aboard a ship and learning about life from a bunch of crude and some obnoxious crewmen. But despite all that growing up stuff he knew right from wrong and turned to God in times of need.

All the pep talks he has been giving himself are nowhere to be had. He wanted to bring a gift this time for the dinner not dessert, as Mrs. Jacquart can bake. He goes to the European baker in town and asks him what would be appropriate to bring for dinner.

"Well hello Mr. Sauvè, how are you today sir, and I am hoping you can help me," says Freddy as he looks at Mr. Sauvè.

"Hello to you too Freddy, I have not seen you for long time. Are you okay or working hard?" asks Mr. Sauvè.

"I was wondering if you could suggest a wonderful dessert to take to the Jacquart family for dinner. You see

Mr. Sauvè I am going there to get permission to court their lovely daughter Anna, she is a very, very pretty young lady," says Freddy beaming fondly.

"I see, then you do not need pastries or cakes my dear young man. You need flowers and a big bouquet for mama and a little bouquet for Anna. You must not insult the mama and daughter when they have cooked and baked all day for this occasion correct?" says Mr. Sauvè hoping that Freddy will try and understand that this is good advice and will surely take the advice he is given.

"I understand what you are saying Mr. Sauvè but where do I get such flowers as you advise, and will I be able to afford them?" asks Freddy more worried and nervous thinking about how can he afford the bouquets of flowers and not be embarrassed also.

"Dear young man do not worry I have a cousin by marriage the florist Tremblay and he can help you with whatever you can afford. Maybe he can make an exception with a discount," says Mr. Sauvè with a smile on his face.

"I would be so grateful to you sir and to your cousin the florist, but are you sure he will give me a discount? If not it is okay too," says Freddy feeling his nerves coming back to normal.

So, Freddy turns and walks out the bakery shop across the street to the florist Mr. Tremblay. He is a nice man and a friendly person and everyone likes to get their flowers here too. Freddy turns the door knob and as he enters in the shop he gets a mixed smell of roses, daises, and sweet petunias too. Freddy loved the smell of flowers it reminded him of his homeland and how he would run in the fields and woods and smell all the different flowers blooming.

As he approaches the counter to ask for Mr. Tremblay, a big man emerges from the back of the shop he looks at Freddy and waits for Freddy to ask a question from him. For he already knows why Freddy is there to shop.

"So young man how may I help you today and do you see anything you might like also?" says Mr. Tremblay trying not to giggle.

"Good Mr. Tremblay, I was told by your cousin the baker Mr. Sauvè that you could maybe help me with a problem of etiquette for me please. Sir I would be most grateful and it is of a great importance I do not go there looking like a donkey with no ears," says Freddy starting to feel nervous again and sweating palms start to form.

"Well then you have come to the right place and I am sure I can help you young Freddy. I am sure we can find something to make it easy for you. We have received a new flower plant this year and everyone likes it, they use it as a center piece for the dinner table. It has beautiful red blossoms and green leaves, and stays alive for the whole two months and then you plant it outside for next year," says Mr. Tremblay hoping he could really help Freddy out with his problem.

"Mr. Tremblay, that sounds really good but I need that plus a small bouquet for Anna too. I must not go there empty handed it would be an insult to the family and Anna," says Freddy really starting to worry and even more nervous than before he entered the shop.

"My dear Freddy, it will not cost so much, let me make you a bouquet for Anna and a plant for the family dinner table okay," says Mr. Tremblay. "Let us say first what can you afford Freddy and we can go from there okay," says Mr. Tremblay.

"Sir, Mr. Tremblay I can only afford to pay five dollars in total and I know that these flowers cost a lot more than that for sure," says Freddy with a sigh of despair in his voice hoping maybe the florist would lower even more his price.

"Let us see I am sure we can say five dollars is enough to purchase a plant and a bouquet of flowers. It is a deal then come by and get here before noon.

"Oh thank you so much sir, and I will be here before noon and will have your dollars for you okay," says Freddy beaming. He could not believe his good fortune that he will be able to present himself as a proper young man to court their daughter.

So, Freddy left the florist shop and went to thank Mr. Sauvè again for his help. So now all he had to do was wait for the day and the beginning of a new courtship. Little did anyone know that Freddy was already in love with Anna and now he could also tell her and let her know. Hopefully she would also feel the same way.

As fate, would have it Anna also fancied Freddy and has fancied him for a little while now. Every since he has been coming to dinners and she sees him practically every time went it would be her turn to bring her brothers their lunch pails. Each sister had a turn to bring the lunch pails even the married ones because they had husbands that worked the mines also.

But Freddy had eyes only for Anna and he was smitten and so was she, but she was nervous too as this was the first young man she has ever courted. To have her parents and brother's permission was something she did not think possible, but she was pleased deep down inside and tried hard not to show it to much. As she did not want to jink it ever. As the days slowly approached Freddy and Anna were both a bundle of nerves too. Even thought they were a few miles apart, they still were nervous about courting and being courted and it was to be a big celebration all around and joyous day to remember.

As the day slowly approaches Freddy thinks to himself what a delicious meal and day it is going to be. With his purchases, he also thought how could he go wrong Mr. Tremblay the florist said it was a "sure fire way" to win the ladies over.

Freddy was already imagining the sweet smells of the delicious dinner he was to eat. He also started to think about the other reason for his being invited to dinner, he was going to get to court Anna with her parents' permission. This pleased him and made him quite nervous at the same time because it was an occasion of real importance to him. He was nervous but he was not going to show it. If at all possible he wanted Anna to see him as confident and bright young man that wanted to court her. Anna also did not want to appear as a foolish young girl either her only problem was the language barrier but she knew her brother would help her. She trusted her family very much and knew that they would be supportive of her in every way. But Freddy he had to rely on himself and in his heart and mind he felt like he was a good baptized Christian man in the eyes of God. Freddy seemed to a little more religious as time passes he still remembers Granny's preaching to the children and it somehow was starting to stick to Freddy. This was good thing as the Jacquart family were religious too especially Mrs. Clementine Jacquart the Matriarch, of the family and the mother. It was something that all her children knew and practiced. The father on the other hand Mr. Jean-Baptiste Jacquart Sr. did not go or do anything religious with his family, but they prayed for him anyway. As Freddy was getting ready he was wondering if Anna truly wanted to be courted by him, if she did not, he was sure she would have said something by now.

As he agonized over this fact Anna was at her home also helping with the last-minute preparations and getting ready herself. Her sisters gave advise as much as they were allowed too as the older ones were married and they were not too sure themselves. Anna had finished her Convent schooling before coming to New Brunswick, Canada so she never engaged in conversation with men unless they were her brothers or her father. This was going to be something of an adventure. Freddy was from another country and so was she and here they meet in a little mining town through way of her two older brothers.

As Freddy approaches the house he is so nervous that he thinks he forgot his voice too. The whole Jacquart family greet him at the door and everyone is thinking the same thing how will these two-young people act tonight. Freddy walks in, as he does he hands a beautiful plant to Mrs. Jacquart and a small lovely bouquet of pink baby roses to Anna. This bouquet was small yes, but it said a lot about his gentlemanly ways and manners too. Mrs. Jacquart accepted the plant and Anna accepted her bouquet as well. They all sat down with the plant and bouquet center table pieces it made the table lovelier this year. The food on the table was delicious as always. As they were starting to eat everyone was glancing at Freddy and Anna waiting for a reaction from either of them. Freddy and Anna were very shy and wanting to be able to say more than hello or good day. Each knew that they other would and could have language problems but it was not going to interfere with them and they wanted to be together despite the odds in their favor. It was a silent dinner until Mr. Jacquart decides it was time he said something.

"Since I am the head of this house and father to Anna, all this time John his son is translating for Freddy, I and my family are happy to give our permission and blessing to Freddy to court my daughter Anna and with my son John as chaperon and translator too," says the father Jacquart as he waits for an answer from Freddy, he looks at his daughter and tries to wonder what she is thinking too.

"Well I am very happy and hope that Anna will be very happy with me too. I will try my very best to learn your language too I have already asked your sons with whom I work with and they are helping me very much. But with my thick English accent it may take some time," says Freddy hoping this will not make the family or Anna change their minds about him. But as it turns out he was scared for nothing as he looks at Anna.

"I am very happy that Freddy wants to court me and I am also happy to learn his language as well and maybe some of his cultures too," says Anna through the translating of her brothers. Anna smiled at Freddy and everyone knew that this was a good match and a very happy one at that.

They proceeded to finish the delicious dinner and enjoy the day and the new beau their friend Freddy was to their sister Anna. They would go on to have a great courtship Anna eventually learning English well enough to communicate with Freddy and he learned a little Belgium but understanding more than he could speak.

The courtship was going along smoothly for about six months and everyone was enjoying seeing the two young love birds together. As fate would have it something or someone again comes along to put a burr in this lovely relationship. And it was certain someone that was not giving up on Freddy just yet. Oh, yes, the ugly eye of jealousy rises again! Miss Nelly hears about Freddy and Anna and she immediately goes crazy and asks her Uncle Sven if he can interfere on her behalf. But Sven has had enough and it has been quite a long time now since she and Freddy parted ways. He knew that Freddy was much happier with Anna than he ever was with Nelly his niece, but despite all this he still loved his niece and hoped this would not make Nelly hate him. Six months had already passed and the Captain Sven was already back from a trip and he was getting ready for another. The cooling box repair man is very good a t his job and this made Captain

Sven more money, so he decided to come back and purchase another cooling box from the same man. When Nelly heard of this she immediately put thoughts in motion wondering how long it would take to get Freddy back from Anna. But Nelly was in for a surprise because little did she know that Freddy and Anna were already in love and she was too late. Besides her Uncle Sven wanted Freddy back on the ship with him whether he courted his niece or not. But Freddy's life had changed. First working in the mines and then meeting Anna and her family. So, he was happy now to have a family again and he did not want to leave. So when her uncle returned and told Nelly Freddy was not leaving Anna, Nelly broke down and sobbed for awhile. Then she lifted her head and dried her eyes and said thank you to her uncle. Captain Sven said goodbye and left but he still felt that Nelly was not taking it as well as she pretended to be. This was a little bit alarming to her uncle but he still had his ship to run and maintain so he decided he would wait and see what happens.

But after a few weeks of waiting for a new cooling box the Captain hears that Freddy has asked Anna Jacquart to be his wife. But her father says she is still too young and Freddy must wait a year. So he is waiting and working in the mines and he also got promoted to Foreman. So, Turk also hearing the same story going around the town he starts to think maybe this is his big chance to try and court Miss

Nelly. The Captain Sven leaves for his next trip the following week and Freddy announces that Anna said yes and he is building her a house in the meantime. The whole Jacquart family is so happy that they give Anna and Freddy a lovely piece of their land and they help him build the house. As Freddy and Anna wait to be married they still court and build their beautiful home for their wedding day.

The Change

Something happens and the people of Fredericton, New Brunswick start to ask the question. Are you enlisting? Do you want to go to war? Yes, there is talk and World War 1 becomes legend. It was a worldwide spread war. It would destroy millions of people and many countries also. But for now, it was just talk but talk that was making more sense with each broadcast it was given. The people everywhere were listening and wondering will it come here? Are we safe in our own homes and country? Or will we have to join the Army, Navy whatever they want us to do just to save our own skins? It was a very trying and depressing time for some but he two young loves just kept going along and plan a wedding anyways despite all the chaos and mayhem about them. It would still be a little while yet for the War to manifest and wreck havoc among the world's population worldwide. It would prove to be a very big thing and people had to take and make everyone notice and know it could happen to them as well as anyone else in the entire world. But Freddy and Anna were still very happy and in love. There was on delay though the wedding had to wait because Anna was not yet fifteen and that was the age her sister got married and another at sixteen. This was the law in the Jacquart home and it was abiding by and that was that. Freddy and Anna decided that yes they would wait and in the meantime Freddy would build their happy home as a wedding present to Anna. But Miss Nelly hears this and she is beside herself now knowing that Freddy is truly going to marry Anna Jacquart, so she goes into a fit that she is noticed for and it does not help. But poor Turk thinking now he has a chance is refused and heartbroken because Nelly has no intention of ever letting Turk court her at all. This is something that she would never let happen and her uncle would just be so mad at her. So in lieu of this wedding happening Nelly does the right thing and tries to forget Freddy and move on with her life. As time goes by for Freddy and Anna they enjoy each other's company and the language barrier becomes more and more less odd to them both. They enjoy going out to picnics to family outings and just taking long walks too. But now that Freddy is promoted to Foreman of the mines he has more work to do and tries to make time to see his lovely Anna, it is hard at times but the two love birds make it work for them. As the time goes by Anna's birthday is about a few months away and so they decided that her birthday is July 26th, they would get married July 24th seeing that her fifteenth birthday is just two days after and Anna was sure her parents would not object at all hopefully. And as for Freddy he just hoped they would say yes to the whole idea....

As the months went by and it seemed ever so slowly for the two love birds, but it would all be worth it in the end. As the months went by it was getting harder for the love birds to wait, but even so they also hope that their home would be built in time too. This was very important to Freddy as he wanted Anna to have the home of her dreams. He also wanted her family to know that no matter what he would always provide for her. He left his home and family and now he was making a new family in another country very different from his own, and Anna was facing the same thing being from another country herself. So, the two had things in common and if they can master the others language they will have it made. As for the wedding, well it will be small but tasteful and Anna's sisters and mother plus Anna herself were going to make the food and as for some spirited drinks the men of the family had it covered. It was going to be a great day and a remembered one too. There was a hitch to all this wedding stuff, Freddy still could not find his baptismal papers saying he was baptized Catholic. So now it was going to be a dilemma as he Catholic priest could not marry them without proof of being baptized Catholic Church. So now Anna and Freddy start to panic and wonder what to do, they try to ask for a special permission from the church itself but they were refused. Upon hearing that Freddy and Anna were having wedding problems the Captain Sven was boned to marry anyone who wished him to do so, provided it was on his ship and they were willing to do so. The ship did not have to be at sea if it was docked in the water. So, Captain Sven went to see Freddy and asked him what he thought of the Captain's idea, at first Freddy was hesitant and pondered the thought for a moment before answering the Captain.

"Captain Sven it is a very generous offer you make to myself and Anna, but I cannot answer for her and her family. And I would not like to come between you and your niece Nelly if for any reason," says Freddy hoping he did not offend the Captain Sven.

"My dear Freddy as you like to be called now, you could never come between myself and Nelly we both know that she is capable to do that all by herself, right?" says the Captain as he clears his throat he starts to say something else. "I believe that you and Anna Jacquart really want to marry soon and live in your beautiful house that you have built for her. Then I propose that you and I pay a visit to her family and ask her parents and Anna what they think of my proposal to you both," says the Captain feeling good about his decision and hope it will help Freddy with not having his baptismal papers.

"That sounds really great Captain but do you think that they will go for the idea and we can get married Anna and I?" says Freddy trying to be hopeful about the whole thing and maybe it just might work too. Freddy thought to himself what harm could it do anyway.

"Freddy my dear boy, it is settled then we shall pay a visit to the Jacquart family and speak with the parents, and the older brothers as they are friends of yours and can translate I do believe," says the Captain seeing the doubt almost leave Freddy's face.

"I am very grateful to you Captain for doing this and may God be on our side," says Freddy as he starts to think of a way to make the Jacquart family let the Captain marry them. But in his heart, he knew that it was not the same as having a priest bless the wedding vows. But as the Captain explained to Freddy that it was not as nearly as scared as a "Holy Wedding" but the Captain was also an "Ordained Minister" himself back in his country Norway. He has not married anyone in a long time and he was looking forward to this joyous occasion, and he could not think of a better couple to perform a wedding ceremony if they will agree. Now all he had to do was convince the Jacquart family that he being a Captain of a ship is not is only credentials, but that he is a "Ordained Minister" seeing as it is not Catholic it is still a recognized religion and it is legal. But Freddy was afraid that Mrs. Jacquart was a firm Catholic and very much into her religion as she tried to instill in her children. Even though Mr. Jacquart was not as religious as his wife he did let her have her say in the religious upbringing of their children. So now Freddy was praying and hoping that God in his infinite Wisdom would help these two young lovers get happily married by the Captain as they could not by a Catholic priest. Then Freddy had an idea he would talk it over with the brother John and Jules to get their reaction, and maybe he then can have knowledge as to how it might all turn out. It was going to be a bit tricky as to how Freddy was to approach the Anna's brothers and asking them in a hinting way what their parents reaction might be especially their mother's opinion on the whole matter at hand. Freddy was sure that that brothers would sort of understand as John also has been bitten by "Cupid's Arrow" and he knew what it was like to not be with the one you love. John has fallen for a lady but she is recently a widow and by law must wait a Mourning Period of a year before even considering any marriage or courting of any kind. This was hard on John because he and the widow Johnson were in love her full name is May-lee Johnson, her deceased husband was Earl Johnson (God rest his soul). He died in the mines a huge shaft fell on him as he tried to climb out of the deep hole he was in and did not make it. So now Mrs. Johnson is a widow with a child to take care of so she mourns her husband and pines for John Jacquart as well Lord forgive her. Her love for John Jacquart happened slowly after her dear husband Earl died. It was about three months later they started talking and they got to know each other and liked each other, and it turn into friendship and blossomed from there. Freddy knowing this about John was hoping he could appeal to John's own dilemma and use as an example of what being apart from your love one can do to you and how much it hurts inside just feel that way. He truly hoped that the brothers would be on the side of their sister and their friend to make their parents see, that having the Captain Sven marry them was not the end of the world and was still in the eyes of God just not a Catholic God. It was going to take some doing but if Freddy ever believed in faith it was now that he need to and fast. Anna on the other hand knew her family and knew how her mother was about her Catholic religion and it means a lot to her, this was going to be tough...

But Freddy was sure that John and Jules would plead his case before their parents for their sister and Freddy. It meant a lot to Anna and Freddy that her brothers would take the task of speaking to their parents for them. But Anna was not too sure about her mother and the religion thing that had to be resolved yet. It will prove to be a hard task at that but for some reason Mrs. Jacquart always listened to her children when they are speaking to her, especially her eldest boy John and sometimes Jules as they are the two eldest boys and have an opinion and thoughts of their own. All in all, it remained to be seen if Mrs. Jacquart would consent to having the Captain Sven perform the wedding ceremony. But the two brothers and Freddy and even Anna put their heads together and tried to come up with a plan that would please everybody concerned. It was hard going to think of something in a religious way for the mother Jacquart to except and be comfortable with also. It was would take some brain storming and a lot if Hail Mary and Our Father prayers to reach a point where everyone would be happy and life could continue as before. Anna was worried that Freddy might like the idea that her mother was very religious. But as Freddy had her brother John explain to her that he understood her mother being religious because, his beloved Granny was the same way and he understood too. So, they tried and tried to come up with a solution to the wedding vows dilemma it was harder than they thought and they tried to come up with something concrete. Freddy asked everyone if it was a good idea to ask the Captain Sven to speak to the Jacquart parents himself, but having John translate as the Captain's French was not very good and he needed help in translating what he knew he wanted to say to them. John and Jules both wondered why the Captain Sven wanted to help them meaning Anna and Freddy. After all, didn't Freddy once court his niece Miss Nelly and would this not be awkward for him in a way? But it seemed that Captain Sven was not so shook up about the situation as the brothers were. What they did not understand was that the Captain Sven loved Freddy as an adopted son. The years they spent on the ship together made them have a mutual admiration for one another almost like family. So, for the Captain Sven feeling awkward about performing the wedding sermon, he could not be more delighted and honored. Now the only thing that could make this wedding not happen is mother Jacquart and her religious beliefs. But Anna knowing her family as she does know that her brothers will find a way for her parents to make their mother and father see that this is a religious wedding sermon just not a Catholic one. But that all religions of different faiths are no less religious in their ways too. Catholic religion is not the only religion that exists in the entire world, but it might as well be for mother Jacquart she saw no other religion and being from another country what was all she had to survive here in Canada. But as time changes things so do people and mother Jacquart is about to enter a new way of life, she will find it hard to adapt but eventually she will try and conform to the new ways of this country called Canada. And she must also learn to speak another language as well. This seemed all to over whelming for her at times even though she finds it difficult to cope at times, she must also remember that she is near her time to birth another Jacquart child who will be the first born in the new country Canada. This is why she held onto her religion all the new changes and her new unborn child and speaking a different language it was at times very stressful too. But her faith kept her going and it would prove to her salvation at these trying times for her to carry on and be brave for her family and herself as well. It was a new beginning here... But even with all that mother Jacquart was true to her faith and letting the Captain Sven marry her daughter to Freddy was a long shot at best. So now they had to find a way to make mother Jacquart see that this was the only way for now. But little did everyone know that Captain Sven had an "Ace card" up his sleeve. But all would be revealed at the meeting with the Jacquart family and things will be said and done for sure.

The older brothers set up a meeting between the Captain and their parents for the following week coming up. This was real nerve racking for Freddy and Anna for the decision for them to marry weighed heavily on the family decision. But Freddy was sure that the Captain Sven would be able to make Anna's parents, see that this was the only option that they had for now. But as always time would tell all and so that was that for now. It would be hard for Anna and Freddy because they wanted so much to be married, as young people in those did and they wanted a family of their own also. So now they just had to wait and see if the Captain Sven and the Jacquart parents can agree on this....

It was along week for Anna and Freddy they still courted during all this fuss about who marries who and why. But then the meeting was finally coming to be and everybody was wondering the same thing; can the Captain Sven make the Jacquart parents see that this is legal and blessed by God also. But only time and the good Lord knew the outcome. As the Captain Sven arrives at the Jacquart home with Freddy he is greeted by the whole family and they all sit down around the same table Freddy and the family share meals on. They sit and wait for the Mr. And Mrs. Jacquart to sit first and then everyone else sat too. It was a little tense in the house but the Captain was sure he knew what he had to do. And if need be he would because of his fondness and admiration for the wonderful man that Freddy has become. And Captain Sven knew that Freddy always wanted a family life. Since he left his homeland Jamaica he has always talked about having his own family again. This was the chance he needed and wanted and Captain Sven wanted this for Freddy with no doubt in his mind and Captain Sven was not leaving this house until he could marry these two-young people or at least find someone who could. But the Captain Sven had a secret and if need be he would use it.

"So John please tell your parents that Freddy has told me about the problem of he and Anna not being able to marry by a priest I hear? And I find this very unsettling to me as I can also perform wedding sermons. And as for Freddy he is a Catholic in his country they were all baptized by the High Church of England. Some were baptized Catholic and some were baptized Anglican. It depended on the plantation owners religion, and so their slaves were baptized the same religion," says the Captain as he looks around the table and seeing two people wanting to be married and trying to be hopeful about it all.

"Well then let me translate all of this to my parents and we shall see and hear what they have to say and how we will try and solve this problem," says the eldest of all of them John as he proceeds to tell his parents. All eyes are on them and only poor Anna can understand at this point. The Captain and Freddy look to Anna and John for facial expressions to try and understand what is going on and how the parents are taking it but from what was being observed the Captain was seeing not a lot of smiles. And just two young people trying and hoping would maybe change the minds and atmosphere in this home this day. As he thought about it again and looking at the sad faces of Anna and Freddy, he knew he had to do something and he had to do it now or else. There was a pause and the Captain took this opportunity to speak again and so he did.

"Excuse me John, but I think that I have something more to add to this conversation it is about me. I am about to reveal to you something very personal to me. You see back in my homeland Norway, I was an "Ordained Minister meaning I am of the Anglican faith. This a religion almost like the Catholic faith the only difference is we do not do the holy sacrifice as the Catholic do. But with that being said we are recognized in the eyes of God and man," says the Captain hoping this will persuade the Jacquart parents to try and see if this is a good way too. But seeing those sad faces was making the Captain sad too.

"Well now Captain Sven if what you are saying is true then I cannot see why you should not perform the sermon. But then again the final answer is from my parents. But I will tell them of this new situation and see if it cannot be more suitable for this family," says John hoping he can persuade his parents to see this is as close to Catholic as can be for now. And he also said a private prayer as he approached his parents with a new proposal and hoping this time they will let his sister and friend marry and be happy.

As they wait for the Jacquart parents to decide the girls bring out food and something to drink for everyone while they wait for the decision to me made and it would not be a hasty decision either. The Jacquart children knew their parent's ways very well and that is what was worrying poor Anna now. And the house that Freddy and her brothers help build was quite near ready and they wanted to move in as a married couple. So now this depended on the parent's decision and if they were okay with the Captain Sven marrying their daughter and not a Catholic priest. The Captain was hoping they would let him perform the sermon he was so looking forward to marrying Freddy and Anna, as he looked at Freddy as a son he never had. This would be an honor and it would be the happiest day for him. The

Captain gave up being a "Minister" because he was not getting enough funds for his Parrish so he tried to work to help his church. But when he could no long help them he went to work on the boats it was to be for a short while. But he came to love it and worked his way up to Captain of his own boat. And the years went by he left the church and gave the position to his next in line.

But Captain Sven always sent money back to that church that he once looked and watched over for years. But seeing as the Jacquart parents know this he was wondering if he did more harm than good. But as they wait to hear the decision from the Jacquart parents they sit and drink in silence hoping not to evoke any bad vibrations and so as not to jeopardize the matter at hand. There they all sat around a big table looking at each other and not knowing what to say at this moment. The atmosphere is tense and quiet which Freddy thought could go either way. As for the Captain Sven telling his story Freddy and Anna hoped that the parents would also take this into consideration for the two-young people who just want to be husband and wife and have a family too. As it was the Jacquart parents who wanted time to think it over. What it meant was to try and convince mother Jacquart the Anglican religion was almost in some ways similar to the Catholic religion. Mean while Anna and Freddy still had to wait a little longer, since Anna's parents asked to have a week to think things over. It was okay with them as they still time to make everything official and binding. It was going to be hard to make the mother Jacquart to consent to this marriage union if she feels it is not of Catholic doing. This prospect made Anna feel that maybe her mother was not going to budge. She prayed and prayed as her mother had taught her to do. Freddy on the other hand was on pins and needles hoping that Mrs. Jacquart will be persuaded to see that this was almost as good as having a priest preside over the sermon. Still everyone had to wait for the week to be up, and at the end of this week everyone will know the answer.

It was proving to be hard and stressful week for the two-young people in love. They were hoping and praying that it will be a positive outcome and all will be happy. It is hard at the best of times to plan a wedding and make sure all is right and well in the world. But this was a time also that gossip and rumors and even some truths were going around about the "War", it was a to be all over the world hitting a lot of European countries too. But as the people were saying to one another it is just a rumor at best, even rumors, gossip can sometimes manifest truths. But for right now Freddy and the Jacquart boys were not thinking of that at all. Everyone had hoped that mother Jacquart would make an exception for Anna and Freddy and not make them wait because certain birth certificates cannot be found. After all, as John and Jules say he grew up on a plantation maybe the people there did not keep records. So maybe Anna's parents would take this into consideration and have some compassion and be more open minded to thought of the Captain Sven doing the wedding sermon and making her happy. But Anna knew it will take a lot of convincing for her mother to see Anna and Freddy's side on this wedding matter. But during all this wait and pressure Freddy and Anna's brothers kept on building her dream house and life went on. When Nelly heard that her uncle wanted to do the wedding vows for Freddy and Anna, she was furious she wanted to scream so loud and so long that she was beside herself. After seeing Nelly in the local General Store and Market Turk still tried to court Nelly and was hopeful, because he had heard that Freddy was marrying Anna Jacquart and building her a house with her brothers. Poor Turk thinking he could court Nelly she never liked from the first time she saw him aboard her uncle's ship. But that Freddy was another thing all together he was handsome not to dark, he turned into a good looking young man, light brown wavy hair skin the color of a light caramel and a physic from all those hauling crates and other physical duties. Freddy turned out to be a handsome gentleman that was about to be married to a pretty strawberry blond girl from Belgium and she stole his heart and poor Nelly does not stand a chance any more. She was also furious with her uncle Sven she was sure he would be on her side and not with them... But her uncle Sven was not worried or impressed by her behavior to him or the situation at all. So now they had to do was wait and see how the Jacquart parents were going to react to the situation and if father Jacquart will be victorious in his wife bending a little in the name of love.

But as the week has now come to an end the Jacquart family sat around the big kitchen table, everyone in their proper seats awaiting the decision that was made by the parents. This proved to be a nerve-racking week for Anna and Freddy they were on pins and needles most of the courting time they had as of late. But as they say true love conquers all and hopefully it will here too. But as the father and mother of this family changed looks, everyone else held their breath especially poor Anna as this was about her impending wedding. She prayed and prayed that her father would be able to soften her mother to the idea of Captain Sven marrying her and Freddy and give her blessing too. But as Anna knew her mother she was asking the impossible in way if a blessing. As they all waited with bated breath the father of the house hold and the head of it too, slowly rose from the table and cleared his throat before speaking and looking at his wife also he took a moment as if to be totally clear on their decision to let the good Captain Sven marry their daughter to Freddy. And as the father decides to speak he looks to John.

"My son would you please honor your father and translate this what I am about to say word for word? Your mother and I have decided that if the good Captain Sven marry your sister and Freddy, that Anna and Freddy must also promise one day to renew their vows but in a Catholic church. And they must also promise to keep searching for the birth certificate proving Freddy is a Catholic also," says the father Jacquart.

"Well I will translate this all as you say father, your every word will be spoken as you wish. And I am sure by the big smile on Anna's face that she is very happy right now."

says John as he turns to Freddy and Captain Sven to tell them the good news too.

"Freddy my friend and Captain Sven, I have some great news for you both. My parents have agreed that the good Captain Sven can do your wedding sermon, but you must promise also that you will never stop looking for your Catholic birth certificate. And when you do you will renew your wedding vows in a Catholic church. This is the only request my parents ask, is this okay with you both and can you keep the promise?" asks John as he looks to his sister Anna and looks at Freddy to see their reaction to all this.

Freddy is the first to speak as he rises from his chair he looks first to the father and then the mother Jacquart knowing that John will also translate for Freddy word for word.

"Mr. and Mrs. Jacquart to have been very kind to me, letting me into your home feeding me and making me always feel welcome. I would also like to say that your wish for me to continue to find my birth certificate I will gladly do. And I would also like to say that your excepting of Captain Sven to do the wedding sermon is very gracious of you both. And please be very sure that I will always take care of Anna and she will be happy," says Freddy as he looks again at Anna's parents for a reaction of some kind.

"Well I have something to say and I am also very happy and honored to be able to perform the wedding sermon for Anna and Freddy and I will give the best wedding sermon that Anna and Freddy deserve. Because their love should be honored also in the eyes of God and Man. It should be blessed and celebrated for all to embrace and rejoice.

As everyone sat down again after they all had their say the Jacquart parents, told their eldest son John that they were satisfied and the wedding was going to be as planned. The nerves were gone and Anna and her sisters started to pick up the pace for the wedding now that it was happening for sure. The Jacquart girls including Anna were very busy preparing for the wedding. As for the men, they were busy too finishing up the last touches to the house they were building in time for the wedding night. It was going to be a glorious wedding and the family and friends were excited for Anna and Freddy.

Everyone but Miss Nelly she was told by her uncle Sven that he was doing the wedding sermon after all. She undoubtedly was not impressed to say the least she even tried to plead profusely with her uncle, not to marry Anna and Freddy and to think of her feelings in all of this. And to make matters even worse Turk asked if she got an invite if he could be her escort for the day. Well that just made her more angry and bitter because she knew there was no way that she was going to be humiliated by those two love birds and her not be loved at all. She deep down would love to be invited but as the bride not a guest in anyway, and especially not escorted by Turk of all the heathens she could not.

This was the last straw for her. Uncle Sven presiding over the wedding sermon and her being asked by Turk to be her escort was just too much for Nelly to bear. She took to her bed and stayed there for days on end. Her parents were worried but knew why she was acting this way. She truly thought that she would one day become Mrs. Alfred Reid, but it was not to be as another woman was about to have that honor and her name was Anna. Freddy made his choice and never regretted it for a moment even with the language barrier between them. But as the time went by they got better at understanding each other. They still pronounced some words different that did not stop them from being in love and wanting to be married to each other despite the pitfalls before them.

Yes, this was a very different love between two people but sometimes opposites do attract and it is a very good thing. Even thought they come from different backgrounds they or had a love that would surpass all odds. For now, the wedding was going as planned and the house almost done. It was good day for everyone who wanted this wedding to be. Even thought poor Miss Nelly hated the idea she was till kind of pleased for her uncle Sven as he very fond of Freddy and was very honored to be giving the wedding sermon for Freddy and Anna. Captain Sven had also come to like the Jacquart family and he was overjoyed when the parents gave their consent to him doing the sermon. It was a little touch and go before the parents decided but it all worked out in the end. Sometimes a little faith and prayer goes along way, just when you think things are not going to happen they do. Anna had learned this from her and tried to show Freddy how it works too. They were the happiest young couple of all Fredericton and the mining town of Minto, New Brunswick. They were going to have the wedding in the church but since Freddy did not have his birth certificate, the Captain suggested they get married on the farm and that way everyone could attend. The Jacquart family agreed and it was settled the wedding was to take place on the farm July 24, 1912 at 10:00AM, two days before Anna's fifteenth birthday. It was going to be a double celebration after all for everyone attending to enjoy and celebrate the happy newlywed couple in their joyous day. It also was going to take some doing in way of preparations. The food was to be done by the Jacquart women and the Jacquart men were to set up the table and chairs on the lovely spot on the farm that Anna picked herself. It was a beautiful place on the farm you could see the lovely oak and spruce trees in the background. And if you listened carefully you could hear the slow water running down the little brook nearby. It was a favorite place where Anna lived to sit and listen to the brook's slow running water and to just sit and be calm and one with all of nature. It was to be a grand celebration for all who were attending, even the Captain was so thrilled and Freddy was also. Now to say that the young soon to be married couple were not nervous either. No Anna had that sorted out she still needed a dress. She would have tried to make one but her wedding was put on hold, so now she would borrow her sisters since her mother's dress was too small. Anna had a bigger bosom than her mother and sisters except for her sister before her Alena, she was just a little smaller than Anna but still she was closer to Anna than the rest. It was settled Alena would lend Anna her wedding dress and that also took care of something borrowed. Anna now just needed shoes and a bouquet to make it all come together. He had another sister help with the shoes this time Irma who had feet the same size as Anna. This Jacquart were a very close knit family and everyone loved one another. And now Freddy was to be a part of this big happy and kind family it felt good in his soul. But despite all this Freddy still thought of the Captain Sven and Harry as his family too. Freddy was in turmoil again he needed a suit so the Captain and Harry got him a suit as a wedding gift to Freddy. He felt so loved and liked that he was ready to burst into tears. His only regret was that he could not have his proper family there. He would have loved for Granny and Louisa, and even the brothers James and John and his beloved Melvina. Yet despite all that he still managed to make a life and home and family for himself. As Freddy pondered his life up to this moment he thought to himself that he had come along way, since that little boy be smuggled on to a ship in the dark of night. Never to see his family or homeland again and not understanding the true reason behind his having to leave so sudden. Not until years later as he starts to matured and realize it was a way to save his life. Knowing Granny as he did she would do anything for him and even if it meant sending him away. Freddy believed that she would rather die than to see Freddy be tortured and abused by his tyrant of a grandfather Old Man Reid. But that was in the pass and now is now and he was a man now, and he was going to marry the most beautiful girl in the world. So now this was his new chapter in life and what a wonderful chapter it is. The townsfolk were all talking about the Jacquart wedding and how wonderful for the family. Everyone was wishing the happy couple well; except Miss Nelly she was teething at the bit she was outrageously furious about the whole wedding thing. She hated Anna for stealing Freddy's heart and hated Freddy for letting her. Sad but true Nelly had to concede that she lost Freddy to Anna Jacquart soon to become Mrs. Alfred Barder Reid. Nelly was so heartbroken she took to her bed again for a longer time than last. This time Nelly knew no matter what she did she would never be able to win Freddy back to her. He was a soon to be married and this was not the behavior of a lady but of a spoiled child not be able to have their own way.

 Unlike Nelly, Anna was not a spoiled child but a grown up in a way that she understood the meaning of hard work and leaving her home and country for another foreign to yourself. Plus, having to learn the language and their customs is not an easy task for some people. But Nelly always had it easy and as she saw it so could Freddy if he had married her instead. But Freddy and Anna were the same they both came to another country they work and find the people different. So now the wedding and the house was finished too it was a blessed day for all. The weather was fresh and good sun shining, birds singing, and butterfly's fluttering around. This was truly a union waiting to be seen in the eyes of God and Man. Freddy has his suit and Anna her dress, the food made the home hooch all ready. The big day finally arrives and everyone is in attendance the farm looks good with all the decorations and paper streamers. The food smelling awesome as always and the hooch fermenting in the still. Yes, this was going to be a heck of a wedding feast and celebration. But the main attraction will be the bride and groom and their wedding vows. And to make it even more special Anna has decided to say her vows in English if she can. The idea of her brother translating her wedding vows was a bit too much for Anna to accept. After all it was her big day and she wanted it to be special like every other girl who dreams of getting married. So now that everything was ready all there was left to do was wait for the next day and get married...

    It was hard sleeping for Anna and Freddy they both knew that this was a lifetime commitment and it was to be taken very seriously. They both knew that this is what they wanted and they were both very happy to get married now that Anna's mother said yes. It was like a miracle happened when Mrs. Jacquart gave her consent Anna felt like her prayers were being answered. And now she was about to be Mrs. Alfred Reid and a married woman like her other sisters except Julia she was still a little young yet. As the sun rose that wonderful day Anna and her family started to get ready for the wedding and the all the family and guest too. Also, this was another reason to celebrate Mr. Jacquart's brother Jean-Pierre who help him get his passage fare to come to Canada, was moving closer to his brother with his family. So now the Jacquart family was expanding and in time to join in the wedding festivities. The Jacquart family was very happy to hear that more their family was joining them in New Brunswick, Canada. So now the wedding guest list just got bigger and more merrier and the family could not be happier. Anna was thrilled to see her cousins and Aunt and Uncle too it was going to be a wonderful wedding and she felt it was being blessed by God already... As Anna was preparing for her wedding getting her dress on and shoes fixing her strawberry blonde curls. She looked around at her sisters and mother and her aunt all of them busy and happy for her. It was a feeling of great joy at that moment Anna felt in her heart. She knew then and there she was also very blessed with this family and was also with a wonderful man she was about to marry. This day was so perfect and it was all hers for today, tomorrow would be someone else but today it was all hers and Freddy and they were the luckiest couple on earth and God was smiling down on them with his heart. No one could have asked for a more perfect day or family and friends, this was a day to celebrate love and family and friendships and all that God has to offer too. Outside the long table was set near the big oak tree. The food was smelling delicious as the guest started to arrive. The flowers were blooming and the summer breeze just blowing nicely.

The ground was laid with tarp painted white for the bride and her father to walk down the makeshift aisle. The seats were arranged so that all the people could see the wedding sermon as it unfolded. The food table was very long as it held upon it two roasted pigs, two big sides of beef and four roasted chickens all cured and marinated for this festive occasion. The sweet smell of Belgian pastries was also very inviting to the nose and palette. The kegs were also full as well as the wine jugs there was also a lemonade for the non-alcoholic drinkers. Anna was so happy and it showed as she was beaming like a bright star in the sky. Freddy was very nervous but he had the Captain Sven and Harry on his side. He was sure they would be his rock in times of need as they always are. The wedding song was being played by some of the guest who were neighbors and friends as well as guests. Some of them played the fiddle and others guitars, violins it made for a good sound and it was very fitting too. Because some of these musician's slash neighbors also have come to know the Jacquart family well and they were all honored to be in attendance and perform for this joyous occasion. The guest settled in as they all were waiting for the bride to appear. It seemed like ages but as soon as the neighbors started to play the door to the house opens and out walks Anna and her father. She is so radiant in her beautiful white wedding dress and her flowing strawberry blonde hair braided on her head to hold her wedding veil. Her father looking quite elegant in his wonderful dark blue suit, and her mother following behind in her beautiful lighter blue dress she wore to match her husband. Her siblings also all decked out in the Sunday best and being ever so happy for their sister Anna. At the makeshift altar, we also see the handsome and dapper looking Freddy with a very nervous grin on his face. He is also wearing a dark gray suit and a lighter gray tie to match. Beside him stands his best man John who introduced him to his lovely bride to be Anna. And in front of him is the Captain Sven who took many hours to decide what attire to wear. It was a beautiful sight to see the wonderful weather and smell of flowers and delicious food. And to see all the happy faces and bearing ones too, and to see how much two young people could be so much in love. And as Anna and her father started down the makeshift aisle and the sound of the fiddles and guitars and violins it was becoming true to Anna and Freddy that they were getting married and it was for keeps.... Everyone rose to their feet and watched Anna and her father walk down the aisle, all the while Freddy smiling at her and Anna at him.

Yes, some said Anna was too young to marry and she should wait a little more, but they did not know that Anna was well matured for her years. Leaving your homeland and living in another country and learning another language makes a person grow up rather quickly. So as far as Anna was concerned she was old enough to be married and she was going to be today!! It was a day she thought would never be and the thought of not marring Freddy was not what she wanted at all. Let them talk she thought she was marring the man of she loves and that is what she truly wanted. To have a life with Freddy and bear his children that is the life she wanted and was going to have it. Marrying Freddy was her life and no one could tell her any different.

As they settled in as married folk they also added to their little family. First came the daughter Flora who born September 19th 1913, and then the birth of a son Reuben born August 1st 1914. This was amazing and wonderful for them both. For Freddy, it was a gift from God and he was so very happy and grateful. He missed his family very much back home in Jamaica, and seeing his own family growing he realizes that he would love to have his family here with him too. They have a good life and plentiful too as Anna has a green thumb and Freddy still works in the mines life is good for them. But even thought by now Anna and Freddy have almost conquered the language barrier, and can manager on their own it is hard to communicate at times. But brother John is still around for now and translates for them occasionally. But all in all, they are happy and the children are thriving on the love and good life that Freddy and Anna have given them. This was their lifestyle now and everyone was happy and the Jacquart family were also very happy that Freddy decided to build their house on the Jacquart property. It was still wonderful to celebrate the holidays thought Freddy with his new family-in-laws. But he still yearned for his family back home hoping he would return someday with his family. But until then he would rejoice in the family he has started to make now. Freddy continues to work in the mines alongside his brothers-in-law now. He enjoyed his life and his children as well, coming home to his family was a blessing he thought and thanked God everyday for this miracle. He had come from another country with nothing and now he has a family a good job and home he had help building. Life could not get any better than this Freddy thought it was what life should be like and live it graciously ad kind to others. He remembered some of Granny's teachings and these teaching would help to serve him thought out his life. He as a child never thought that his life would turn out this way, and he never dreamed that he would find love and have a family of his own. You can never map out your life as you want it to be thought Freddy, but you can try and make your life good and peaceful thought Freddy if you truly want to... Sometimes things are not in your control and situations arise, decisions to make and conversations to be had. Yes, life was different for a family man but in the end, we all survive for another day. But the everyday day to day life routine was okay and everyone adapted to it. But there was talk of a worldwide war and soon some men were going to be asked to enlist. For Freddy and his brothers-in-law, it was just talk but every day at the mines, the men would talk about it constantly. It was all everyone was talking about now, if it was to be worldwide then their men, husbands and sons could be called to "Arms." It was something the Jacquart family feared too, what if their sons and Freddy were called to "Arms" and must go to war. It was a fear of all the Jacquart women especially Anna who could find herself alone with two small children. But for now, it was just talk and everyone was secretly hoping that it would stay just talk and nothing more. But as the time wore on the talk did not die down and now suspicions were running high. The town folk were getting anxious and very leery about the "World War" not affecting them. It was almost certain they thought as they were under British Regime if England goes to war, then Canada will be asked to fight in this war and bear "Arms" as all the women were fearing from the start. Would it come to that or not? July 1914 England declares war and now Canadian men and some women are being enlisted to the WW1 of the century. It was the doing of Prime Minister of England at the time and seeing as Canada was under the "British Rule" the men and some women were to enlist. It was hard for Freddy because he saw his brothers-in-law get ready to enlist. But Freddy has obligations and some married men were not asked to enlist, but Freddy was a British citizen all his life. Being a British citizen made it possible for Freddy to stay in Canada and have a very good life. He felt it was his duty to try and enlist to fight for the country that helped him have a better life. He discussed it to lengths with Anna as much as he could make her understand. He wanted to join the Army and serve his country he felt it was his duty to serve and give back. Anna finally gave in after a few days of thinking about, I wonder where she got that from thought Freddy. But she said yes and that was good enough for him, he went and enlisted with the Jacquart brothers and they all came home happy as clams. This was a proud day again for the Jacquart family they now had three male members from their family just enlisted. It was again the talk of the town as was Freddy and Anna's wedding. But it was a small community and everyone knew what everyone else was doing. Anna was still uncomfortable about her husband and brothers going off to war. But as Freddy and her brothers pointed out to her, she has her parents and sisters and younger brothers nearby if she needs them at anytime. She felt alone and scared with two small children by herself. She thought about it and decided that she could handle this on her own, she also had the help of her remaining family. It was a comfort to know that they were there at an anytime day or night to help her in any way they can. But the thought of them going to fight a war against strangers and would or will they come back alive? It was a hard call and now it was done so all they could do now was pray like they never prayed in their lives and ask God for help. Mrs. Jacquart with her religion she prayed every day until they were shipped out to Nova Scotia to start training camp and how to fight a war.

    The whole town had a parade for the men and some women who enlisted to go fight a war for "World Peace". It was a wonderful parade with banners and the men and some women marching in their Army uniforms. It was a proud and sad day for the townspeople and the Jacquart family. Yes, they were proud of their sons and Freddy going off to war but at what price would they have to sacrifice for them to come home safe and sound. Prayers were good but were prayers enough the last church sermon was about asking God and all the angels to bring our sons, husbands and some daughters home safe to us dear God. It was going to be very unsettling for the people and the

Jacquarts until their sons and Freddy come back home safe and sound.

World War I

The war started August 4, 1914, but Freddy and his brothers-in-law could not enlist until November 1, 1914. They had to have boot camp training and the boat to Nova Scotia only took so many enlisted men and some women at a time. Some women first because they were nurses and badly needed for the wounded soldiers. It would prove to be an experience for Freddy and his brothers-in-law it would change how they see the world. Yes, Freddy, John and Jules would see the world at its worse and at its best. They finally set sail on a September almost sunny day they were going to become "Soldiers in "WW1." It was very different than what they thought they lived in "barracks" which contained cots for beds and they were lined up against each wall. They were in a row of twenty across each wall. Every man was a signed they his own cot and he also had a foot locker for his personal stuff with a heavy lock. The women had their own "barracks" but everyone shared the mess hall where they had all their meals. The boot camp was not easy it was hard training survival skills on how to stay alive. They also learned how to use a bayonet and gun and not to miss to many times as their lives depended on it. The food was not all that great but Freddy thought to himself he had better meals on the ship. But then they were not here for the food or the accommodations either. They were here to learn survival skills in how to fight a war and come out of it alive. It was a grueling training process and it required a lot of skill and common sense, most of all the will to survive and go back home to their love ones. But even thought this was hard on them these men and some women still forged on and became one of the first "Black Soldiers" the war has ever seen. Yes, they were the "First and damn proud to be "Soldiers" and to fight for the country so love so much. It would be a little more gruel training before they would see real combat on the front lines. It would be another six months before seeing any frontline fighting. It meant more outdoor training and more of their awful food and nit seeing the family back home. This was the hardest part for most of them, it was hard to be away from their loved ones. They missed their wives and husbands and children and parents too. But the ones who could read and write could keep in contact with them from time to time. But others like Freddy who had little schooling it was a problem. But lucky for him he had his brothers-in-law to help for now so he was okay with it. They would write for him to Anna and their parents telling them of their experiences at boot camps and how the food is not like their mothers'. It was nice to have a letter come to them and that they could still feel like they are still connected to their families even if they are far away. It was already a long time and know one new when the war would end. Everyone was sure of the start of it but the end was still a mystery to be won. Freddy and the Jacquart brothers were eager to get to battle and win this war once and for all and go back home soon. It was a cold winter that year and the men were learning how to live in harsh conditions. There were some men and some women who did not make the soldier they thought they could become. As for Freddy and his brothers-in-law they were use to hard work and long hours. Having a farm and working in the mines made for long days and hours. They did not find it that hard except for being away from home so long at a time.

This reminded Freddy of when he left his homeland so very long ago. So now he had to do it all over again but h this time at the end of it all he would be home again. He longed for battle to serve his country as did his brothers -in-law. They could enlist because the war was starting in Ypres Belgium, so they went to help Canada and fight for their country as well. The recruited men were from all over Canada, Nova Scotia, Ontario and New Brunswick and even some from U.S.A. April 22, 1915, Canada sees first major action at Ypres. April 9,1917 the Canadians take Vimy Ridge. But in between all this the men made wood and barbwire fences to keep enemies from invading at night. They also dug out and lived in "trenches" where they slept, and ate and the other trenches were called the "latrines" for bathroom purposes. Still they had to endure harsh weather and at times the food which they called "rations" was not were not enough to go around. Some men were lucky they had families that would send "care packages" to them. Freddy, John, and Jules were lucky as the Jacquart family sent what they could to them and it was almost enough to keep them going. The bad thing was they could get sick and some soldiers did they caught like lice and "Shell shock" or their favorite 'Mustard Gas". Now the "shell shock they sent you home and waited for you to be cured before sending you back. Bu the "mustard gas" well that was different it caused blindness and maybe Cancer later or the ultimate death... But living in the trenches did this to them and let us not forget if they got wounded well it was amputation right then and there. Some were lucky with their wounds other not so lucky. Being on the front lines was no picnic it had Freddy and other soldiers wondering why the hell did they enlist. But then Freddy thought to himself he was there for his new-found country and home to be in peace. He did not like the fact that he had to kill people and they in turn could kill him too. But then he started to see men die beside him and around him and he knew this was really "war time" and these soldiers and their enemies were shooting for keeps. This thing called war is bad and a lot of lives would be lost and maybe forgotten hopefully not. It was hard for Freddy in the beginning but then he became a very good soldier and did his best to stay alive to be able to go home to his family. But for some of the other soldiers it would not be the case some would not make it home at all. Freddy became friends with some of these men and to see and know that may die or at best get wounded made Freddy kind of sad. But the thought of his brothers-in-law not making it back home was worse. The days and night of hearing bullets fly above and around you constantly and having lice and rats infect your food and your body. If you got even a common cold, it could turn into a disease very quickly. Because of these conditions some of the soldiers were not able to with stand pressure either. But it was like living in "Hell on Earth" the conditions appalling and unfit at times for mankind. You see the men had to live in these dug out mud rat and lice infested holes at times for days and night that turned into weeks and months. The winters come and the harsh winds at times turn bitter cold. But during all this disaster and death and almost starvation at times these Canadian soldiers kept their front line and were able to take over the Vimy Ridge. It was not easy by any means it was along hard and most horrible war. It was also the first war the whole world had ever seen and the people of the world hoped it would be the last of its kind. And because Canada fought for England it truly achieved Nation Status, for the sixths-six thousand that gave their lives and the one hundred and seventy-two thousand wounded, it was this immense sacrifice that to Canada's separate on the Peace Treaty. The Canadian soldiers were a very brave bunch of men and some women, the women were mostly nurses in this war and without them some men would not have made it home safe. But the war was to go on and until one country would win, it was hard for Freddy to understand the killing part of war. Yes, they were trained and had seminars about how it would be, but being told and being in the thick of it was totally different and not all what one would expect. But still war was not what anyone wanted and so it was still a battle of who will win this one? Freddy tried to keep his spirits up getting mail and the occasional care package, Freddy was not doing too bad. His brothers-in-law were transferred about four months later they went to another battalion and this make Freddy sad to see them be deployed elsewhere. They were going into Belgium to help there as it was their homeland and they were needed. Canada was there to help the Belgians and so were the Jacquart boys and they wished Freddy all the best and him them. They all promised to meet back home on the farm in Minto and resume their lives once more. It would prove to be awhile yet before going home to their families. The war would last for a few years and it would take many lives on both sides. But someone had to win it hopefully it would be the good guys. And as for Freddy he was on the good team his soldiers and "brothers in arms" wanted to defeat the enemy and go home victorious. The soldiers that built just fences did not see too much action, but Freddy's group did and it was not pretty. The smell of rotting flesh from the dead and the wounded moaning in pain, and fighting of the rats for food and keeping the lice from your body. In between all that there were gun shots whizzing by and men dropping like flies. Oh yes, this war was a bloody war taking lives and prisoners wounding men and some women making life miserable and lonely at times. Freddy saw all this and all he wanted to do was win this damn war and go home to his family. But the enemy was not going to make it that easy they also wanted to win and they were not going to go away quietly either. It was a bloody battlefield and more bloodshed to come so it seemed to Freddy. He was starting to wonder if he would ever see his wife and children again. It was a war that was starting to seem unnecessary and futile so say the least. Freddy was hearing whispers of the war coming to an end but by the way the enemy was shooting it was not to be that soon. There biggest problem was taking over the Passchendaele, near the Vimy Ridge. They had taken the Vimy Ridge but taking Passchendaele was going to be tough. But then the

Canadian soldiers got their second wind and climbed up the Vimy Ridge and Captured Passchendaele and entered the Mons November 11 1918 which became the "Remembrance Day." This is where Freddy and a few of his comrades got wounded. Freddy got shot in the leg and managed to make it back to the latrine and his battalion. But some of the others were not as lucky some lost limbs, eyes and some just did not make it. The Canadian soldiers won the war but at what price. These men were going home to a life they have not had in four years. It was like going home for the first tine to some of them. For Freddy, it was going home wounded but alive and thankful to God he was still alive When he was able he inquired about the Jacquart brothers over in Belgium he was told that they were okay and would be going home soon too. But before they sent Freddy was sent home he received a "Medal of Honor for being wounded in the line of fire and still fighting for his country. The soldiers were sent home in the spring of 1919 to civilian life. Some could not cope when sent home this was because of the "Shell shock" they experienced it made them dizzy, irritable and headaches also mental difficulties. These men were hospitalized and some recovered others were never the same again. Freddy arrived back to his family in June 10, 1919 and Anna and their children were happy to see him. His in-laws asked about the war and if their sons were okay, Freddy said they were okay and should be home soon. He did not want to talk about the war, he was not happy when he had to. It was not something Freddy liked or bragged about even if he got a medal. It was something he wanted to put behind him for now and try and get his old job back and live again normally. Soon came word that the Jacquart boys were finished with their tour of duty. But the was just one difference Jules was staying behind in Belgium for awhile he found his school sweetheart and wanted to marry her and bring her to Canada. He would not be returning for awhile just yet not without his new bride. The family rejoiced in having John and Freddy home for now. They had a celebration everyone came to greet the soldiers home from war and to see the Freddy's medal. It was a joyous time especially for Anna as she had her husband safe and sound back with her and the children. Flora and Reuben were happy to see their father. They had pictures of him in his uniform so they knew who he was. The whole town had a parade for all the returning soldiers and it was wonderful was a lot of food and wine and beer and lemonade for the non-drinkers. There was also dancing as the farmer Mr. Walsh let them use his barn for a real country hoe down. The fiddles and banjos and violins were strumming that day and night everyone rejoiced and celebrated the return of the soldiers who so bravely fought to keep their country Canada safe to live in once more. Anna was very proud of Freddy his medal and the fact that he came home like he said he would. Their life could now go back to the way it was and life was good again. Freddy also went back to the mines it was a little hard at first because of his wounded leg that had healed but he had fixed by a war doctor and it was not the best at times. Freddy managed to get his old job back and never complained about the shooting pains either. But this was off and on pain but at these times he would feel more pain than usual. This would go on for awhile and eventually Freddy knew he had to have it seen to properly by the town doctor soon as possible. He sees the town doctor who only comes to Fredericton and Minto every month. Freddy suffered a bit till he could see the good doctor. The doctor told him that he could help for now but sooner or later, he would have to see a real doctor from a big city like Moncton, New Brunswick. But for now, he sent Freddy home with some pain medicine and told him to keep it wrapped up at night with a hot towel, and keep it elevated as much as he can whenever possible. This would prove to be a little hard for Freddy because working in the mines consisted of standing for a lot of hours at a time. He never complained but Anna saw it in face and eyes at times the pain he was feeling. His family was happy to have him home the children were very happy as well. Freddy loved his family and adored his children and they him. Everything was going well, and soon things would be back to the way they were before the war. Even thought Freddy came home from the war with a medal it was not something he talked or bragged about at all. He never engaged in war talk with the other soldiers he was not comfortable with the war talk at all. He did not like the fact that he had to kill and bomb innocent people. Killing the enemy, he could make sense of at times, but the killing and bombing of innocent people all in the name of war was not all what he expected. To be honest Freddy did not know what to expect being a soldier entailed. He was certain when he was at boot camp but then when he was faced with being on the front lines. And then facing the war and in all its carnage and death and watching men die around him it was at times too much to bear. For this reason, Freddy tells himself he abstains from talking or engaging in conversation about the war. Anna was worried that Freddy was not handling be back from the war, at night sometimes he would have night mares and Anna would ask and he would just say nothing. It would last for awhile but then his nightmares ended and he was alright again. But his leg was another story he had pain now and then but it was bearable and he never complained to anyone at all. Freddy was a proud man and had to make his own way in life, never having anyone at his side until now. He had his family, his friends and his in-laws but sometimes just sometimes he missed his other family back home in Jamaica. He still managed to survive and make a new life for himself and now raise a family and live a wonderful life. It was a long hard way back to civilian life for Freddy and some of the other soldiers to adapt to their previous lives before the war, some adapted well others came home shell shocked and or wounded. The shell shock soldiers were hospitalized and treated for headaches, dizziness and paranoia. It affects some families and the government compensated them till they could be well again. Unfortunately, some poor soldier never got better and this was very devastating for the families of these soldiers. Freddy counted his blessing because he came wounded yes, but he was still able to provide for his family. And to still be alive that was very important to him, and to Anna and the children. The Jacquart family were just as happy that that their sons and son-in-law all came home safe and sound. But still they also felt bad for the other soldier that were not as lucky and the other parents who were not lucky too. Every Sunday at Mass the Jacquart family and Freddy would pray for all the soldiers that were home and aboard. It was a war that all the world prayed would not happen again and everyone could live peacefully and kind.

 Being back home was good for Freddy as he missed being away from home so long. He had a friend write letters for him as he had very little schooling and he knew the Anna would like to know how he was doing. He never told her about the war at all it was a dark place that he sooner would like to forget and not be reminded. His life with his family resumed as usual and it was good again to be back to his normal life. It was hard going at first but he eventually adapted and returned to the mines again with the same position as before Foreman. He did have a hard time trying to adjust at times but he still made it through and tried to forget the demons of war that haunted him. It was a known fact that soldiers of war did suffer from trauma and even depression from being at war and leaving their families behind. Those were lucky ones who made it home, and the ones who did not well they were mourned and buried. Freddy was lucky enough not to come with "shell shock disease" it was a hard on the soldiers who did have it they had to be hospitalized. This war was not whatever boy and man who enlisted thought it would be. They did not know what to expect and for sure they did not think it would be as horrible as it was. But for the soldiers that survived they had their own personal demons to contend with and try to fit back to the life they had before going to war. It was a hard transition for some and others well, they had demons too but not all the returning soldiers were eventually back to themselves. Freddy never liked to talk about the war and even less about his medal for his war wound. He always felt that even though he fought for his country that he did not like the killing part. But as he knew in his heart he had to kill or be killed himself. It was survival of the fittest and ever soldier on that battle field knew that going in. Yes, they had boot camp training but it was not as being there live and being in the mix, and seeing it firsthand was a rude awaking for some of these men. They came home either badly bruised or wounded or even worse dead. It was a time of reflecting on what was important and being blessed that they were still alive for some and that they fought to keep their families and homeland safe.... But now let us not forget the wives and mothers and sisters that were left behind to worry and wonder if they would ever see their love ones again. It was a little hard for Anna she had two children and she dreaded the fact that if Freddy returned dead how would she explain to a now six and five-year-old children that daddy died in the war. But her prayers were answered and Freddy returned home safely and only a wounded leg and a "Medal" for his bravery. Anna and her family were very proud that Freddy got a "Medal" but Freddy did not rejoice in their happiness, for him it only meant that he fought a war and killed other soldiers. The friendships that were built on this war was also a tragedy because the soldiers became friends and the next thing you know they could be shipped away or dead it just depended on the day in question. It was a hard way to see the world and what the people were capable of doing in times of war. Freddy often thought of his comrades that lost their lives and how he could make it home. He was very grateful and because of this Freddy started to take his religious upbringing more serious than before. He knew in his heart that his praying to God kept him sane enough to stay alive and return home again. It would take Freddy some time to adjust to his normal life again and with the help of his family and God, he could overcome these obstacles and demons that plagued him. Despite all that he still was very happy to be home and safe to enjoy his life with his family once again. He would rejoice and get back to the life he had before the war and make his family happy. It was hard after the war to put the pieces back together and make everything the way it was. Wars do ruin countries, families and the minds of soldiers who fought in them. It is the starting over and asking oneself "Was it really worth it?" Freddy never regretted fighting for his country and family but he did not like having to kill other soldiers he did not know. But if the truth be told he knew in his heart that they would have killed him and his soldier friends if need be. It was a horrible five years in the making and hopefully the people thought that it would never happen again. But as we all know time will tell all and all would be revealed. Freddy dreaded the thought that this could ever happen again and he prayed every day since he came back, that this war would be the end and everyone would live peacefully again all around the world. Life went on as usual and everyone tried to keep their spirits hopeful and every Sunday in church the congregation, would pray and pray that this awful war they had known would never be man's downfall again. The good people of New Brunswick were very hopeful and went about their daily routine and tried not to think of how the war almost tore their world apart. Yes, for some it did by their love ones that were at war came home dead, but for those who did not it was still for them because they had to look to look these poor families in the face and wonder if they blamed them for being alive and not their men folk. It was a very trying time and the people did have to learn to adapt all over again. This war was senseless and selfish too.

Freddy went back to the mines some soldiers were not able to go back to work. Others that were did the same job as before. But not all the families were lucky enough to have their love one's home with them. It was a trying and sorrowful time this war made boys come back as men and men come back angry or not all. It was a war that affected countries all over, Freddy saw some of it first-hand and did not always approve of the methods used. But life had to go on and still be lived even though it was hard to know that you left many a soldier on the battle field some knew some you did not. Freddy resumed his life again he went to work in the mines and he was happy with that. The Jacquart family were happy that Jean-Babtisite Jr., came home and Jules he stayed on in Belgium. Jules found himself a pretty little Belgian girl named Maria and he planned to marry her too. But all in all, life was almost normal and happy and for now. Life would be good for awhile but now there was a rumor that the Big Depression was about to come and everyone would lose their jobs, homes and even their businesses. It was another scary time for the people they were just getting over the effects of the war and now this depression rumor. It was going to the ruin of many countries as well as the people of these countries. They say it is to be chaos and mayhem and not everyone will survive. People again are fearing the worse as with the war. But Freddy is reassured that for now the mines are safe. Freddy cannot help wondering how the war had affected his homeland Jamaica and his people, his family. To this day he has not heard of any word from home since he left as a boy. He had his friend the Captain Sven find out for him but to no avail was there any information about his family. It made him sad once again to know he may never see his family or homeland again. But as the years went by and wounds healed life got to be a little better and so did the moral in a way of the community. Anna and the children were happy to have Freddy home with them a proper family enjoying life. But this would last for a few years and again the rumor of sorts, spreading talk about the great depression about to come about. People wondering if it because of the war but the by now has been over for almost twenty years. It would just be rumor but still people are weary now of rumors. Freddy takes it in stride and does not fret at all. He has the mine job and what he can grow on the farm as well. So, for now all is well and good and he can enjoy life with his family. For when he was in the army he missed his family and now he was happy to be home at last. But this good life would eventually come to an end because the rumor of the Depression becomes true and the mines are closing slowly. Everyday business is dropping and people are getting scared all over again. It is causing some countries to panic and others to be in chaos and mayhem. It proved to be a great depression and it was hurting the whole world just like the war did. But Freddy wondered what will this do the countries and the economy how are people supposed to live through this dilemma and survive without any or no damages to the world and the people in it. This was a cause for alarm and to be on their guards for this was going to be a depression of all depressions. If this were to happen it would take down countries, people and empires, all will or could be destroyed. Freddy and Anna especially Anna worried a lot about their family's future. But for now, says Freddy all is okay and tells Anna for now do not worry we will be okay. And for now, Anna's fears are put to rest and she goes on with her life, family and not worrying about depression. Life in general was pretty good and considering the war has now been over for at least five years. But as luck would have it the good life was coming to an end for some others a disaster. Families and businesses were all destined to fail some who had jobs and farms, would feel the sting of having less. But the people who were rich would feel shame and destitution, where as the poor people would just feel destitution. It was a bunch of talk but still these kinds of talk, rumors if you will can escalate even at the best of times. For now, people were listening to the news and reading the newspapers to see if the rumors were true. It would be just rumors for awhile until the economy starts to dwindle and people were buying less. It was just a matter of time for the big "Depression Era" hit the entire world over. Yes, it hit the "Stock Exchange Building," "Wall Street" before hitting the rest of the world. It was chaos and mayhem at its best for the world to see. Companies went bankrupt and people lost their homes, their jobs and some even committed suicide. The world was at a lost and everyone in it man, woman, and child from the very old to the very young were suffering. But now it was a shift in pecking order meaning there was no more High-class or Middle-class or lower-class. Everyone was feeling the 'Depression Era" in different ways, some lost it all while others just lost. Social standing was not much of an issue during these times and it did not hold much bearing either... But despite all these pit falls ahead of Freddy and Anna they still forged on and to stay strong for their family. But it was obvious that the "Depression Era" was about to fall upon the country Canada and its people will also feel the pain and hunger like some already know. But Freddy also that there was talk of the mines closing for the coal was not selling so great now. Freddy decided he must have a plan before the mines close so his family will not suffer. He knew that Anna's older sister Alena was living in Montreal and it was a half day's ride by train. Her older sister left New Brunswick with her husband who got a better job in Montreal. Freddy asked Anna to write her sister Alena and ask if there were any jobs available in Montreal. It took about a month to get an answer back but her sister's husband Michel says yes, he can have Freddy work with him in the packing plant. That night Freddy and Anna talk in great length about the move to Montreal. It would mean Anna leaving her mother and father and what about the children Flora and Reuben almost teenagers now. And what about the rest of the family her brothers and aunts, uncles, and cousins. But then she understood that this would be better than being too poor to keep her family together. It would prove to be trying times for the whole human race. The lives of many are affected by this catastrophe and bring ruin to all the world. But even with these odds against him Freddy made the decision to move his family to Montreal and hope for a better life. But as fate would have it at times when we plan there is a higher power steering us elsewhere. As fate would have it Anna's father who had been feeling sick took a turn for the worst, and now her mother would be alone to care for him. Anna told Freddy to go on ahead without her for now and she would follow behind later. She could not leave her mother alone to care for her father and hopeful he would get better quickly. Freddy left behind his family Anna and the children but vowing to send for them soon as he is settled in Montreal. It was a tearful good bye for everyone and especially for Anna being apart was not good for anyone... Anna stayed and helped her mother with her sick father but during this time also, the children did not want to leave when it would be time to go to Montreal. Freddy Jr. was going to follow his parents as he was still a child but the older two Flora and Reuben wanted to stay behind with their grandparents, as they had friends and school and did not want to change anything. This was how things stayed as time passed on Anna's father got worse and he eventually died in his sleep and painless. And because he suffered so it was a blessing he died in his sleep peacefully. Freddy came back for the funeral and to bring his family to Montreal. The train ride there was good. Anna and Freddy Jr. got to see the scenery all the way there. Freddy had a home for them already, but there was something missing he did not like his job. He talked it over with Anna and asked her what she thought, Anna said to give her time and she will give him an answer. She set about finding work, school for Freddy Jr. and a job for herself. She searched the want ads and found a job working at the Royal Victoria Hospital laundry. But still it was not nearly enough wages to make ends meet. It was the "Great Depression Era" it was a bad time for everyone around the world. The day the "Stock Market" feel they named it Black Tuesday, it was a day that families lost pay checks and homes other lost companies, some even took their own lives. But Freddy and his family managed to get by and they had little but worked hard to get it. The "Depression Era" would last a long time before things got any better, but as fate would have it Anna meet a lovely Jewish lady that volunteered at the hospital. Her name was Emily Bernstein and her husband was named Saul. Anna and became close friends and Anna told one day that Freddy was not happy with his job, and they were expecting another child on the way in August. Now they had only been in Montreal for almost two years and still found times to be tough. But as time went on it Anna was getting more tired now she was in her mid-thirties by now and another child was hard. Between Reuben and Freddy Jr. there was the war so the births were spread out. And now almost twelve years later she is expecting again. It was a blessing in disguise for the family but Freddy was so very happy and so was Anna. But the fact that Freddy did not like his job was worrying Anna at lot. One day again Anna and were having coffee and talking and happened to mention in passing, that her husband Saul was looking for a valet of sorts and would Freddy be interested. Anna said she would ask him and see what he says she was very hopeful that her Freddy would be happy to change jobs. His reason was this packaging was fine but then he was changes over to delivery and it was hard loading and unloading with his wounded leg from the army. He would come home nights with swollen ankles and feet. this after a time became unbearable for Freddy to endure and for Anna to see. It was making her feel bad to see her husband in such agony practically night after night. Anna decided after their supper she would ask Freddy if he would like to change jobs and become a valet to a Montreal Judge Oh yes, Mr. Saul Bernstein a highly respected retired judge but a good one in his day. He was also looking forward to meeting Freddy if he decides to take the job. And Anna knew her husband would be perfect for the job because he dressed always like a gentleman does. Freddy and Anna both decided that Freddy would be better working for the judge and his legs would not hurt as much. Also, Freddy had a sense of style always did even as a poor boy back home. This was a perfect fit and Anna was getting bigger as her pregnancy was developing. She would have to leave the hospital soon as she would not be able to the laundry, and at her age it could become dangerous for the baby and the mother. But during these times there was no maternity leave pay so she was taking a chance that her job would still be there waiting for her. Unfortunately, she had to take the time off and take of the child and herself. So even with the new job for Freddy it was going to be harder to manage with two mouths to feed now. But even thought times were tough this was a blessing another child a new life even if it meant being a little strapped for a little while longer. It would work itself out and Anna and Freddy were at least grateful that the older two children were with their grandmother helping on her farm. These were hard times for all everybody around the world. It would prove to be soup kitchens for some and for others charity hostels and some just bum on the streets for hand outs if any to be had...

But luckily Anna and Freddy had the Bernstein's to help especially after they gave Freddy the job of valet to the retired Judge. It was good because now Freddy Jr. was getting bigger and needed new clothes and school supplies soon. And, it was easier on Anna so close to the birth which she was praying and hoping very hard to have a safe and healthy baby. Anna was having a hard pregnancy she would vomit practically vomit all day long and feel nauseous too. But this new job would be a little financially better for them and for Freddy Sr. health wise as his legs and ankles did not swell as much anymore. The Judge and Freddy Sr. got along quite well as they both like to look dapper and gentlemanly at all times. Anna also had her older sister Irma and her husband Michel would help when they could as they had four children of their own This Depression Era hit the whole world hard every country was not left unsaved, some people were penniless, homeless and even suicidal. This would be the way of the world for a long time to come. As Freddy Sr. worked for the Judge he became somewhat close to him and told him of his childhood in Jamaica and how he had to leave his home as a child. Also, the Judge told him of his day's a s a lawyer then court judge, and of how he loved up hold the law and put bad people away for good. Anna was so happy that it turned out well for her family. The families would also luncheon together on occasion and it was at these times Freddy Jr. loved to go for he got to eat cake, cookies and sometimes ice cream. But he had to eat all his lunch first. The Bernstein's did not have children so they spoiled Freddy Jr. a little, and bought the baby a bassinet as they knew it was hard for the Reid family. It was hard for Anna too for she feared at her age to be having a child could prove a little bit dangerous. She prayed hard every day and night knowing that God hears her, and Freddy prayed too knowing the same thing. This was a time for families and friends to come together also what was saving the Reid family was that they could keep their food rations. It was hard and cruel times but with the lo9ve and support of family and friends they managed to survive for the most part. It was an never-ending battle some days wondering if the food rations and the little food you did have left would be enough to feed your family. But with the new arrival of a baby proved to make their lives to more bearable with the promise of hope and love for this new baby to be born. Freddy Sr. was secretly hoping for a girl as he had only one and two sons it would even it out, he prayed every night in hopes that the Lord would hear him and grant his prayer. Anna's prayers were different she prayed her baby would be born healthy and happy and have everything the child needed. But as we know only time would tell and until then life would go on. For this was the life they were dealt and they would rise to the challenge and defeat the odds at all cost no matter what. But time went on as usual and Anna and Freddy awaiting the arrival of the new baby, and Freddy Jr. getting ready for High School his first year. As summer was coming to an end the birth was getting close now the end of August or there about. It was a hot summer and the weather was cooling down a bit and making it things work little easier for Anna to manage. She had nausea and 's vomiting all through her pregnancy and still working part-time, they needed the money for when the baby arrived she would have to be off work for a few months at least. She was hoping maybe a year if possible but if not well, she would find a way to make to work for the family. Freddy was quite happy working for the Judge and the Judge was just as happy with Freddy's work as well. The two families were happy with their lives despite the depression all around them. Yet even when they were asked

Anna and Freddy why another child? they answered why not. In Belgium, they have a saying Le Mal pour faire de bon, meaning good can come from bad (roughly speaking). To them it was not having the baby that worried them but how to give the child what it needs. But then they realized that the Bernstein's were helping too and it was a lesser burden to carry. This child was loved before it was even born this was to be the golden child for Freddy. He felt so connected to this unborn child of his and was wondering if this child would feel the same. Anna was counting the days now and was starting to show her ankles were swollen and her breasts were hurting more than usual. It was hard for her this pregnancy as she was much younger for the other three children. Despite her age and how hard it was this time she never complained for this was her golden child too her last baby, and she knew in her heart it was a little girl. Anna did not tell anyone of what she felt if a boy or girl, she did not want to be mistaken and raise anyone's hopes. But as the blessed day was nearing she was getting sicker by the day, and it was worrying Freddy as she was not like this for the other three. But the doctor reassured them that it was normal and not every pregnancy is the same. They went home from the doctor's office and waited for the newest Reid child to arrive. Then it happened Anna's water broke in the morning and she was rushed to the hospital. It was a long delivery. There were complications of sorts in the delivery room the doctor feared for mother and child. But God listens to mother's prayers and he guided the doctor's hand with the metal forceps steady in hand and ever so gently prying the baby by its forehead, and hearing the child crying loudly for being brought out this way as if she was angry. Yes, a girl they were so happy and grateful that their child was born healthy and not having to worry if she would be born deformed. It was a great relief to the parents and other family members. Now Anna had to recuperate and get her strength back to return home with her new daughter.

They kept their promise to give the girl child the name Emely after Mrs. Bernstein the Judge's wife. but it would be a middle name. Freddy wanted the child to have a different first name so they decided they would think on it first before the child would be baptized. By the Catholic church they had six weeks and then they must be baptized before God and man.

In the mean time Freddy asked the Judge for extra shifts or maybe even odd jobs around their house. It was going to be tough for Freddy Jr. starting High School and a new baby girl. Freddy was so excited that he had a new baby girl, he doted on her and spoiled her like crazy. But in fairness so did her mother and older brother Reuben and older sister Flora when they would visit the family. This little girl was everyone's little darling and she loved it, but she was not spoiled rotten after all this was the Depression and there was not that much to be had. Still for a little baby girl new to this world she was doing just fine. Except for the little scar she would have forever on her forehead by the metal forceps used in her birth. Yet she was a pretty little baby rosy cheeks, and soft golden curls and gray-green eyes that sparkled when she smiled or laughed. She was a happy baby too and oh so very smart. She was always watching from her pram or crib with her eyes, as if they were wondering around the room. She would giggle and coo as most babies do but as far as crying goes she hardly cried for nothing anyways.

In all she was a good baby and was loved and enjoyed by her family. The Bernstein's helped with the bassinet and baby clothing and other things for the child. This certainly was a big help to Anna and Freddy who were thankful to the Bernstein's. Seeing as the Bernstein's did not have children of their own they liked to spoil Freddy Jr. and the new baby girl. After all she was Mrs. Bernstein's name sake. It was like a blessing from God the help and support the Bernstein's were giving to them. Depression Era was hard on everyone world wide it did not discriminate every man, woman and child was affected by this terrible blow to world economy and quality of life for the people of the world.

But there was no change in sight and people were wondering if this was the way their lives were to stay forever. But now there was a christening to prepare for as now the time has come to baptize the new baby girl. Freddy and Anna have decided what to name their new baby girl and add to the name Emily. The day finally comes everyone is a t the church and the priest stands by the Holy Fountain, gathered around the parents and Anna's sister Alena and her husband Henri a policeman who just got promoted to Captain. Could this day get any better Anna's sister and her husband were thrilled to be asked as God parents. So now as the priest anoints the baby girl he asks for the name of the child and her God parents. And as h the priest makes the sigh of the Cross across the little girl's forehead blessing her scar as well. He says these words. "In the of the Father the Son and Holy Ghost, I baptize thee Alena Emily Reid, daughter of Anna and Alfred Reid. And God parents Alena and Henri Desaire." And with that being said she is now officially Alena Emely Reid and the newest member of the Reid family.

WWI & Lena

It is the year 1936 and Freddy has now lost his friend and employer as the Judge Bernstein passed away. It left Anna and Freddy very sad, even little Alena Emely missed them.

Mrs. Bernstein went to stay with a niece she had living in Toronto, Ontario but, she kept in touch with the Reid family and never forgot her namesake either.

Freddy who is now jobless tries to find work anywhere he can, doing whatever he can in the way of work. He worried everyday about how to provide for his family. He took any odd job he could get and during these times it was mighty hard. He would dig ditches and wash dishes for local diners when he could get the work, and he would even shovel horse manure if needed. Freddy was not afraid of hard work even if he was a little older now.

It was still a depression era and it was not looking like the economy was about to change anytime soon. But Freddy came along way and had fought against all odds so he was not about to give up now. There was even talk of a war but to Freddy it was just a rumor to keep the peoples mind off the depression.

It seemed that people who had riches now found themselves poor and the poor; well some were homeless. This depression era was making living unbearable for some while others just lost their will and ended their lives. It was tragic for the family and friends that were left behind.

But through it all the Reid family preserved and stayed strong together and prayed as a family.

Thankfully, Mrs. Gold who was a friend to the late Judge Bernstein and his wife remembered Anna and offered her a job house cleaning. Even though it was just part-time Anna accepted gladly as these were hard times and every little bit helped. Plus, she could have her daughter Lena of four years with her. She hated the thought of having to leave her with strangers. Anna and Freddy never left Lena with a babysitter. It was either one of them or both or a family member sometimes like her brother Freddy Jr.

Little Lena was happy and a little spoiled but she was never rude or disrespectful to anyone. She loved her family and her older siblings doted on her as she was the baby. She also loved going to work with her mother. She would help with the polishing of the silver cutlery, and sometimes dusting the furniture when she could.

As the Reid's worked and Freddy Jr. worked hard in school and Lena flourished. There were times when Freddy Sr. had no work and they had to depend solely on Anna's part-time job. But even in these days and nights when they also had little firewood to warm the house up. It was in these times that the family prayed and kept their faith.

Then one day out of the blue his brother-in-law Michel, Alena's husband calls Freddy and asks him if he would be interested in working for the packing company. Freddy said yes and thanked him as he knew that God had answered his prayers and would help him provide for this family.

It was not easy she had a hard birth with Lena and still had a hard time walking on some days. Back then they would call it "Milk Legs" meaning that her breast milk leaked into her legs. Thankfully she did not have too much and it was not to painful at times. She never complained once and went about her life as usual taking care of her family and working at her job. She knew that someday she would have problems down the line but for now she had to stay strong for any obstacles that would come her way. It was a time for reflection, unity, and strength. Some of the population felt misery, shame and even contempt towards one another.

But then Freddy Jr. announces that he would like to further his education and if they could help. But as it stands it was hard for his family also. But then he remembered his classmate saying that his dad needed help on the farm, as he was leaving for college on a Scholarship. Freddy Jr. went to see Mr. Jones and he told Freddy it didn't pay much but he had free room and board. This was great Freddy thought to himself he could save for school too and not be a burden to his family. When Freddy Sr. heard the news he was so happy that he told all his friends and neighbors. Anna was also happy for her son she knew he liked school and she was delighted too that he would go further with his studies. It was a trying time for some but for the Reid's now it was a good time. Even Lena was happy even though she was just a child her parents tried to protect her, she was not aware yet of the Depression Era. But as it progressed into more years even the small children were aware of the limited things people could have, an standing in line for food stamps and having little to eat all the time. But this is what they grew up in for now and hearing everyday it will get better, but it did not seem that way. The radio would broadcast Presidents of other countries and Prime Ministers all saying the same thing. Asking the people of the world to pray and have faith things will change for the better. But this blind faith they are asking the world population is a hard to believe when you see children crying from hunger and the poor begging in the streets and old men and some women digging ditches and shovel manure just to eat. This was a very hard time but one had to be strong and have faith that it will get better. Until then people did what they had to do some begged some borrowed and some even steal. Whatever was required to keep the family feed, clothed and sheltered that was what people did. Freddy was a proud man by nature but he knew when he had to put his pride aside for the greater good that being his family. It was harder on him and Anna as they were not very young anymore but they still could do a hard day's work no doubt. Also, now Anna was asked by the Jones to do some cooking for them, she got to take home the leftovers which was a great help at home. But despite it all Freddy and Anna wished the economy would pick up and this dreaded Depression would leave and everybody could work and provide for their families better. This was something Anna prayed on every night before bed. She would like to give her children an education to better their life and the world could get back to normal again. As the Depression wore on there was still talk about another war and how it would make the economy worldwide so much better. But as usual everyone thought it was just talk it seemed that everywhere people went it was the topic of the day. The population around the world were still feeling the effects of World War 1 and the Depression. Almost twenty years later since World War 1 ended and now there is talk of World War11. But as the years went by things around the world were not any better and the economy was not any different. People still begging, borrowing, or stealing whichever help them to get by. Sometime even good people end up doing stupid things to survive the harsh lives they were forced to live. A midst of all this Freddy and his family managed to survive they did find it hard near the end of the month, and would only feed Lena and Freddy Jr. if he was at home. Freddy and Anna would miss meals so their children did not have to miss any and that is because their children cane first. It was hard times but seeing as Freddy Sr. did any job it was not so hard at times for his family. But the talk of another war worried the people especially soldiers who have went to war, and saw what it can do and how damaging it can be when they return home. But if things remain the same just talk for now and if the economy did not make a speedy recovery for all mankind. It could lead to another all-out war and the whole would suffer again tremendously. But the shaky government wants war thinking it will help the economy rise again.

 It was a scary thought for some to think they would lose sons, husbands, and brothers to a war that benefited who really? Freddy was hoping that another war would not be the solution but, he was just one man hoping to see the world heal without another war if possible. Still the depression went on and people were getting more and more depressed.

 Soon Lena would be starting first grade and she was looking forward to being with other children. It was a trying and sorrowful time. It was disparaging everywhere one looked. Some people tried and somehow survived while others gave in to easy and found it hard to adapt. Freddy and his family had hard times but they tried to manage and for the most part they did just that. Even though they did all this it was still a hard life and one had to be strong especially with young children, who still do not understand what is happening around them. Unfortunately, the children who did understand found it hard also to adapt and to be thankful for what they have. Some of the teenagers like Freddy Jr. who had a little part-time job didn't complain too much. Yes, everyone had hardships and hard times but, it was something everyone was experiencing around the world even the Reid family.

As the depression era lingers on so does the feeling of depression for the whole world poor and not so rich alike. And even in the harsh winters of these times when coal was scarce Freddy would exchange favors with the neighbors for coal. Just so his family could stay warm and comfortable. The winters in Montreal could be very cold and harsh. That is how Freddy's neighborhood survived the depression because everyone helped their fellowman and neighbor whenever possible.

But this would not last forever as the talk of war was increasingly becoming more fact than talk. It was said that the war would bring back the economy to where it was before. But the populace the people of the world were not so easily convinced that the war would build up the economy to where it was before. But it would be nice to be able to work and provide for their families and have dignity again. Freddy did what he could but it was getting harder and harder as each year rolled around. But this only lasted for another few years as it was that the war was about begin and this time Europe was at it is time again. Only this time Germany wanted full control of the World. This did not sit well with the rest of the world either it was foolish to think that one country should or could rule the entire World. There it was the ruling that the world was going back to war. As it turned out it was to begin September 1, 1939 and the recruiting was to start immediately as some parts of Europe were already assembled and waiting for orders to attack.

    Freddy knew he would enlist as he did the first time but now he was a little older, and wondered if this could be a strike against him. If this was the case, then he just had to try and then know for himself at least.

    He did not care for the killing part as he was not fond of taking lives of strangers. But still he had wanted to defend his country, the one he now called home for many years. He also knew that his family would not be very thrilled with the idea of him going back to war. He did not want to leave them either but duty calls and he had to answer.

    He wanted to talk with Anna first about it as she was going to be left alone with the children. Hopefully his family would be supportive and understand why he had to enlist again.

He decides that he will talk with Anna after supper that night. As the family sat around to eat a merger supper, Freddy thinks of how he will approach Anna with the idea of going back to war again. This was a hard decision for Freddy to make but he knew he needed the support and love of this family like he did the last time. After supper Freddy and Anna had a long chat about him re-enlisting in the army.

"Well Anna, I hope I have your blessing and support as you once gave me before and that you will try to understand why I want to re-enlist again," says Freddy hoping she will understand why he must go back to war if they will take him this time. Because he has gotten older now.

"I understand Freddy and hope you can do something for me. Come back to us and not get wounded again if you can help it," says Anna as she looks into his eyes for comfort.

"I will try and keep this promise to you and anyways with the age I am they just might keep me on home ground," says Freddy trying hard to reassure Anna and himself.

"Well there Freddy Reid I see that you have already made up your mind so then it is settled and we will tell the children tomorrow morning at breakfast is that okay with you?" asks Anna as she hopes they have done the right thing by letting Freddy re-enlist again.

The next morning, they all sat down at breakfast as a family and the children were told that their father was wanting to re-enlist in the war. As it was Freddy Jr. who was aware of the war as he was a young man now being twelve years older than Lena who was only eight years old by now. Lena was still a little girl being sheltered from the horrors of the war itself.

So, it was decided, Freddy Sr. would re-enlist into the war, but this time he was more prepared for the outcome of it all. Freddy was confident that his Army record spoke for itself, as he got wounded saving a fellow soldier. It was something he never wanted to talk about but it was there in his Army file and he got a "Medal of Valor" for this heroic stance he made. Unfortunately, it would be stolen in later years.

But Freddy wanted to defend this country Canada., which has embraced him and has let him raise a family here too. Even thought he calls Canada home now he will never forget his homeland Jamaica. As he enters to re-enlist he is hoping that they will accept him and let him defend this country he has come to love.

He signs papers but they tell him he must wait two weeks and return for confirmation, because Freddy did not have a phone so he had to go in person. This was a long two weeks for him to wait but in the meantime, he kept on working and finding odd jobs.

Freddy Jr. who just finished his schooling went to work for a company called "Marconi." They made weapon parts for the Army and were hiring men and women to work on the assembly line, it was hard at first but then Freddy Jr. got the hang of it. The faster you were the better. A lot of people went to work for Marconi but it was not enough. The company was still in need of employees to make as many weapon parts as much and as fast as possible.

Anna was wanting to go to work there too but, who would be home to mind Lena? With Freddy Sr. gone to war the money would be okay but, it would still be tight. The only change would be no more food stamps and real milk. Freddy Jr. working and her sister and her sister's family were all working at "Marconi Company" too. She had a choice to make stay home or go to work. She would wait and see what turned out with Freddy Sr.'s confirmation letter and then she could and would decide from there. She was worried she couldn't find a reliable person to watch over her baby girl Lena. But for now, she did not have to worry and would cross that bridge when she came to it. This would make life a little easier thought Anna, but she would worry too much about Lena and who would mind her. She also had the option of putting Lena in the convent and to be taught by the "nuns," and Anna knew they would watch over her baby girl.

But this would be her last resort because Lena was always with her family, and Anna was worried how she would react with strangers. Anna herself was taught by "nuns" back in her homeland Belgium and she enjoyed their teachings but, her Lena was another story; spoiled a little by her father and older siblings which worried her mother a lot. It was a big decision on Anna's part and she would have to weigh out the pros and cons of the situation at hand. But she still had two weeks left for the confirmation of Freddy getting back into the army or not. It depended on how the army was to decide and then she could make a firm decision herself and not worry anymore for whatever reason.

The two weeks finally came and Freddy got confirmation of him being reenlisted into the Canadian Army. So now Anna made her decision and Lena was sent to the Convent of Franciscan of Sisters and later to a convent in Riguad, Quebec. The "Riguad Convent" was not one of Lena's favorite places to be she was a little by this time 1942, she was not enjoying the strict rules and regulations being instilled upon her. But for the families' sake and hers she tried to adapt as much as she could. The army had Freddy doing guard duty guarding the prisoners of war and he had to travel all around Canada to different

Prison camps. His first assignment was to go to New Brunswick since he had lived there already and knew the province quiet well. Freddy got this posting because of his war injury and he would not be able to run or fight in battle if need be. The other only position they could give him as he was a "Decorated Soldier" and that held respect in army terms. He was happy in a way as he now older and looking forward to the end of wars for all mankind alike. You see Freddy fought for this country to defend it not to see how many enemies he had to kill for that to be true. They say wars change some men and make men out of little boys but all it does is take lives and homes and destroy countries. Freddy was happy that he got a guarding post and could stand and guard he would do this for a is awhile. Freddy guarded the prisoners for all around Canada for the first three years of the war. As it seemed the ending of the war was not soon coming and now Freddy was having problems standing for long periods of time. He was transferred to a hospital in New Brunswick because when he got his leg injury in the first world war, they still had his medical records on files. They tried helping him but it was obvious that he could no longer just stand and guard the prisoners of war. Freddy was worried now what would he do for work but as luck would have it the army offered Freddy a job in the "Officers Mess Hall" he would start off slow and see if he liked it. Freddy said yes and upon his release from the hospital. Freddy was discharged and he was transferred once again to this time Ottawa, he liked Ottawa because it was just a train ride to Montreal. He would sometimes get time off and be able to see his family once in awhile. Lena liked her visits when Freddy and then family were all together, Lena was Freddy's little princess and he adored her a lot. Lena also had a bond with her father and with her mother, and her older siblings also joined in spoiling her a little too. But thankfully Lena did not take this for granted because she knew that the love she had from her family was worth more than any new dresses, shoes or hair ribbons she could ever want or need. Also during visits from her father Freddy, they would sit and talk about his beloved home Jamaica and how he missed it so much and all the family he had to leave behind. Freddy would talk about his homeland with tears in eyes each time it made Lena very sad. Freddy enjoyed working in the Officers Mess Hall he started off peeling potatoes, carrots and onions, but this lasted for a short while because Freddy started to cook with the spices his Granny would use back home in Jamaica. He was soon promoted to soups-chef meaning he helped the chef prepare the food for the Officers.

    Freddy would do this job even until the war ended on September 2,1945, but it would take at least another year until the prisoners of war were returned to their homelands.

1946

The prisoners of war are returned home to their countries. Freddy is sent once again to the hospital this time in Ottawa. Anna and Lena visit him in the "Veteran's Hospital" and he tells them that he has been released from the Army with a small pension. Anna says it is okay and Lena is relieved because now her father can stay home and she can leave the convent for good. But is months until Freddy can walk and go home again to his family. Anna is happy to have her husband home again with her and the children especially Lena she misses her daddy so very much. He finally comes home and Lena gets to leave the "Convent" for good. Freddy stays home and now he cleans and cooks now too Anna is very surprised. Lena is very happy to be home and have her daddy with her for always. Freddy is happy too but something is missing he needs to work, this is all he knows from birth. Freddy has worked all his life and never knew what was unemployment or welfare. He only knew that if a man wanted to provide for his family then he had to work no matter what. He decided to start and look for work. Lena was attending a local Catholic school nearby and he would walk the pavement everyday looking for any kind of work. It was frustrating for Freddy to not find work after the army even though he had a small pension for now it still was not enough. But he still walked everyday and when he could afford it he would take the bus. Lena seeing the frustration in her father's eyes made her want to work too. But Freddy and Anna would not hear of it all, so Lena said okay and continued with school for now she thought. Then one day Freddy happens to meet on of the friends of Judge Bernstein his past employer. His name was Michael Taylor; he was head of management for the "Berman Building" one of the biggest in Montreal now. Mr. Taylor was very happy to see Freddy again and asked him if he could join him of a cup of coffee. Freddy said he would be delighted and they went to a nearby restaurant called "Dunn's" it was famous for its smoked meat sandwiches. They walked in and ordered their coffee and started to talk. It had been a long time for both and they missed Judge Bernstein. They sat there looking at each other and thinking about the Judge in their own way. Each man having their own fond memories of the man that they both so admired. Michael was happy that he ran into Freddy because he knew that Freddy was having hard times and he needed a new elevator operator and he wanted Freddy for the job.

"Well Freddy it is so nice to see you again and have this time to chat with you," says Michael. Hoping that when he asks Freddy his next question he will say yes.

"Yes, it is very nice to see you again too Mr. Taylor and I am happy to see you and that life has been kind to you," says Freddy as he sips his coffee and smiles at Michael.

"Well there is this matter I am having and maybe you can help me solve my problem?" says Michael as he looks at Freddy with a smile.

"What seems to be your problem Mr. Taylor and can I help you in any way possible?" says Freddy wondering what could Mr. Taylor be talking about.

"It is like this Freddy, I need an elevator man for my building and I need one soon," says Michael hoping Freddy says yes.

"I am very pleased that you would offer me this job but, as you know my leg is a little weak, and I cannot stand for too long a time," says Freddy hoping this does not change Mr. Taylor's mind.

"I do not see this as a problem you have a small stool inside the elevator, you only stand to open and shut the door. It would be a good fit I do believe," says Michael gladly now that Freddy has accepted the job.

"When do I start Mr. Taylor and what are my duties?" asks Freddy to be sure he heard right.

"You can start this Monday coming. I will meet you in my office and give all the information you need alright," says Michael Taylor happier now than beforehand.

As both men say their good-byes, Freddy goes home and tells Anna of his good fortune of meeting Michael Taylor and the job offer he was given too. This meant for the family that things would and could get better. Lena was also very happy now she could go to public school and leave the convent for good. This was a joyous time for the Reid family and it meant with the two pay cheques coming in, and with Anna still working Freddy Jr. could return and finish his schooling. Anna and Freddy Sr. were so happy that their money problems would be a little better now.

Monday morning came and Freddy is getting ready for his new job at the Berman Building. As they sit to have breakfast Anna looks at him and says with happiness and relief in her voice, "my husband I am so happy and proud of you that you have found a good job and your running into Mr. Taylor is a true blessing. As my mama always said pray and God listens." As she pours the coffee Freddy listens to her speaking and answers in kind.

"Yes my dear wife, it is a blessing that we have received from the Lord and He will always keep us in his light," says Freddy as he looks at his wife adoringly.

"I am so happy and hopeful that this job will do this family a lot of good and we will all be better for it," says Anna as she has sparkle back in her eyes and hope in her heart.

"Well my dear Anna this is a turning point for me, as I was afraid that because of my leg that it would be hard to find work again. But God blessed us with Mr. Taylor and his job offer, I will not let this family or Mr. Taylor down," says Freddy very determinedly.

Freddy kept his promise and went to work in the elevators of the Berman Building in downtown Montreal. As promised there was a stool for him to rest at times if needed. Freddy quite enjoyed his new job and was happy to be working again.

The year is now 1949 early summer in June to be exact and Lena does not want to return to school in the Fall. She begs her father to let her work with him at the Berman Building since there are many factories in this building. Freddy is hesitant but as he cannot refuse Lena anything or almost, he gives in and asks Mr. Taylor if Lena can work there just for the summer. Lena's parents are hoping that after she sees how hard it is to work she might change her mind and return to school and finish. But Lena is very happy and cannot wait to start but little does she know that she must start at the bottom and prove her worth. Freddy says ok and waits to see his daughter's reaction to work.

It is Freddy and Anna's hope that all their children finish school and learn as much as possible, because of the little amount of education both parents had. Freddy had very little schooling and Anna just a little more. So far as the Freddy and Anna were concerned education was important and with it many doors could be opened as opposed to closed.

But Lena was not having any of it and she was determined to go to work at any cost, even if it meant no schooling to further her chances in life. Being seventeen Lena thought she knew the world now and she had it all figured out. But it was her first try at working in the big world and she was determined to go to work and her mind was made up.

But what she was not sure of was the job that was in store for her. It would not be something she had imagined either it would change her perceptive of working really quick. But after all it was a job and it had to be done right. It was still going to be challenging for her and maybe be humbling for her being a teenager and all.

It was settled she would start to work after her school finished the end of June. She was asked and shown how to separate all the buttons that were needed for the sweaters being made. It was not the glamorous job she thought to have but it was work and she did not mind to much. But as the floor manager told her if she worked hard she could get promotions to other jobs. This was great news for Lena now she thought she could have all the thinks she wanted. The day came for her to start working at a factory called Helen Harper. They manufactured woolen sweaters of all kinds. She knew she start at the bottom and her within the company. Lena continues to work for Helen Harper Company and starts to enjoy working and making her own spending money. She also contributed a little to the household as she wanted to do her part too. Her parents were very happy that she had already adopted this attitude from the beginning. This would make her more responsible and mature. It would also teach her the value of money, hopefully.

Lena was spoiled not rotten spoiled but loving spoiled and she had a lot to learn about life in general. She went from home to convent then back home, it was a change that she accepted and dealt with. As time went by the job got easier and Lena was doing great she was getting the hang of the job and enjoyed the pay checks she got from it each week.

As the Depression Era was ending more jobs were being created and the economy was looking better for all concerned. It was a good sign for the whole world.-But thankfully it was ending and the people had hope again. It looked like the Reid family was getting stronger and better as they fought the Depression and won. Yes, it was a trying time for everyone but as a family they persevered and triumph.

It would be a time in their lives that all would remember for a long time to come. Freddy enjoyed his new job and the fact that he could keep an eye on his daughter making sure she did not falter in any way possible. But as we know fathers and daughters sometimes have a special bond and so it should be.

But Lena's parents were happy in a sense that she could have a job near her father and could be protected also. But this was not what Lena wanted but she accepted it knowing her parents did this out of love for her.

But as the summer flew by Lena was enjoying working and did not want to return to school anymore. She was not like her brother Freddy Jr. he wanted to finish school and maybe go to college.

But only time could and would tell what and how lives were to change with the Depression at an end and the economy picking up slowly but surely. It was a time to be hopeful and know life was going to get better for everyone in the entire world.

Freddy and his family were thankful and did not take this new beginning for granted, because they knew too well how easily life can change for the worst or the best. It was a lesson that everyone had learned and understood. Hard times are very scary but sometimes they can get better with hard work and love of a family.

Things would slowly get better thought Freddy and he was patient and knew it would in time. Till then he would take care of his family and be happy for his blessings.

Freddy was hopeful that now his family's life and his would get better day by day, and it made him happy and grateful and very hopeful indeed.

Sometimes God does answer prayers and helps us find our way, that was what Freddy's dear Granny would always say to him. He never forgot her precious words or her teachings either. It carried him through his life always especially during war times. Freddy thought to himself his family was going to survive and so would he right along with them.

As the summer is also coming to an end Lena still wants to keep working and making her own money but her parents do not want her to quit school. Lena protests and cries and pouts until Freddy cannot help but give into her and let Lena leave school.

Anna was not to thrilled about the idea but she knew how Lena had her father on her side always. Freddy did lay some ground rules that she had to keep her job and pay room and board now too. Lena agreed to the terms of the house and Freddy's rules and so she could continue to work and leave school.

Lena soon got a promotion and was now learning to take inventory instead of sorting buttons. She enjoyed this part of the job more than sorting buttons. This was a new challenge for Lena and she accepted it whole hardheartedly but it was not easy. She got up early in the morning and sometimes she worked late. It was tough at times to get up but she did it all the same as she thought of the pay check and what she could do with it. She could pay room and board at home and had money left over for herself. She was getting things that a young girl of this era wanted and needed. She was even able to buy gifts for her family.

Freddy was proud of her and watched her mature into a beautiful young woman that was his daughter. Freddy as also happy because he could keep an eye on his baby girl and make sure she did not dawdle and goof around at work, like some of the other young girls and boys that worked there. It looked like everything was going to turn out okay and he was happy with the arrangement. It was going to work out just fine he thought.

Anna had her doubts. She wanted Lena to have an education that was better than hers or Freddy and she worried that Lena may never finish her schooling.

Lena was not worried at all. She wanted to work and that was what she would do. She would learn all she could about the "Helen Harper Company." It was a learning experience in life of sorts and Lena embraced it with open arms. For Lena was like her father in many ways. She had his spirit and his strong will and liked a good challenge now and then.

Freddy and Lena had a very special bond, for she was his last child his baby girl and he sort of spoiled her a bit more than the others and at times it showed. Yet Lena did not abuse this bond with her father as she loved both her parents and her siblings equally and they loved her the same way. Lena was a very loved young lady and because of this she had the common sense to know and understand the teaching of her parents and siblings. The Reid family had a lot of love for one another and they were happy with each other through good and bad times at all costs.

1949

Lena has been working for awhile now and has saved a far bit of money, but she also has lovely new clothes too. This was Lena's passion, she loved clothes as a child. She would cut out the ladies in magazines and dressed them in different outfits. She also had an eye for fashion and liked putting different outfits together.

It is summer time now and the Legion Branch 55 was having a picnic for all the members and their families. So of course, Freddy packed up his family Anna, Lena and himself and they went to this Legion picnic. It was held in Long Sault, Quebec as they had the best beaches and picnic grounds. There was a lot of people some were members and some just family member's.

There was one family in particle that was about to be involved with the Reid's, but little did they know of it at the time. There was a good looking young man with brown skin that approached Lena and asked her what her name was. She replied to him, "Lena" and she asked him his. He said, "Malcolm," but they call me Junior. His family was there because his uncle Cecil was in the Army and he invited his brother Carl and his wife Margaret and their children.

Of course, Freddy was watching from a distance and was not to happy to see his "little girl" being pursued by a young man he did not know. But that soon changed as Lena brought Malcolm's parents to meet her parents. They were a little taken back at how Lena was not shy with these people. They were also surprised to see that they were very nice people and down to earth like them.

Mr. Carl Izeard, as he gave his name, worked on the railroads where he was Porter for the train company "Canadian Railways." His wife Margaret was a "Char Lady" meaning she cleaned other rich women's homes. So, Freddy thought they were just hard working people like himself and his wife. They chatted about the picnic and how it was a nice gesture on the part of the Legion 55.

"Well Mr. Reid I see that our children seem to be getting along and that is just fine with my wife and I," says Carl Izeard as he looks at the kids.

"I see what you mean and may I call you Carl? And please call me Freddy and my wife is name Anna," says Freddy with a smile.

'Well then you can call me Carl and my wife is named Margaret but we all call her Margie," says Carl to Freddy.

"Mr. Reid sir, may I have your permission to take Lena for a walk, we will not be alone sir," says Malcolm as he points to his siblings. He motions for them to come over and say hello to Lena's family. As they are approaching Freddy looks at them with a smile.

"Mr. and Mrs. Reid may I introduce to you my sister Shirley and brother Donald," says Malcolm as he looks at Freddy hoping he will say yes.

"Hello Mr. And Mrs. Reid we are very happy to meet Lena's parents you have a very nice daughter," says Shirley.

"Hello sir and Mrs. Reid very happy to make your acquaintance and you have a real nice daughter too and I think my brother does too," says Donald always the kidder. He was the joker of the family and like to play harmless jokes on people.

"Well thank you both for the compliments and I see that your parents raised you all well too," says Freddy as he is amazed that these children are well-behaved.

As Anna and Margie can see what was transpiring before them decided they should all eat together and get to know the families better. For even if the fathers did not want to see it the mothers did and knew what to do to be very sure of what was happening. As the mothers were setting up the food both with their picnic baskets they also noticed that there was enough food for an Army. They did not fear for there were two men and two young men with healthy appetites and all the food would not be wasted for sure.

As they ate the fine picnic food and talked and got to know each other better it turned out to be a great day after all for both families.

Lena and Malcolm finally went for that walk they wanted and Malcolm was wondering the whole time if he should ask her if she would like him to call on her sometime for a movie or maybe dinner. As they walked and talked Malcolm was working up the courage to ask Lena on a proper date. Lena also was wondering if Malcolm was going to ask her out on a date and where would they go. It was a wonder for both and it was also something they both wanted. The only remaining question was if Malcolm was going to ask Lena out or not and what will she say?

"Lena, I would like to ask you something and please do not be offended in any way," says Malcolm finally having the courage to ask. "But would you like to go out with me sometime to a movie or dinner of just for a walk in the park?"

"Yes Malcolm that would be fine. A movie, dinner or a walk in the park all sound nice," says Lena happy that he finally asked her out.

"Well how about the movies next Saturday? We could double date with my brother Donny as we call him and his girlfriend Diane. She is a French girl but she speaks English but you also speak French, so it should be a fun time for all," says Malcolm also happy that Lena said yes.

"Yes I speak French from my time at school and my mother is Belgian as you know so her English is good but with an accent for sure, and I am sure it will be fun to go to a movie with your brother and his girlfriend," says Lena as she smiles at Malcolm.

"Ok then shall we say about six o'clock? The movie starts at seven o'clock to be in time for the opening credits and get refreshments too," says Malcolm really happy now that he got the courage to ask Lena out for a date.

It was going to be a good night now all he had to do was ask his brother Donny if he and Diane would like to join them for the movies. He was hoping that his brother did not have plans already made and that he would say yes.

As they start to walk back to the picnic tables and their families Malcolm sees his brother Donny walking towards him, Malcolm thinks to himself no time like the present to ask him to double date. Donny was not an easy person to convince at times and Malcolm was hoping that this would not be one of those times. He had to approach his brother easily and not make him feel he had to either.

"Donny do you and Diane have any plans next Saturday and would you like to double date with Lena and I to go the movies? asks Malcolm hoping his brother will say yes.

"I am not sure yet, I would have to ask Diane maybe she would like to do something else if she has the day off. You know she works weekends sometimes just like today," says Donny not sure what his girlfriend might say about all this.

"I really like this girl and would appreciate you doing this for me brother to brother, and she is really nice and sweet so please can you ask Diane if she would go also thank you brother Donny," says Malcolm hoping he played his cards right with him and made his point.

"I will ask Diane and let you know later. I am seeing her later tonight so I can ask her then okay, that is all I can promise you for now."

Meanwhile Lena has returned to the picnic site where her parents and Malcolm's family are sitting and talking still. As she sits down she decides to tell her parents about Malcolm asking her out on a date. She is hoping that her father will not get to bent out of sorts and make Malcolm feel uncomfortable and her uneasy about the whole thing. She knew he would protest but she was ready for him.

"Dad, I have been asked out on a date to the movies by Malcolm and we will be double dating with his brother Donny and his girlfriend Diane," says Lena waiting to see how her father and mother react to the news she just said to everyone at the picnic table. The both set of parents look at one another and exchange questioning looks. They just went for a walk and now talk of a double date.

"Well I guess it would be okay since it is a double date," says Margie the boy's mother looking at her husband for approval too.

"I am not so sure about this but knowing my daughter as I do she will want to go anyway, so I also say okay but she must be home at a decent hour," says Freddy looking at his wife wondering what she is thinking about all this.

"I say it is settled then the children go out on a double date next Saturday and we will see how it goes from there," says Carl as he looks over at Lena's parents hoping they agree with him. Freddy gives him a nod as if to say he agrees and the wives just look on knowing it was okay too. So now it was settled, Saturday they would have their double date and see what happens from there. It was going to be fun for them. It was funny for Lena just meeting a young man and going on a date, but the funniest thing of it all is that Malcolm is a Black man like her father only much darker. Her father was not upset about it but a little weary at best.

Yes, he meets the parents and they are very hard working nice people and raised their children well but this was his baby girl and he was not ready for her to leave home and marry just yet. He wanted her home as long as he could keep her there. She was his last child at home and he was not ready for her to leave just yet. Anna felt the same but she knew her daughter had a strong will like her father and she knew what she wanted and would go for it like her father.

This is why at times they butted heads and Anna had to referee, she did not like getting in the middle all the time but when it was necessary she would. But it was not too often they butted heads but it looked to Anna as if they might if this dating thing goes any further than just movies and dinners. So as always Anna prayed on it and waited to see what would happen and if it was a good thing they said yes to Lena about Malcolm. Lena was very anxious as she waited for Saturday to finally roll around, she was hoping to see a movie that was a little romantic and dramatic too.

She was also happy of the fact that it would be a double date because Donny and Diane both agreed to go to the movies with them. It made it easier for her to be just them and no parents around to keep a watchful eye on them all the time. Saturday night arrives and Malcolm, Donny and Diane pick up Lena at her home in the borrowed car from their Uncle Cecil. The say good evening to her parents and assure them that Lena would be home at a reasonable time and she would be safe as Donny is a very good driver. Freddy and Anna wished them all a good time and off they went into Uncle Cecil's car and to the movies.

It was not a long drive to the movies but it seemed like one for Lena. She was excited and nervous all at the same time. It was her first real double date and she was having fun, and enjoying the company of Malcolm, Donny and Diane. She turned out to be a nice girl too.

The movie was a good movie about people finding love. It was called "An Affair to Remember." It was quite good and the boys were real sports about the whole thing. It turned out to be a good night all around. Lena was hoping that Malcolm would ask her out again and that she had a real nice time too. Malcolm was hoping on his side that if he did ask her out again she would say yes. So now only time would tell and if this new friendship would become more than that in the future.

Two weeks went by and Malcolm finally called Lena and asked her out again but only just them no double dating. She said yes she would and was happy he called. He told her about a party his aunt was having and would she like to attend. She said that it sounded like fun and was happy to be invited but she could not stay out to late as her parents would worry too much. Malcolm said okay and they made a time to meet.

Malcolm borrowed his uncle's car again and picked up Lena.

As they arrived at the party Malcolm introduced Lena to his Aunt Beatrice. It was her birthday party, and she was very happy to finally meet Lena after hearing so much about her. Beatrice was Malcolm's mother Margaret's sister and they were very close and they talked a lot about Malcolm meeting Lena Reid.

The party was great. The food, the music, and the people were just wonderful. Lena was having a grand time and was happy she came.

She also got to see Mr. and Mrs. Izeard again and they asked about her parents. Lena said they were well and they would like to meet with them again sometime soon.

As the party was ending Malcolm again asked his uncle for his car and along with his brother drove the young ladies home. Before saying good night, Malcolm asked if Lena would like to go out again sometime. She said she would think about it as she had a lot to do with work and her family. He said okay but, would call her the next week following just in case, she said fine and they said their goodnights.

After Malcolm's Aunt Beatrice's birthday party Lena and Malcolm started to date more. It was a slow start but Lena and Malcolm eventually started dating seriously. Malcolm was finding himself in love with Lena and he was hoping she was in love too. It was looking like it might even be as serious as wedding bells.

By now they had been dating for almost a year and Malcolm wanted to marry Lena but, he knew he had to ask her parents for her hand in marriage. He also knew that Lena was the apple of her father's eye and it was not going to be easy to ask him at all. Malcolm was sure if Lena felt the same as him she would convince her father of this marriage.

Her mother on the other hand was more gentle and understood young love as she was young when she married her husband. That was then and this is now and times have changed. The world was different now and life was better all around. Malcolm knowing all this still had to ask the most important person of all Lena and hope she will say "yes."

Malcolm had a good job setting jewels and other precious stones into rings, bracelets and necklaces. It was a small jewelry store but he made good wages and could afford to marry and have a good life too. With Lena working at the factory they could make ends meet. That is until the children come along, then Malcolm was prepared to take a second job and Lena would stay home. That would be in the future; for now, he had to find the courage to ask Freddy Reid for his daughter's hand in marriage and ask Lena if she will be his wife.

It was a big decision for Malcolm to make but, he knew he had to act fast before all his courage faded away and he lost his nerve. It was almost Christmas time so he thought it would be the opportune moment to ask Lena to marry him and ask her father for her hand in marriage too.

He was thinking of asking his parents to invite Lena's family for Christmas Eve dinner at his parent's home and make it official for both families. This way he thought it would be easier for him to pop the question and take some pressure off him. Malcolm hoped his parents would say yes and after he tells them why he was sure they would be all for it.

It was going to be a Christmas to remember for both families alike and hopefully a joyous one also. He knew that Lena cared for him deeply and in her own way loved him too but he had to ask her to marry him. She was all he ever wanted in a girlfriend and now he wanted her to be his wife and share a lifetime with him.

He had a little over two months to prepare and keep the faith that it will all work out for the best. In the meantime, they would keep dating and let their love blossom as time goes by. The two-month wait was going to be a bit tough because Malcolm wanted to propose right away but he knew that Christmas would be a better time and give him more time to get to know Freddy Reid.

Two months seemed like a long time but it would fly by fast and before Malcolm knew it would be asking the love of his life to be his wife. He would also try and win Lena's father and mother over to his side and hope for the best when he proposes to Lena.

Donald and Diane knew of Malcolm's plan but kept it a secret for they wanted to see the look on Lena's face when Malcolm proposes to her. Everything would be revealed at

Christmas time. In the meantime, it was to remain a secret until Malcolm was ready to ask Lena.

Every time they were together it was hard for Malcolm to contain himself and not ask Lena right then and there. But he also knew that he had to do this as a gentleman and properly for Lena deserved that and more. He also knew that it would upset his parents as well as Lena's especially her father Freddy Reid a very proud man to say the least. He kept his cool and stuck to his plan and waited for his opportune time and place to "pop the question."

It was a good idea because at Christmas time everyone is full of love and joy and goodwill towards men. Malcolm was hoping that Freddy would be feeling this and a whole lot more. Until then he waited till he could ask his question and get an answer. It would be a very special day in his life and hopefully for Lena's too.

Married life he knew was something they would have to work at and of course they being young and not of legal age would need consent from parents on both sides. This too weighed heavily on his mind as he knew fathers did not like to give consent for their daughters to marry before legal age.

With all this Malcolm also prayed as he was always in church as a child, his parents sang in the church choir. He knew the power of pray and how it could work wonders he also knew that it took time and strong believing and yes faith too. With all this he stayed strong and determined not to back away from his quest for he was a man with a mission and he was not giving up at all. After all he had to ask to know for sure the outcome and then and only then would he be sure of his decision. And respectably Lena would have to say yes if she did love and want to marry him and spend a lifetime with him too.

He had a lot to think about and decisions to make and wonder how to approach Alfred Reid about asking for his daughter's hand in marriage. Malcolm knew he was brought up right and a gentleman must ask the parents first and then the young lady in question. It was not something he thought of lightly but something of great importance and after all it was his life too.

Christmas Eve has finally arrived and the Reid and Izeard families all got together at the Izeard home for a great meal. Malcolm is nervous and his brother Donald notices and so does Diane but they say nothing as they were sworn to secrecy.

Malcolm realizing that the time had arrived and he must find the real courage now and ask Lena's parent's permission to marry her. As for him he knew his family would say yes as they just adored Lena. He thought that he would wait till after the lovely dinner his mother prepared and everyone was feeling full and happy. He also wanted wait till his father and Freddy had a few drinks of whiskey as he thought it might help the situation. He wished for a whiskey himself the "Dutch Courage" as they say. He knew what he needed was a clear head and heart for this situation before him.

The family sat around a big Christmas Eve dinner and laughed, talked and even made some jokes. So far so good thought Malcolm. Lena was looking so pretty and her golden hair shone so bright. He thought to himself if this beauty says yes to my proposal of marriage I will be the happiest man alive for sure.

Donny and Diane were bursting with anticipation with wonder if Lena will say yes and more so to see the reaction of the parents on both sides to Malcolm's proposal to Lena. It was going to be a memorable Christmas for both families and for Lena and Malcolm too. Malcolm thought it was going well but the day was dragging on as he was starting to get nervous, but his brother gave him moral support as they were very close and always had each other's back.

So now all Malcolm had to do was wait for his moment and then just ask the question and hopefully he would get his answer he wants from everyone concerned. They say Christmas can be magical and sometimes miracles occur. Maybe this was one of those times thought Malcolm as he hoped deep down inside it was going to be.

Malcolm looked around the room and say everyone there he either loved or liked a lot and that he thought was a good omen and he was holdings onto that. As they sit around the table and wait for dessert and coffee Malcolm ponders the thought of when he should ask the question. Should he wait for everyone to sit down at the table for dessert and coffee or just before they leave?

After all the pep talk his brother and Diane gave him he just had to be brave and ask. As the parents started to sit down Donny and Diane took their seats Andy gave an encouraging look towards Malcolm.

"Ahem ahem," as Malcolm clears his throat and gaining more courage. "I have an announcement to make but first we need permission meaning Lena and I. Lena, it would be an honor for me if you would agree to be my bride and spend the rest of your life being my wife," says Malcolm looking at Lena and back at her parents. Scanning the table trying to feel the mood. He could see Donny and Diane giving smiles of approval as they just adore Lena, but it was his parents and Lena's that had to approve. There was a quite hush and no one spoke for what seemed like a long time.

Finally, Freddy looks at his wife before he says anything letting Mr. Carl Izeard to be the first to answer his son's request. "Well I must say Margaret and I did not see this coming at all. It is not to say that we are not thrilled either, but I think Lena's parents should be the first to decide. I am so sorry, Lena should they be the first as her answer says it all really," says Carl hoping he did not over step his bounds, or spoke out of turn either.

"I must say that I agree with you Carl, we must wait and see what my Lena says," says Freddy looking at his wife as if to say I can deal with this.

Before she answers Lena looks at everyone one by one. First her father, mother and then Carl, Margaret, Donny and Diane. Lastly she looks towards Malcolm and sees his face, wondering what she will answer to his proposal.

"Well I must say this is a different kind of proposal but, I can see that it does serve a dual purpose, ask my parents' permission and proposing to me. And my answer to all of this is yes and I hope we have all the parent's blessings and permission," says Lena really looking at her father this time only hoping he understands completely. Again, a moment of silence as all eyes are on Freddy and he feels the heat for sure.

"All I can say is that these two are so young and they should wait a little more, but in saying that we can see it is falling upon their deaf ears. If my wife agrees and Carl and Margaret agree then they can marry. But not too soon I hope, I have to save some money up first;" says Freddy seeing the look on his daughter's face knowing if he did not give his consent she would be furious at him forever and he didn't want to do that to her either.

"So it is settled then that Lena and Malcolm can get

married. My wife and I are thrilled and give you our blessing and permission too," says Carl with a big happy smile.

"I am so very happy that you and my son are getting married. We welcome you to the family and hope both families can be friends also," says Margaret after listening to everyone and staying silent till now.

"I also would like to say something. I am also happy to have your son as a part of my family," says Anna with a smile.

It was settled they would get married and in a church but it meant that Lena could not marry in a Catholic Church because Malcolm was Protestant. Lena was prepared and did not sweat the outcome because she was getting married and that was that. So now they had to find a church make arrangements and invite guests.

Lena's Godfather, Police Chief of Montreal, Mr. Henri Deseare, told Lena as his wedding gift to her he would pay for the wedding of her choice. Lena was beside herself with joy, it was like a dream come true.

She could not wait to tell Malcolm of the good news and hoped he would be thrilled too but, they still had to set a date. Lena did not want to get married in the Winter or the Fall. They would figure it out and then let their parents and Lena's Godfather know on what date they have decided.

There was so much to do. Lena was not aware of all the arranging and preparing this would take, it was a bit overwhelming at best. But as she thought about it the more she realized it was her wedding and one she would never forget so it had to be perfect.

Perfect even if it is wasn't in a Catholic Church. Sometimes we cannot get what we want when we want it. Lena knew it mattered to her parents but, she made them realize that God is everywhere and in every Church. Just because they sing hymns different and preach the sermons different it is still a "House of God," and we all pray the same in the end; on bended knees and hands folded in prayer.

Donny was to be Malcolm's best man, and Lena's best friend Helen was her maid of honor. Diane and Malcolm's little sister Shirley, would be the bride maids. The ushers were two of Malcolm's cousins; Willie and Hugh Izeard. This was going to be a wonderful wedding.

Lena and Malcolm did not want a very big wedding, just close family and friends. However, it turned out that Malcolm had a bigger family in Montreal than Lena did. It did not matter for it was okay and she understood, as some of her relatives from New Brunswick would come, as well as, her older brother Reuben and his little family and her older sister Flora and her husband.

In all it was going to be a wonderful wedding with

family and friends and lots of good food and spirits for everyone to enjoy. It was going to be a special day and everyone was going to have a wonderful time.

It was only the middle of January so Lena and Malcolm both decided on a May wedding. Spring in the air and flowers blooming everywhere and the sweet smell of the spring air. It was a great month to get married and is what they will do. As the months went by Lena and her mother and Margaret who was soon to be her mother-in-law helped with the wedding preparations.

Since they still wanted a church wedding they found a Reverend Este to perform the ceremony. Freddy was not too pleased that his baby girl was not being married in a Catholic Church but none the less she was being married in a church anyway.

Lena and her mother both prayed for sunny blue skies and birds chirping in the trees, and a little breeze in the air. It was a day the young lovebirds would not forget. As everyone entered the "Union United Church" in St. Henri a part of Montreal's west end, the organ music was playing a wonderful hymn till it was time for the bride to enter.

After her maid of honour and bridesmaid's s entered, Lena was lead into the church by her father as the music to the Wedding March played. Malcolm turns as he hears the familiar tune on the organ and sees Lena and her father coming up the aisle, and he just smiles from ear to ear, thinking to himself, "Wow she is beautiful for real," and waits till she arrives to meet him at the altar.

Everyone sits down and the Reverend Este begins as he looks over the crowd in the church, seeing new and old faces and liking the atmosphere in the church today.

"Dearly beloved family and friends we are here today to witness the holy matrimony of Lena Reid and Malcolm Izeard, who have asked to be married before God and family and friends. Before we begin who does give this bride to be hand in marriage?" says the Reverend Este as he awaits an answer.

"I do Reverend give my daughter's hand in marriage," says Freddy as he looks at Lena for the last time as his little girl who is about to be married.

"Well then Malcolm Izeard do you take Lena Reid as your lawfully wedded wife in sickness and health, for richer or poorer and forsaking all others?" asks the Reverend Este.

"I do," says Malcolm a little nervous and a lot happy.

"And do you Lena Reid, take Malcolm Izeard as your lawfully wedded husband, in sickness and health, for richer or poorer, and forsaking all others?" he asks again.

"I do," says Lena as she looks over at Malcolm giving him a big smile.

"Well then I now pronounce you both man and wife, you may kiss the bride," says the Reverend.

Everyone starts to stand up and clap as the newlyweds walk down the aisle. Everyone smiled, there was some crying and the parents are just beaming on both sides. It truly was a glorious day and Lena and Malcolm could not be happier. They both felt blessed on the wonderful day they shared with family and friends.

Now everyone was outside and throwing the traditional rice at the newly wedded couple as they made their way to the Belgian Hall for a wedding party with lots of food and drink and music too. Lena was amazed at how beautiful everything was and Malcolm was pleased as well he thought it to be great.

The cake stole the show away from the gourmet foods and desserts. It was a cake to behold in all its splendour. It was a beautiful Belgian made wedding cake Mr. Deseare ordered from his favorite bakery shop ``La Patriste Belge."` It was one of the finest bakeries in Montreal and it was going to be a perfect cake for a perfect day. It would be a cake made to perfection and so sweet and delicious just looking at it. It was three layers high and had a layer of chocolate, vanilla and butterscotch. Everyone marvelled at it and said it was just beautiful to see and they were all anxious to taste it too.

Lena was so thankful to her family, her Godfather and her new in-laws for all their help and support to make this day wonderful. It was a day she would never forget or wanted to forget either. It was a truly bless day all around for the happy newlyweds.

Their guests enjoyed and embraced the magical day that was their wedding. Lena and Malcolm were very happy and joyful and full of hope and promise of their lives together. They both had dreams and hopes of what their marriage and life together will be like, also they wanted children and Lena was that Malcolm felt the same way as she about children. It was going to be a happy marriage and life for them to share for now and always.

They had a lovely honeymoon at St. Sauvier, a popular ski resort. In the spring and summer, it is a vacation spot for newlyweds and young couples to enjoy. They had a week there and it was just beautiful with plush green grass all around and a wonderful view of the lake where they could go for a stroll. It was nice and they enjoyed every minute of it.

After the week was over it was back to the old grind of work and seeing what married life was like for them. Lena went back to her job as well as Malcolm both starting to realize that this was for real now and no turning back to their parents anymore. This meant they were adults now and had to deal with their own problems and see how it was to be all grown up.

Now they had been married a year or more and it was okay by Lena and Malcolm. One day Lena found out she was pregnant and due in November. Their parents on both sides were ecstatic although Freddy and Anna already had grandchildren in New Brunswick. Their son Freddy Jr.'s wife gave birth about three years before Lena got married. To them it was not so new but to Freddy and Anna it was a new blessing to the family.

    For the Izeard's, this would be their very first grandchild and they were over the moon and so very happy. In fact, both sets of parents were very happy and Lena was just overjoyed to becoming a mother. As for Malcolm, he was beside himself with joy and wondering if he would make a great father.

    Still they had to wait for the birth to know if it will be a "girl or boy" and what to name the child. They had to make plans and Lena could not work for much longer. As soon as she was showing working in a factory would be too much with all the dust and fumes in the building. For now, she could work until her sixth month and then she would have to take it easy for awhile. It was to be tough when Lena would have to finish working but, it would be all worth it when the new baby arrives and makes everybody happy to greet this new life that was growing inside of Lena that was created by her and Malcolm's love.

    Also, what was nice was they would be able to experience the child's first Christmas soon after the birth. It was just a great blessing and a miracle in a way as Lena was told by her doctor that she may have trouble conceiving. But now she knew that she could and was just so very happy. It was a marvel and she embraced it every day and talked to the child that was growing inside of her. She could not wait to meet her new born baby and hold her or him and see it's little face and hear the word "Mommy" for the first time. They say all babies say "dada" but, not Lena's child her baby will be saying mommy before dada.

She was a little worried about one thing seeing as the child will be born in November and since it is cold, she worried the baby would be born with a cold. Her mother laughed and said not to worry, babies are tougher than you would think so just enjoy this time and be happy not to worry.

But she had other concerns too, such as, how to change a diaper or make a bottle or just plain take care of a child so small and fragile. She need not worry because Malcolm being the eldest in his family, often helped his mother with his baby sister Shirley and knew what to do, so that was covered at least. For now, Lena's worries were put to rest and she could just concentrate on keeping well and healthy for the child.

Little did she realize that a new born is a lot of work and a lot of late night feedings and changing not to mention other things like teething or colic. Yes, she had a lot to learn but her maternal instincts will guide her and she had her mother and mother-in-law at the ready for any advice or help. Lena felt so lucky to have two such wonderful women to be by her side and that she could lean on if needed.

Yes, in all, it was going to be okay and Lena and Malcolm will bring a new life to the family and the child will be loved and cherished and taught all good things from parents and grandparents alike.

The child was to be born in late November and Lena was hoping for a girl which is perfectly natural. It was a very happy time for Lena as she awaited her child's birth. The days were long and the nights longer just waiting for this child, Lena was also learning a lot of how the caring of babies was major work for the first couple of years. But that did not make her nervous or anxious at all she wanted to be a mother and if it meant all this and more so be it she was ready. As for Malcolm being a father he already knew from helping with his siblings that it was not always easy. The real challenge will be when the child arrives and then it will be for real not just a wish.

The month's roll by and finally it is November and Lena goes into labour. As she is taken into hospital in the ambulance her mother goes with her. Malcolm and Freddy are still at work but Freddy gets there first and asks to see his daughter and grandchild.

On the evening of November 28, 1951 Freddy and Anna are told they have a beautiful baby granddaughter and she is healthy and has a lot of pretty light brown hair. Freddy and Anna started to cry. it was a miracle and blessing all in one. Lena was the most over joyed new mother there ever was she finally had her child. As she looked down at this pretty light brown haired child with olive tone skin she gave thanks to God for this precious baby girl.

She was anxious to bring the baby girl home and have her Christened, but first as she was being presented to the family awaiting to see her. Freddy put his arms out first and held the female child. He smiled at her and had tears in his eyes. He was overjoyed to see his baby girl have a baby girl of her own.

When Malcolm arrives with his family he sees Freddy holding his daughter and puts his arms out for the child. As Malcolm looks down upon his first-born child he has tears in his eyes as he realizes this is for real and so is this baby.

Everyone is asked to leave so that mother and baby can rest but they all promise Lena to be back the next day. Lena now left alone with her new baby girl she holds her and thinks to herself this is my child, my little girl and I will name her. I will give her a name that will be her own and it will be a name she can be proud of and live by.

For now, Lena just wanted to enjoy her baby girl and be happy she is finally here and healthy. As time goes by Lena has her daughter baptized and as she promised she picks the child's name. The little girl grew up to be very sweet and pretty and she was a good child and kind and caring too. Now she is about sixteen months old and has a new brother on the way. Yes, after Lena's first birth the doctor who delivered her daughter told her she had a blockage and that is why she had a hard time conceiving children. But after the birth of her first child the doctor repaired the blockage and now she is fine to conceive like other women. This is why and how Lena is about to have a second child.

On April 3, 1953 Lena gives birth to a son and feels blessed to have two children and one of each sex. This boy child was baptized Malcolm Izeard Jr, of course after his father. It made for a joyous family. The in-laws and Lena's parents were both ecstatic about the fact of two grandchildren. As for the Izeard's this was their only grandchildren but for the Reid's it was not but the fact that they were Lena's babies it was just like the children were the only grandkids they had.

The first Christmas they had with both children was something special now that there were two babies they just spoiled them to no end. Lena loved the attention her children were getting but she did not want them to grow up and think everything was to be given to them.

She asked everyone politely if they could not spoil the children as much. As they were the parents and seeing as she is the mother she wanted her children to have good values in life. She knew that by asking this it would hurt their feelings but now she was a mother and she also knew about being a spoiled child what it would or could lead to. Everyone said yes and it was settled. As time went on Lena enjoyed being a mother but Malcolm not so much as a father. He could not go out with his buddies like before and Lena could not go either so it was hard to get away from the children and have some fun. It was getting to Malcolm. Lena was becoming aware of Malcolm's restlessness and was getting more worried as the days and nights went by. She knew he would go out after work and come home late sometimes it did not bother her at first but then it became very apparent that this was not the life Malcolm thought he wanted. One day Malcolm comes to Lena and tells her he has a job offer in Alaska laying down pipe lines for the James Bay Company. She says ok and asks how long he will be gone.

"Well I am not sure Lena but, you know that this life is not what I want and I do not think I will return to you and the children. I will send you monthly checks for the house, the children and you but I want a divorce and as soon as possible," says Malcolm feeling like a heel and a bad person all at the same time.

"Well then let me tell you Malcolm Izeard Sr., I have had a suspicion for a while now and knew this day would come. So yes, you want a divorce fine but, I GET

CUSTODY OF MY CHILDREN! And furthermore;" she controls her temper at this point, "the checks better be on time too."

Trying not to show him her tears she maintains her composure and cannot believe he was leaving just like that. As he packs to leave Lena tries to think of what will happen to her and the children. Will he send the check to help support their children? She also thought of asking for her old job back at the Helen Harper factory since she kept in touch with some of the girls there.

It was going to be hard but, she knew she had to be strong for her children and make sure this did not scar them in anyway shape or form. The real dilemma was going to be telling her parents and in-laws. How would everyone react? She knew for sure that her father Alfred "Freddy" Reid wasn't going to stand for this at all and her mother Anna was going to cry. As for Malcolm's family, they would be appalled at how childish their son was acting.

Malcolm Sr. told his parents that it was all too overwhelming for him; two children and still young and that he had to leave this marriage and be on his own. Lena agreed to the divorce on her terms and he had to agree.

Yes, poor Lena had a lot to think about but, she would take it one day at a time for after all was she Freddy Reid's daughter. She just had to think of all the obstacles her father endured to come to this country alone and to succeed, she too would succeed and overcome this hurdle in her life. She had a long road ahead of her but she was made of good stock and knew she would pull through somehow. By the grace of God go I as she often heard her father say during difficult times. She was thankful that her children were still too young to understand, but one day she would explain the whole story to them but for right now it would have to wait. She knew she had a hard road ahead but for her children she would survive and make sure her children were loved and protected at any cost. It was her duty as a mother to protect and love her children even if it was alone.

Alfred and I

The year is 1954 and Lena is managing well, and as for the pay checks Malcolm promised they came alright but not as frequently as he said. By now Lena has moved in with her parents and after a lot of "I told you so" from her father he finally had to let her alone with that because her mother was happy her daughter came home.

It was not easy for Lena except for the fact that she got her old job back but was worried about a baby-sitter. As she prayed God answered her prayers. Anna had to stop working because her legs were giving her problems and standing all day in the laundry room of the hospital was too much for her. She decided to take care of her grandchildren for her daughter, you see Anna did not like the idea of strangers taking care of her grandchildren so she wanted to do it.

The little girl and boy were becoming very attached to their grandparents and seeing as Freddy was the girl's Godfather and Anna the boy's Godmother it just made more sense for them to help Lena and her children. After all she is their daughter and she needed their help and they adored these two children to no end and would protect them at any cost. It was a struggle for Lena but, she never once said she regretted having to care for these children alone.

As the years went by Malcolm Sr. kept his part of the divorce agreement and sent money for the children. But he also wanted visitation rights to see them but, Lena was worried that he would see them like the checks he sent "once in awhile." Lena went to court and had his parents as mediators so that her children could see their father with his parent's supervision only. It made things easier for Lena and her peace of mind. It was okay with the children too for they loved being around their other grandparents.

This issue was resolved and everyone was satisfied. It turned out to be just as Lena thought it would be. Freddy and Anna were not too pleased as Freddy had a lot of, "I told you so,'" and Lena had to live with that.

Anna on the other hand was just happy that her daughter was happy and her grandchildren were with her and Freddy. It was hard to accept for Lena in the beginning because she believed in marriage, but Malcolm Sr. was not as sure and it broke her heart.

But Lena had her children and her parents so with all that she would survive and rise above it all. Yes, it was going to be hard, a single mother living at home with her parents, but she could get her old job back and Anna stayed home with the children till they were to start school.

This would last for a little while until Lena meets a fine young man at a party and would soon be his bride and he would accept her children as well. This would upset Freddy and Anna to no end as they would not let the children go that easily.

Lena goes to a surprise birthday party for a good co-worker of hers. To her surprise she meets a very nice young man by the name of Abdul Mohammed, he was dark skinned and of East Indian and Guyanese decent. He worked as a Railroad Porter and some weekends he drove a taxi with his brothers. Abdul came from a big family of eight children and like Lena he was the youngest. She liked him from the start and they made plans to meet again.

Lena told him from the beginning that she had two small children and that did not phase Abdul in the least. He was looking forward to meeting her family and especially her children. Lena was kind of wondering how her father would take to her meeting someone else, but she was still young and she should not waste her life away by just sitting at home always alone.

Her mother Anna also worried she would always stay alone and when Lena told her about meeting Abdul Anna was happy but as Lena spoke she did worry how her husband Freddy Reid would react to his daughter meeting another man. Freddy was not ready to have his baby girl leave home and Anna was not ready to have the children leave either.

It was going to be a real sight to see when everyone would finally meet. Lena was hoping that this would be a happy event for all this time. She had to be sure that Abdul understood her position that the fact was she had two small children ages four years old and two and a half years old the girl being the oldest one.

As they grew fonder of each other Abdul adored her children and liked her parents too. After a year of courting Lena, and Abdul got married on August 21,1956, which was two days before Lena's twenty-fourth birthday. It was a small wedding at the Court House, with just close family and friends. Lena was happier with Abdul than she had been with Malcolm Jr. Even thought their marriage did not last long, she still had two beautiful babies from that union.

Life with two small kids was getting better as she had the support of her family and Abdul who just loved his little family. They lived with Lena's parents for awhile until they had a child of their own. Their son Abdul Jr. was born on August 8, 1957.

Lena's parents thought it would be wiser for her and Abdul to start their new family first, and then bring the older two into the family. Lena protested at first but Abdul made her see the obvious that her parents had become very attached to her older children even though they had other grandchildren Lena's were closer to them.

This arrangement lasted for a little while. When Abdul worked on the trains as a Porter or as a cab driver on the weekends, Lena would take her older children for weekends so they all could get to know each other better. It was breaking her heart to live so far away from her older kids so she had to move closer and Abdul understood now having two children of his own. He treated them all equal and made sure that they knew they were brothers and sister.

Lena eventually moved closer to her parents and became the Custodian for her parents and the other tenants. It was a good thing for Lena and her parents and her older children too. On June 12, 1963 Lena gave birth to another son. They named him Goram after Abdul's brother who he was very close to and made him the boy's Godfather. Now Lena and Abdul had all four children together. Although the older two stilled lived upstairs in a separate house from their mother and siblings. Lena was just downstairs and always on hand if they needed her in anyway.

Now this is all fine until the older two children become teenagers and the year is 1967 the year of Expo 67. It was a year that every teenager at that time was going to Man and His World as it was called back then but it was for Place des Nations Arena where they had bands playing every weekend.

It was loud and great light show a lot of screaming teenagers having fun. But the catch was that it all ended at 2 a.m. and seeing that Malcolm Jr., whose sister nicknamed him Jay Jay when they were very little. Because even though their grandmother Anna tried to hide the fact that would come late from there.

One night, Anna fell asleep and Freddy and Lena were up talking when the teens came home late and it was not pretty. They got caught and no grandma to shield them this time. Of course, Freddy strict as he was new but he figured if they were together it was okay to a point. But now he had to save face in front of his daughter and act very mad.

You must remember too that Freddy and Anna did not want to lose the teenagers in anyway shape or form. Freddy taught them their prayers and how to push themselves on the swings. How many nights did he and Anna stay up with their granddaughter when she would have severe asthma attacks and Freddy carried her on his back so she could make it to the bathroom All the while tears in the grandparent's eyes feeling the child's pain. They loved these grandchildren of theirs' but it is not to say that they did not love their other grandchildren as well.

The teens got grounded by Lena and knew their mother would make sure they did their punishment. For them it was no more bands for at least two weeks, which to a teenager during summer vacation is downright mean.

Even having Lena's children living with them Freddy and his wife they also saw Freddy Jr.'s family from time to time. Lena's children and Freddy Jr.'s children love being with each other. For he had four girls and one boy and

Lena's two older ones, but they all got along well. Freddy Jr even took the older two children to his house for sleepovers. His wife Vera just loved Lena and her children and everyone just loved Abdul and how well he fit into the family. But none were as happy as Lena to see that her children had a decent role model for a father as well as her father.

It helped to make the children all feel the same and connected even if they had different fathers. It was a little harder for the girl as she felt her biological father did not want her. It had been almost two or three years since she and her brother had any word from him. So, in her teenage mind she thought okay then so be it and life goes on or so she thought.

This worked for a little while and then she wondered why, but then she thought again that she had her grandfather and stepfather that loved her so much so now she felt better with herself. She had a grandfather who from birth was always there. A grandmother who doted on her and her brother and they both were loved so much.

As well as all the other grandchildren Freddy and Anna had there was the Izeard side of their family. The teenagers were the only grandchildren on this side and the first two. They had two other grandchildren but they never saw them again after their son Donald divorced his wife.

Malcolm Jr. and his sister were the only two on this side and here too they were loved. Their father's parents tried to make it up to them for having a missing father, growing up they often heard their grandfather Carl Izeard say that their son did not deserve their two children.

Despite all that Lena never stopped Carl and Margaret Izeard from seeing their grandchildren. She also remembers the times they pitched in and helped her too. Yes, Lena and her children were blessed and her parents were always by their sides. She remembers all those times her daughter was with asthma and had to go to the emergency and how her parents would take the child no matter the time of day or night seeing as she had little ones at home. And seeing as Abdul was always working on the railway or Diamond Taxi. Lena was very lucky to have her parents nearby and she felt very blessed. But don't think it was all hearts and roses. There were hard times too.

There was a time when Abdul injured his back from working on the "Via Railway Trains" as a Porter and he made a bad move and hurt himself badly in doing so. For about six weeks or more it was hard times for Lena and her family. Back in those days there was no sick pay unless you were hospitalized. To top it off it was near Christmas and the family was worried, but Anna as always prayed whenever she was distressed. Freddy also attended church every Sunday and because he gave to the charity box, he won a very big Christmas basket with all the trimmings. It was a great surprise and everyone prayed and gave thanks to God the Almighty. Yes, Anna and her prayers were always saving the family and the teenagers under their roof from harm.

But in all fairness, the teenagers were good kids and loved their grandparents to no end and Freddy and Anna loved them just as much. These children have been with them practically from birth and have been with them ever since.

Freddy was the first to hold the girl grandchild and then his grandson Malcolm Jr. was born in his house while Lena was visiting them.

Now also that the older two were teenagers it was another story all together. It started with the girl having boys and girls sit on the stairs at night just hanging out, but Freddy Reid was not having any of this. He would get a bucket of cold water and pour on them from the balcony above. Well that did not sit well with the teens so they never sat there again. But itdev was horrifying for the girl as she was so embarrassed by the whole situation. When you are a teenage girl trying to impress a teenage boy and that happens, it does not get more embarrassing than that. But that did not stop the boys coming around anyway. It was good for the families to be close by each other and for moral support too...

But then the years go by and now the girl meets a boy they fall in love and she becomes pregnant. But she is still in high school and too young to be a mother. She has options either to marry, give the child up or abort it. But the girl being as she is saying no to the abortion and no to the adoption. But she says she will marry the father as she loves him and wants her child to know their father too.

The wedding took place on September 6, 1969 and it was a small and lovely ceremony in the church. Lena's daughter gave birth to a baby girl on January 15, 1970. She was born with light skin and lots of hair like her mother and they named her Cynthia Shirley. Both the child's mother and father just loved her to bits.

Unfortunately, the two young parents knew it was not going to be good for them. The marriage would only last for three years and they finally separated and then divorced in October 1973. The girl was sad for her child as she wanted so much for her to be raised by both parents as she never was.

Since Lena and Abdul brought the children up together it did give them a stable and loving environment to live in. Abdul always made it a rule to treat the two older children as his own and made sure his boys understood that. He also was very good with Lena's parents and this made Lena very happy, even when her father Freddy would try and find fault at times. It was because Freddy cherished his baby daughter, he loved all his children but, Lena was the last one at home with him, as he and Anna never got the chance to raise their older children. They were raised by Anna's parents and now history repeats itself, as they were raising Lena's older children. But as it stands now they would be helping their granddaughter raise their great-granddaughter as well.

Because of her divorce Lena's daughter and granddaughter stayed with Lena's parents as they had more room and wanted to help. As Freddy put it straight out there, "she is my grandchild and her child is my Goddaughter and flesh and blood too. They will stay with Anna and I and no more discussion about it." They stayed with Lena's parents and no more was said.

This is how it was to be and yes, Freddy's granddaughter, Goddaughter, and Great-Granddaughter all stayed together. And Lena was not too far away either living just downstairs seeing as she and Abdul took the custodian job to be near the older two.

Then one day Freddy asks his granddaughter to please sit down and have a chat with him. He knows that she is somewhat of a woman now but, she must know his rules as well. He tries to find a way that will not make her feel childish at all.

"My dearest granddaughter, you now have a child and she needs to know that her mother will always be there for her no matter what," Freddy says as he looks to her and waits for a reaction to his question.

"Well Grandpa you are right as always and I am sure that I will be the best mother I can be, you see I have a great family support team and I know that all of you will guide me in the right direction."

As I look at him fondly we both know that I will certainly try and get it right. It was not easy but with my whole family around me it was not that hard. My little girl who the family called Cindy and was a real joy. She was spoiled by her grandparents and great-grandparents, but she also knew that being a spoiled brat would not help her cause either. Cindy and I stayed with my grandparents for a little while until I decided to move out on my own, which did not sit too well with my grandparents. They thought I was still too young to be on my own with my child.

July 24, 1974, marked the day that Anna and Freddy had married sixty years before. They renewed their vows and had a wonderful party. The Prime Minister of Canada and the Queen of England sent them congratulations cards. I was told it was a nice wedding too, all the family from New Brunswick came to celebrate and friends were there to help celebrate. Unfortunately, I missed their first one and now this one because my little girl had a tummy ache and I stayed home. But I did not miss the party as we had a small get together at my grandparent's home. It was a grand time and I enjoyed myself a lot.

Cindy is now five years old and almost ready for school, and her father takes her every second weekend. Still Freddy and Anna deep down wanted us to stay longer. Cindy and I brought joy to them and they did not feel so alone. You see Cindy and I went to live with my grandparents when she was only two years old and they bonded with her immediately.

Now it is five years later and I live alone with my daughter. During those first few months Lena my mother would make unscheduled house calls to check up on me. She knew I could handle it alone but my mother just had to be sure. It made me a little angry at first but then I understood by putting myself in my mother's place.

Then Anna got very sick she went to the doctor's a lot. They said she had diabetes but she did not seem to mind that. But then she got worse and the doctors now said she had suffered mild heart attacks in her sleep. We watched her as much as we could for any signs. As we were aware of the signs for diabetes, but heart attacks not so sure. We all knew she was not coming home as she was sick this time around. We all waited and prayed.

Anna never came back home. She died March 15, 1978 and was buried three days later at Reid's Funeral Home. It is ironic that where she was to be shown and later buried was by the funeral home that bear the same last name.

It was a dismal day and everyone at the funeral home was mourning Anna Jacquart Reid. Some were crying and some were just sitting quietly. Myself, I was off in a corner crying a bucket of tears knowing that I would never hear or see my grandmother again. It was also very hard on my grandfather Freddy. He was beside himself with grief, and kept asking God why did He have to take his wife and not him.

It was heartbreaking for me to see my grandfather mourn my grandmother's death. They were the two people in my life that have always been there for me and now only one remains. Yes, I still had my parents but, by now I am calling Abdul daddy ever since my daughter was about a year old. The only grandfather she has ever known was my stepfather.

My other grandparents came and paid their respects, as well as, my Uncle Donny and Aunt Shirley. It was amazing in a way to see that some relatives aside from my Uncle Reuben and Aunt Flora that also showed for their mother's funeral. Also, all the friends she had and their families too.

Freddy and Lena were slowly healing over Anna's death when we all get the news that my Aunt Flora has cancer and has not long to live. My mother Lena and I went to the hospital to see her older sister. She was just lying in her bed looking very old, tired, and ready to die. My Aunt Flora died on March 29, 1979 a little more than a year after her mother.

So now here we are again mourning the loss of a daughter, sister, aunt, mother, and a wife. Just as her mother was before her when she died. It was hard for my grandfather Freddy to lose his wife and eldest daughter; his first born, all in the space of one year and two weeks.

But out of all these death, my brother Abdul Jr. who had gotten married a year before Anna died, announces that he and his wife Tina are expecting a child in September. The child is born September 22, 1978, it is a boy and they name him Abdul III.

It was a glorious time for at least Freddy got to see his daughter's first grandson be born. He knew in his heart that Anna would have loved to see this little boy too. But even the gift of a new life did not make him mourn his beloved Anna any less.

Lena and Abdul both had jobs now and I was taking care of my family. My grandfather Freddy now eighty years old and not wanting to live alone, decided to go live with his eldest son Reuben in Minto, New Brunswick. This arrangement did not fair too well with my uncle's wife Olga as she was not as compassionate as we all thought. She wanted things her way and for the most part thought my grandfather Freddy was a burden.

My grandfather would call every week almost in tears saying he wanted to come back home. In July 1980, my mother and I went to New Brunswick to visit him and we saw for ourselves that he was not happy. My mother made the arrangements for my grandfather to be brought back to Montreal. By now my child was ten years old and a little bit self sufficient and independent of me.

My mother and I decided that we would take care of my grandfather, and he would live with her and my stepfather Abdul who did not even bat an eyelash at the suggestion. He was all for it too. Then Freddy came home the next year after we made all the necessary arrangements for his return. He flourished being with my mother and I and he felt more at home.

I remember one time when my mother had to be hospitalized for a little while, and I would go over in the morning and stay with him. I had a job at the time but it started at noon, so I could care for him while my mother was away. My dad worked too but seeing as he started early he finished early as well and was home by two thirty in the afternoon. So, my grandfather was not left alone too much.

On the days that we spent together, he would talk about his beloved Jamaica that he missed so much. He would talk about his Granny, his mother and his siblings especially his lovely sister Melvina. He would tell me about God and how he loved being a Christian man. How he loved his family and how he loved his Lena. Some would say that she was his favourite. As her daughter, it made me sort of his favourite too. He talked about how he would miss us all when he went to heaven to meet Anna his beloved wife.

My grandfather was a worldly man. He traveled all over during the war, and he even talked a little about it but never too much. We loved those days when he and I would sit and talk about life. Freddy Reid was a man with little education but made sure that his children received a good education along with my brother and I.

Because of his age he lost his eye sight and the doctors said it was a good thing that he was with his family. He managed with having us around and he did well even thought blind by now. He still knew who I was and he held his side of the conversation too.

Yes, growing up with Freddy Reid at times was hard. He was a real old school kind of man. Despite all of that he was also a very kind and loving grandfather and father to all his kin. He was a man who overcame great odds to stay alive.

He was smuggled on a boat to be saved from abuse and torture, never to see his home again which he always longed to see again. He would near the end of his days cry a lot and reminisce about his beloved home Jamaica. But also, let it be known that my grandfather and Lena's father was very proud to be a Canadian and to have fought in the two World Wars.

He was very proud of his religion and being a Catholic man. Which makes me remember for a very long time when my grandpa Freddy took me to his church. One day I saw all these

little boys and girls going to church as if it they were going to a wedding. My grandpa and mother explained to me that I could not go because they were going to their Confirmation which is a ceremony for Catholic children only and as I was not Catholic but Protestant. One day my mother said he should let me learn about my own religion. After that I did not attend many Catholic church services with my grandpa. I was very sad but eventually got over it.

There was one of grandpa's sons Gordie Reid who would have us over to his home. His wife Gladys was a wonderful loving woman and always made us feel at home. I remember as a teenager babysitting for them on occasion. They always stayed in touch too and had us over as much as possible depending on Freddy's health.

I remember in August 1984 Gladys and Gordie had a family reunion at their home and we were all there. My Uncle Reuben and all Gordie's kids from his first marriage where there. I had just met them that day, I knew about them but never meet them before that day. At this reunion, there was five generations. Grandpa Freddy, his son

Reuben and Rueben's son Gordie and Gordie's son Mark and Mark's little girl Susan. It was a wonderful thing for Freddy Reid. He was so happy to be there just knowing he had all these children of his. By now the blindness had progressed but he still had his pride. He would walk blind with his walker and bathe at the bathroom sink every day. Twice a week my dad would bath and shave him too.

    He would still do his daily things like listen to the radio for his favourite things like listening to church sermons as he could no longer attend church itself. He also loved his hockey and wrestling too. The one thing he could not play anymore was his favourite card game Cribbage. So me or my brother Malcolm Jr would play his card hand for him and he would be in his glory. Yes, even thought he could not see he still had all his facilities and knew what was what. My grandfather was a man of little education but was worldly just the same and taught my brother and I a lot of things through the years. He taught me about life and religion and how the world worked for you or against you.

    But it was a little hard on my mother as she had to work but fortunately she worked at a hospital two blocks from her home. I lived only a few blocks from my parents. This worked out good for all of us and Freddy was happy to be with his family too. He was happy because he was with his baby girl again and they had a bond as well as myself with my grandfather. He was not just a man he was father, grandfather and Godfather to me. Until my stepfather came along he was the only father I knew and even after my stepdad came in to my life my grandfather was a strong father figure.

My grandfather was a proud man. Even blind he did what he could for himself and we are all very proud to be of Alfred Barder Reid's blood. Yes, he has other family all over Canada but I was very close to my grandparents on both sides, but the Reid grandparents were not just grandparents for me they were my other PARENTS as well. Freddy was happy and content with his life with us and he would also have other relatives visit him from time to time.

As time went on he got sick with pneumonia and he had to be hospitalized. He was there for a few days maybe a week. He came home and was okay for awhile but about six months later he caught it again and this time it is worse. He goes back in the hospital and this time the doctors are not hopeful. He stays there and my mother, dad, siblings and I all go to visit him. We see him slowly going down and it is not good. As he gets weaker he asks us to all come to the hospital. He takes each of our hands and he says good-bye one by one. My mother and I were the last ones to have him hold our hands. It was a very sad day and my mother and I wept uncontrollably. We knew that he was going to his maker as he would often say to us.

One day before his final breath I visited him on my own and as he is talking to me he strokes my hair and mentions to me that I got it cut. You see my grandfather believed that women should have long hair and men short hair. It just amazed me how he knew with no eyesight.

This was a man that forged many obstacles to stay alive. He surpassed abuse, illness, and even being sent away to make his own way in life. He even joined the Army twice. You see this is just not a story about a man. It is a story about a Great Man that loved and lived for his family. He always made sure we were protected. He was a strict man yes but fair and loving in his ways. At times, as a child I did not understand why but as an adult I do now.